THE CHAMBER OF ETERNITY

JAMES E WISHER

CHAPTER 1

After setting sail from Markane City, Eddred and his companions had set a southerly course. The journey to the City of Coins took only a week and saw them rounding the coast of Rolan before crossing the strait that separated Etheria from the Dead Lands. A hundred miles of water kept the monsters that called the Dead Lands home from traveling north and bringing their endless hunger to another continent.

Now that the city was at hand, he needed to focus. Wallowing in sadness would do no one any good. He took several deep breaths and led the way down the gangplank and into the city.

Except for a few hours before and after noon, the City of Coins existed in perpetual shadows cast by the titanic walls that protected it from the undead horrors plaguing the rest of the continent. It seemed to Eddred that the shadows would quickly become oppressive. Of course, given the heat, maybe having constant shade was a blessing.

All around him, hundreds of people shouted and haggled

over everything imaginable. From food and clothes to slaves and drugs, you could buy anything here. Assuming you had the coin.

Lucky for him, the gold Lord Valtan provided would purchase everything they needed with plenty to spare. After sailing away from Markane and the city's thousands of dead, a deep melancholy had settled over the crew—understandable given that most of them had lost every member of their family. Eddred was no exception to this. The evil magic unleashed on Markane's capital had claimed his queen's life as surely as it did the poorest urchin.

Only the immortal Arcane Lord Valtan had survived. Eddred actually pitied the man, forced to live surrounded by the dead. Since his magic bound him to the city, Valtan had no choice but to remain behind. The task of avenging his people and retaking the continent from Garenland fell to Eddred. Deep down he doubted he was up to the task, but there was no one else to carry it out.

"Where, exactly, are we going?" Prince Uther asked.

The son of the former king of Straken stalked along beside Eddred, his gaze darting around the busy market like he expected to be attacked at any moment. Given how many times Uther had escaped near death at the hands of those hunting him, Eddred didn't blame the man for being anxious. He still wore the same battered and dirty tunic and trousers he had on when they picked him up at South Barrier Island.

"Nowhere exact. After being cooped up on the ship for weeks, I decided to have a look around the city. It's going to take at least a week to resupply and I wanted to give the men a few days of shore leave before we began the long journey across the ocean."

Uther grunted. Clearly sightseeing wasn't his cup of tea.

"Are we certain this fabled continent is even there? Maybe we'll sail for six months and end up in the Celestial Empire."

"Oh, it's there. Valtan assured me he's visited Colt's Land many times. I even found nautical charts among the coins he gave us to guide us right to one of their cities on the eastern coast. Whether we can convince the people there to help us defeat Garenland is another matter altogether."

Uther glanced at him. "Surely once you tell them of the threat Garenland represents, any right-minded person will want to defeat them."

"Don't know. There was a time I would have believed Markane lay beyond the concerns of the continent and we are far closer to Garenland than the people of Colt's Land." It pained Eddred to remember how naive he'd once been. "Time will tell."

A few minutes of walking brought them to the edge of the city's bazaar. The tents gave way to multistory buildings made of light-tan stone. Instead of windows, most of the buildings had only curtains.

They passed businesses of all sorts: inns, taverns, and cafes where people lounged in their flowing robes, drank coffee and tea, and smoked from hookahs. They rounded a corner and practically slammed into a gaggle of nearly naked women. The nature of the sprawling, three-story building behind them needed no explanation.

After their initial surprise at the men's arrival, the prostitutes immediately went to work. Touching and smiling and generally doing whatever they could to convince Uther and Eddred to join them inside.

For Eddred's part, the death of his wife remained too fresh to even consider sampling the wares on display. Uther had no such qualms.

"I'll meet you later at the ship." With those parting words the prince of Straken was happily led off by a pair of bronze goddesses that would make any man weak in the knees.

Eddred quickly disengaged from the pouting whores and made himself scarce. Perhaps a drink at one of the cafes would soothe him. The whole point of this tour was to distract him from his troubles and so far he'd failed miserably at the task.

He settled on a small place a hundred yards or so from the whorehouse. The cafe only had six outdoor tables, two of which were already occupied. No servers waited to direct him so he selected a seat as far from the others as possible.

Eddred had barely settled down when a girl about thirteen dressed in a simple white robe hurried over and asked, "Something to drink, sir?" She had a different accent, but was still easily understandable. One of the advantages of a world once ruled by an interconnected empire: no language barriers.

"Yes, thank you. Whatever your most popular item is will be fine."

The serving girl bowed and hurried away. Half a minute later she returned with a steaming cup of tea. "One copper coin, please."

"My treat." A slender woman, her face hidden by a veil and her body disguised by a flowing black robe, handed the girl a silver coin. "One for me as well. You can keep the rest."

"Thank you, miss." The girl bowed to the stranger and went to fetch her drink.

The woman settled into the seat across from Eddred. All he could see were her eyes, dark, mysterious orbs surrounded by shadows. If the rest of her matched her eyes, she was a beauty indeed, though not the sort of companion he wanted at the moment. Still, he had no desire to offend the woman and she'd done nothing to suggest she did the same sort of work as the earlier women. Perhaps it would be best to let her make the first move.

The serving girl returned with a second cup of tea then took her leave. When she'd gone his mysterious companion said, "I can see your curiosity, King Eddred."

He nearly dropped the delicate cup in his hand. His eyes darted around, seeking a trap but finding nothing. He never should have ordered his guards to remain behind. Damn it! He'd wanted to give them a break and now this.

"Calm yourself," the woman said. "I mean you no harm. I've simply come to make a business proposal." She must have read his expression because she laughed, a luscious chuckle that shook her shoulders and gave a hint of the curves under her robe. "Not that sort of proposition. You have a problem. Or rather two problems, Wolfric, ruler of Garenland and his advisor, Otto Shenk. For the right price, my guild can remove them for you."

Eddred took a moment to gather himself. This woman, whoever she was, knew far too much about him and his situation for comfort. He knew traders occasionally came from the city to trade with the kingdoms; he didn't know they had an intelligence network.

"Your guild," he said at last. "Assassins?"

"Indeed. And you needn't look around so furtively when you say it. The Coiled Serpent has paid all its dues to the city council. As long as we conclude our business outside the city walls, everything we do here is legal."

While he had no particular qualms about killing Wolfric and Otto, the idea of simply hiring murderers to do it seemed wrong. Still, it couldn't hurt to learn more.

He took a sip of tea to wet his suddenly dry lips and asked, "How much?"

Her laugh was softer this time. "Right to the point. I appreciate your directness. Around here everything is always subtle, dancing around the real issue. An emperor and a powerful wizard are far from easy targets. We'd need two hundred pounds of gold up front and the same amount again when the job is done."

He nearly choked on his tea. All the treasure Valtan had given him wouldn't even cover the down payment. However, he could get the coin if he really had to. Plenty of wealth remained in Markane and the dead had no use for gold.

Again she read him like an open book. "No need to answer now. The guildmaster tasked me with making contact, nothing more." She placed a bronze coin engraved with a coiled cobra on the table. "Take this. Should you at any time wish to further discuss the matter, show the coin to any merchant in the city. Word will reach us and I will make contact."

She stood to go and Eddred asked, "What's your name?"

"Naja. Goodbye, Eddred of Markane. May heaven watch over you on your journey."

He watched her until she disappeared into the crowd. The coin felt cool in his hand and had more heft than he expected. Assassins. How had it come to this? Hopefully, with the help of the people of Colt's Land, he wouldn't have to resort to something so desperate.

On the other hand, it wouldn't hurt to be prepared. He'd contact Valtan when he returned to the ship and see if he would begin collecting the necessary payment.

CHAPTER 2

Otto found Wolfric lounging with his new harem. A spare bedroom had been converted into a pleasure chamber based on an illustration Wolfric had found in one of his books. Pillows and cushions covered a variety of couches. Two girls lounged on one side, their sheer silk costumes leaving little to the imagination. The third cuddled with a shirtless Wolfric. Some spicy incense filled the air. Otto conjured an ethereal fan to blow it away from his face.

Wherever Sin found the young women, they couldn't have been working their trade for very long. None of them had that worn-out, world-weary gaze that he'd come to associate with the more jaded members of society.

They were certainly attractive enough, but he was starting to think the new emperor enjoyed his diversions a little too much. The nobles now had orders not to come to court unless they had serious problems and the merchants had similar instructions. While Wolfric's stress had gone down considerably, he risked losing the respect of those he ruled.

Fortunately, most of them were terrified of Otto and his war wizards, so that kept the risk of an uprising to a minimum. The fact that profits and taxes were filling both groups' coffers helped as well.

"Otto!" Wolfric said when he finally tore his gaze away from his companion. "Join us, please. Girls, a drink for my dear friend."

Otto raised a hand and the two unoccupied whores froze. Sin had made it very clear to all of them that while pleasing Wolfric was their primary task, Otto was their true master.

"Thank you, Your Majesty, but it's time for our meeting. I'll be sailing in a couple days and I wanted to go over the final arrangements now in case you have any questions."

"Is it that time already?" Wolfric rolled out of bed, hunted around, and finally found a robe to sling over his shoulders. "Very well. Lead the way."

The two men left the playroom behind. Outside, a quartet of royal guards fell in around them. A short walk brought them to the communication chamber Otto had set up just off the throne room. There wasn't much in the way of furniture, just a table, a handful of chairs, and a cabinet loaded with carafes. The only item of real note was the gold-framed mirror Otto had seized from the Wizards Guild. It allowed for communication over long distances and would help him keep track of the empire while across the ocean.

Draken, one of Otto's trusted lieutenants, bowed when they entered. After Draken had helped rescue Otto from the Wizards Guild, he had proven himself both loyal and skilled. He had now taken Enoch's place as Otto's second-in-command. Hopefully he would prove more trustworthy than Otto's late teacher.

"Your Majesty, Lord Shenk," Draken said.

"What was his name again?" Wolfric asked.

"Draken, Your Majesty," the wizard said.

"He will be serving as your advisor and guard while I'm away chasing Eddred," Otto said. "Rest assured, Draken has my full confidence. You will have no cause for complaint where he's concerned. Should you need to contact me, I've instructed him on the use of the mirror."

"Yes, I'm sure he's very competent," Wolfric said. "The empire has been so quiet lately I doubt there will be any problems while you're gone. Are you certain you can't just send someone else, a diplomat or something? That's their job after all."

"If it were simply a matter of establishing contact with the people of Colt's Land, then a diplomat would serve, but countering Eddred's lies will require someone higher up in the government. Since we dare not risk your life on the treacherous crossing, it falls to me."

"Of course it does. You are always going out of your way for the empire, my friend." Wolfric clasped Otto's upper arm. "I'll hold things down here, never fear. I am the emperor, right?"

"You certainly are." Otto smiled. He'd begun to wonder, as Wolfric became less and less dependable, whether madness ran in the Von Garen line. Having to deal with a mad emperor would make his work more difficult. "I think we've gone over everything this past week. Do you have any other concerns before I leave?"

Wolfric shook his head. "No, no, we'll all be fine. Rest assured, the empire will stay just as you left it. After all the work we've done, it wouldn't do to let things fall apart now."

"No, it wouldn't. I'm sure you're keen to return to your ladies," Otto said, careful to keep any sign of contempt out of his voice. "I have a couple other matters to discuss with Draken then I'm off for Lux."

"Safe journey, Otto," Wolfric said.

"Thank you, my friend. Don't worry, I'll be back before you know it."

Otto bowed and Wolfric took his leave. When the clanking of the guards' boots had gone he turned to Draken. Just in case, he conjured a barrier to keep anyone from eavesdropping.

"You see what's become of him," Otto said. "I wish I'd never suggested that stupid harem. I thought it would be a diversion, not a full-time occupation. He seemed to lose interest in ruling as soon as we fully established the empire."

Draken shrugged. "I'll make sure he doesn't do anything foolish and the other war wizards will keep an eye on the nobles. With the guild broken and no other real threats on the continent, the empire should be safe enough even with its ruler in less than full control of himself."

"Well enough. Contact me if you need to, but remember, I can't travel back and forth at a whim. Don't make me regret trusting you."

"I don't know if I ever told you this," Draken said. "But my brother was one of those you freed in Rolan. He would have died like an animal in a cage without your help. My life is yours, never doubt it."

Otto smiled, finally reassured that he could leave the empire and not have all his gains wiped out in his absence.

࿂

Otto arrived at the warehouse that served as the base of operations for his intelligence network half an hour after his discussion with Wolfric. The team had done some improvements on the outside, replacing siding, painting, and generally making the place presentable. Not that most people would ever see more than the outside.

He took a deep breath and pulled the door open. While his anxiety hadn't fully abated, he had made peace with leaving things in the hands of his subordinates for however long it took for him to find the Chamber of Eternity. Hopefully that would be months, not years.

As soon as he stepped inside, the stink from whatever alchemical concoction Ulf was working on wafted over him. They still hadn't improved the ventilation enough to keep the smell under control and at this point he seriously doubted they ever would.

The magical armor knelt in a neat row against the wall. Hans and his squad were busy packing their gear. They would be coming along on the journey as his personal guards.

"Master!" Corina came charging his way. The girl had finally gained a few pounds and no longer resembled a scarecrow. She wore a black and gold war wizard's robe and her mithril ring gleamed on her right hand. The pack on her back looked nearly as heavy as she was.

She had a bright smile as she skidded to a stop beside him. "I'm all ready to go. Thank you again for letting me come on the trip."

"You're welcome." He'd agreed mostly to shut her up since she'd done nothing but beg to come along from the moment she found out he planned to leave. Also, showing that he had sufficient skill to train an apprentice might help offset his youth.

Hans and his men slung their packs over their shoulders and joined them. They each saluted fist to heart. Unlike many of their missions, they wore a proper black and gold uniform of the Imperial Legion. They were on an official mission and needed to look the part.

"Ready to depart, Lord Shenk," Hans said.

"Good, let's head to the portal."

"What about your stuff?" Corina asked.

"I sent everything ahead days ago. It's all loaded on the ship." Otto waved to Ulf and the group set out. He'd already given Sin and Allen their orders. Mostly to just keep doing what they were doing and alert Draken to any problems.

As they walked through the quiet streets toward the portal, Hans said, "Are you certain it wouldn't be better for us to go then alert you with the rune coin?"

"I wish we could do it that way, but hitting a moving target while one with the ether is still beyond my ability. You'd have to make landfall before you called me and I'm sure the people of Colt's Land will want to talk before they allow us to dock. No, I have no choice but to endure the journey with you. Hopefully, it goes smoothly."

Hans still didn't look happy. Otto wasn't terribly happy himself, but after discussing the matter with Lord Karonin, he'd decided it just wasn't worth the risk. If the empire had still been at war, maybe, but with things finally calm, he decided to take the safe path. Otto had enough books to last six months already on board, so at least boredom shouldn't be an issue.

When they reached the portal fort, the guards waved them right through. A line of five merchant wagons had already formed and several drivers grumbled at them jumping the line. Otto ignored them. The next scheduled opening was for Rolan. Lux didn't come up for hours and he had no desire to wait.

A tap from his control rod, its tip charged with ether, activated the connection to Lux. Hans lunged through ahead of him as though expecting an ambush on the other side. Otto appreciated that he took his job seriously, but they were emerging in another fortress controlled by Garenland soldiers. The odds of an ambush didn't bear mentioning.

But if it made the good sergeant feel better, Otto wouldn't complain. Hans asked for little enough in exchange for his loyalty, letting him do his job seemed a small thing.

Otto and Corina stepped through next. Random colored lines of ether filled his vision for a moment then they were on the other side. They moved quickly out of the way to make room for the other soldiers. Hans stood a few feet away, seeming relaxed, but ready. No doubt seeing the soldiers on duty and no sign of an enemy had calmed him down. Despite Otto telling Hans more than once that Otto getting kidnapped by the Wizards Guild wasn't his fault, the sergeant still took it as a personal failure.

"No matter how many times I see that I'll never get used to it," Corina said. "The ether usually looks so swirly, the straight lines just seem wrong."

"The ether is naturally chaotic," Otto said. "At its core, wizardry is about imposing order on that chaos to make it do what you want. The portals embody that principle on a huge scale. Magic is about order. To be the best wizard you can be, keep that in mind with everything you do."

"Yes, Master." Corina's smile indicated that she didn't take his words as seriously as she should, but as her power grew so would her understanding.

When the last of the squad emerged, Otto deactivated the portal. Hans led the way through the fort's open gate. On the Lux side no wagons waited, but a single wizard in gray robes stood to one side of the gate, a heavy pack on her back.

The wizard's eyes widened when she looked at Otto and she bowed. Probably one of the independent crystal makers headed off to trade. He waved and put her out of his mind. It pleased him to see the wizards he freed making good use of their new rights. It would take time, maybe generations, but eventually people would come to understand that wizards were really just people trying to live their lives.

Crystal City, the capital of Lux, seemed quiet enough as they made their way from the portal to the dock where Captain Wainwright and his ship sat at dock. The port only had a handful of vessels docked alongside theirs. Otto hadn't noticed it on his previous visits, but a plaque attached to the front of the ship bore the name *Sea Star* engraved on it.

Beside him, Corina stared past the ship and out across the waves. Was this her first visit to the ocean? He couldn't remember and that annoyed him.

"Quite a view," Otto said. "In a few days we'll be so far out to sea that you won't even be able to see land."

She clutched his arm. "What if it sinks?"

"Then we drown. Even if you could swim... Can you swim?"

"No. Not much need for it on the plains." Her nails were digging into his arm. Otto conjured a barrier of ether to ease the pressure.

"Well, it wouldn't matter if you knew how. Once we're far enough offshore, you'll run out of strength before you get back. Assuming the sharks don't eat you first."

"What's a shark?" Corina asked.

Hans and his men were listening closely as well. He hadn't even thought to ask if any of them knew how to swim.

"A shark is a big fish with lots of teeth. They'll eat anything they can find. Some types are more aggressive than others. Don't worry, we're not going to sink. This is a good ship with a competent crew. They'll carry us where we need to go and back again without a problem." Otto glanced over at the ship and noticed a figure in a blue canvas shirt and pants, his beard neatly trimmed, standing at the rail. "Captain Wainwright. I trust all is ready?"

"Aye, Lord Shenk. We were just waiting for you. Come aboard."

When Otto and his merry band reached the top of the gangplank, the captain nodded to one side.

"Go below and get settled," Otto said. "I'll join you in a moment."

Hans saluted and led the others to a set of stairs that went below deck.

"What's on your mind, Captain?" Otto asked.

"Generally, when we're at sea, the captain's in charge of all matters aboard ship. I'm thinking that might not work so well with you."

"Tell you what. I won't tell you or your crew how to do your jobs and you leave me and my people alone, unless it's a matter of safety for the ship. Fair enough?"

"Aye, my lord. That's just the sort of arrangement I was hoping for. Since we're not hauling any freight, you all will find plenty of room to spread out. I arranged a private cabin for you right next to my own. It's small enough, but on a ship you have to make do."

"If you'd seen the size of the room I grew up in, you wouldn't be worried. Rest assured, Captain, I'm not a pampered nobleman that's going to complain every few hours about the conditions. Just get us where we need to go as quickly as possible."

"That shouldn't be a problem with them charts you provided. I expect to make the trip in two months, maybe less."

Otto nodded. That matched his own calculations. "Is there anything else you need from me?"

"Nope. We'll be underway within the hour. Make yourself at home."

A ship wouldn't have been his first choice of homes, but at least it was friendlier than either of his real homes.

CHAPTER 3

Annamaria paced back and forth in her room, rocking Abby in the hopes that she'd stop crying. Even an hour of quiet would be welcome. She didn't know what had her little girl so cranky, but for the last three days she hadn't slept for more than an hour or two at a time before she woke up crying again. Both the midwife and a priestess had come in to take a look at her, but both claimed there was no underlying illness. Sometimes, they said, babies were just fussy.

That wonderful bit of news did nothing to help Annamaria, and the lack of sleep was doing even less for her mood. Otto at least no longer troubled her. In fact, before he left, they had hardly spoken a dozen words. He also wanted nothing to do with Abby, which was no shock given her real father's identity.

She let out a long sigh. Oh, Lothair, you certainly did complicate my life before getting yourself killed.

Sometimes, a little piece of her wished he had just disappeared into the city and never returned. Yes, her life with Otto wouldn't have been what she dreamed of, but it might at least have been tolerable. Now she had a baby with no father to help her, a husband that hated her and that she in turn despised, and only a chambermaid with whom to share her secrets.

A soft knock on the door brought her up short. She shifted Abby to her left arm and said, "What is it?"

The door opened and Mimi, her personal maid, stuck her head in. She'd let her hair grow out a little over the last month and it framed her heart-shaped face nicely.

"Lady Shenk is here, miss."

"Otto's mother?" Annamaria's heart raced for a moment. What could her mother-in-law be doing here? "Did she say what she wanted?"

"To meet her granddaughter I assume. She's downstairs chatting with Master Edwyn. Judging from her luggage, she's planning to stay a spell."

"Did she come alone?" All Annamaria needed now was for the nastier members of Otto's family to be hanging around underfoot.

"She had four guards with her, but no other family members," Mimi said.

Annamaria blew out a breath of relief. Katharina, at least, she could handle. "I'll be down in a moment."

Mimi withdrew and she set Abby back in her cradle. A quick look in the mirror revealed a tired, haggard woman. Her eyes were dark and bloodshot, her clothes wrinkled and slept in, and the less said about her hair the better.

As she considered taking time to change, Abby started wailing again. Annamaria scooped the little one up and went for the door. If she was too much of a mess then too bad. At least she hadn't collapsed in exhaustion.

The stairs weren't far from her room and soon enough Annamaria reached the dining room. Katharina stood as she approached and smiled the same kind, welcoming smile she'd offered when Annamaria arrived at Castle Shenk the first time. That look of warm acceptance nearly sent Annamaria into tears.

How long had it been since anyone looked at her like that? Not since Lothair was killed.

"My dear, you look all in." Katharina crossed the room and held out her arms.

Even after a week plus of traveling she looked perfect, every inch the noblewoman in her dark-red gown, her hair upswept and held by silver pins. She made Annamaria feel like a country maid.

Annamaria passed Abby over to her without hesitation and after a few bounces she stopped crying. Maybe Katharina was a wizard too. The silence felt brittle, like the crying was about to resume at any moment. Annamaria had learned not to trust these peaceful moments.

"And where is my son?" Katharina asked. "I assumed Otto would at least come out and greet me."

"Otto's off on some mission for Wolfric... I mean Emperor Von Garen," Annamaria said. "I got the impression he wouldn't be back for some time."

"Typical Shenk man," Katharina said. "Always the first in line for a fight, but when a baby needs taking care of they're nowhere to be found. He didn't tell you about his task?"

"No. Otto tells me very little about his work for the emperor. I suppose he can't exactly go around spilling secrets." Not that he would have told her in any case.

Katharina shook her head. "That won't do at all. A marriage is built on trust and that comes from honesty. Arnwolf, for all his faults, never keeps secrets from me. Whatever was happening in the barony, whether good or bad, I always knew.

When Otto returns, I'll have a long talk with him about trusting his wife. After all, if he can't trust you, who can he trust?"

It took all of Annamaria's willpower to keep her expression neutral. If Katharina ever found out what she'd done, heaven only knew how she might react. At the very least, chiding Otto about trust would be the farthest thing from her mind.

"Why don't you get a nap, dear? I'll look after Abby for you."

"I won't argue," Annamaria said. "If you'll excuse me."

As she made her way back to her bedroom, Annamaria heard her father asking if Katharina wouldn't like something to eat. Typical Father—when in doubt, have a snack. She wished she could solve her own problems so easily.

CHAPTER 4

The journey across the ocean, while tedious, passed without any issues beyond a couple bouts of stomach flu among Eddred's crew. He assumed some of the unfamiliar foods they picked up in the City of Coins had brought about the illness. Some sort of egg concoction mixed with vinegar had set Eddred's insides roiling, so he was in no position to criticize.

As he stood now in the ship's bow, the wind in his hair, looking out at a pair of approaching ships, none of those details mattered. He would soon make contact with the people of Colt's Land. The first person to do so in seven-hundred-plus years. Under normal circumstances, that would be a momentous event. But now, with his mission to convince them to help fight a war, getting this first step right was paramount. Move too aggressively and he risked looking like the villain and if he seemed too weak, he risked looking like a lost cause.

Technically, Eddred had been trained to handle diplomacy, but he usually had Valtan's reputation and the fear that provoked to aid him. This nation sat well beyond the Arcane

Lord's reach and any threats would no doubt see them turned back or, worse, sent to the bottom of the ocean. He dearly wished for anyone or anything that might show him the right way.

Minutes passed and his prayer remained unanswered. The approaching ships were close enough now that he could make out their single masts and square-rigged sails. What really caught his attention were the ballistae mounted in the sloop's bows. Both were cocked and loaded with a heavy, iron-tipped harpoon.

When they were a hundred yards away, a greatly amplified voice said, "Lower your sails and prepare to be boarded."

"Orders, Your Majesty?" Captain Carter asked from his position at the helm.

"Do as they say," Eddred said. "These are the people we're here to meet. We don't want to start a fight."

The sailors hastened to climb into the rigging and take down the ship's many sails. Eddred ignored the process and focused on the still-approaching sloops. There must be wizards on board to amplify a voice like that.

He squinted, trying to make out the telltale aura of a wizard working the ether. Either they were still too far away or he lacked the skill to see that far; whichever it was, he couldn't tell which of the twenty or so sailors was the wizard.

Speaking of wizards, Lilly and Adam, his personal bodyguards, came to stand beside him. "Should we expect trouble, Majesty?" Adam asked.

Eddred smiled. "Always. But unless it's a life-or-death situation, don't react. Remember, we're here to ask for these people's help."

"Understood, Majesty," Lilly said.

When the sloops finally came alongside, one of the crew

tossed down a rope ladder. Eddred went to greet whoever ended up coming aboard. A soldier dressed in a hardened leather breastplate and white trousers boarded first. Eddred pegged his age at twenty-five tops. The clean-shaven youth glared around at the sailors watching him, his hand never straying far from the hilt of a short, curved sword that looked brand new. Not a hardened warrior then.

A moment later another sailor that looked like a brother to the first scrambled up the ladder followed by an older man about forty who wore a blue shirt instead of armor. He had a gold insignia of some sort over his right breast.

This would be the man in charge.

"Welcome aboard," Eddred said.

"You are the captain of this vessel?" the older man asked. Like the people of the City of Coins, his accent was different, but still understandable.

"No. My name is Eddred, king of Markane. I have crossed the ocean to speak with your rulers on a matter of grave importance."

"A bold claim. My name is Captain Kendy of the Bandon City Coast Guard. My duty is to search any ship approaching the city and determine if they pose a threat. If I decide you don't, a pilot will be assigned to guide your ship to the city dock. The harbormaster will then hear your story and decide whether to pass it along to the city council and Lord Governor. You will be confined to your ship until given permission to disembark. Understood?"

"Perfectly. Please, feel free to look around. We have nothing to hide."

"I will, sir." Captain Kendy snapped his fingers and the soldiers fell in beside him.

For the next hour, he stuck his nose into every corner of

the ship, including Eddred's private quarters, the crew's foot-lockers, and the bilge. Kendy was thorough, Eddred had to give him that. But there was nothing to find beyond food and their modest remaining funds.

At last Kendy said, "I can't say if you are who you claim, but you're clearly neither pirates nor smugglers. That gets you to the dock. Jameson!"

A portly sailor older than the captain labored his way up the ladder and saluted. "Captain?"

"You're on guide duty. Take them to guest berth seven. I'll have a team ready to meet you."

"Righto, sir."

It was a testament to the crew's training that they followed the fat sailor's instructions without complaint. Not that he didn't know his business. After two hours and with a little help from a large rowboat crewed by the burliest men Eddred had ever seen this side of Straken, they were tied up at a dock well away from the main area of the city's port.

Eddred easily counted thirty huge, three-masted ships tied up further away. Beyond the waterfront, hundreds of two- and three-story buildings jutted up. The city's massive portal towered above the buildings. And beyond that, he could see a wall probably fifty feet high. His best guess made Bandon City smaller than Garen but considerably larger than Lux.

Jameson dusted off his hands and left the helm. He sauntered over to the rail where Eddred stood. "Welcome to Bandon City. Here come the harbormaster and his men now. I'll leave you in their care. Best of luck to you, sir. She's a fine ship."

Two crewmen put the gangplank over the side and Jameson ambled on down, pausing only to toss an indifferent salute to the group of ten men approaching.

THE CHAMBER OF ETERNITY

Eddred turned his attention to the new arrivals. Nine were clearly soldiers, armed with double-edged swords, small round shields, and wearing mail suits. The tenth man was older, with a well-trimmed gray beard and a blue and white tunic with a small set of gold scales embroidered on the right breast. He carried a closed leather book with him.

"So this lot will decide our fate." Eddred had been so focused on the harbormaster and his men that he hadn't noticed Uther slip up beside him.

"Seems like. You know, I'm not sure what I expected, but so far everyone's very polite and accommodating. I'm trying not to get my hopes up, but if the rulers of this place are as reasonable as the sailors, we might yet succeed."

Uther grunted. "Being polite is one thing. Volunteering to fight a war is another. I say they'll hear you out then send us on our way empty-handed."

The group stopped at the foot of the gangplank and before Eddred could reply the older man looked up and said, "Permission to come aboard?"

"Granted. Please join us."

"Thank you, sir." The older man led the way up the slightly swaying gangplank, moving just as easily as if he stood on level ground. "As I'm sure you guessed, I'm Bandon's harbormaster. Captain Kendy has told me quite a story about you. I've read about Markane of course, home of the last living Arcane Lord. The journey must have been difficult."

"Tedious, but the weather was fine. King Eddred of Markane." He held out his hand.

The harbormaster grinned, grasped his wrist, and shook. "Paxton, good to meet you, sir. Never shook the hand of a king, quite an honor."

If he knew the state of Markane at the moment, he

wouldn't have been so impressed.

"So I understand you want to talk to the city fathers. Now I don't like to be nosy, but it's my job to screen out anyone that might waste their time. I don't suppose you crossed the ocean on some minor matter, but I still need to ask you to tell your tale."

Eddred nodded. "Certainly. The continent, you would know it as Etheria, has been conquered and Markane nearly destroyed. I've come seeking help—soldiers, wizards, anything you can offer."

Paxton frowned. "I see. Don't think you'll get the answer you want, but I'll take your message to the council. Until the reply, stay on your ship. Some of the locals will be around in time to sell you fresh food and whatever else you might want at an only modestly outrageous price. Feel free to trade. As long as you behave yourselves there won't be any trouble. My boys will stay nearby just in case. Good day."

And as quickly as he'd come, the harbormaster took his leave.

"How long do you think they'll make us wait?" Uther asked. The prince had been silent during Paxton's visit, but his eyes never stopped moving as he studied the soldiers that came with him.

"Depends how hard they want to flex their muscles. A week minimum, probably more. I suggest we settle in and get comfortable. We're going to be here awhile."

∽

It turned out that Eddred was overly pessimistic when he guessed at least a week. Two days after their arrival,

Paxton returned with a fresh complement of soldiers and without his book.

He met the older man at the gangplank and asked, "Do you need more details?"

"Nope. I delivered your message and the city council and lord governor agreed to talk to you. This is just a preliminary hearing. They want to meet you, hear your story for themselves, you know, that kind of thing. I suspect they'll talk it over for a spell before deciding whether or not to summon the ambassador corps."

"Ambassador corps?" Eddred asked.

"Yeah, the representatives of the other nine city-states." Paxton scratched his head. "I'm not really up on all the politics, but let's just say things are complicated. None of the city-states would dare risk helping you unless all the others agreed to pledge the same amount of aid. Anyway, I'm sure the council can explain things better than I can. Come on, you can bring one guard, but that's it."

Eddred's wizard bodyguards had been standing back while he talked, but now they hurried forward.

"Our duty is to protect the king at all times," Lilly said.

"That's right," Adam said. "What if an assassin tries to kill him on the way to the meeting?"

Paxton chuckled. "Outside wizards aren't allowed in the meeting hall anyway, so you two might as well stay here. Allowing a guard is a show of good faith. I assure you, if the lord governor decides to kill you all, two wizards won't be able to stop him."

Eddred turned to Uther. "Care to take a walk?"

"Your Majesty!" Lilly said. "You can't just go in blind. Heaven only knows what they might try."

"How can we trust them to help us if we won't trust them

to hold a peaceful conversation?" Eddred shook his head. "I appreciate your concern, both of you, but if this is how it has to be, then this is how it will be. Stay here and keep an eye on the ship. I have every confidence our hosts will guide me safely to my destination and back again."

"That's the spirit." Paxton led the way back down the plank and Eddred and Uther followed.

As soon as they reached the boardwalk, the nine soldiers fell in around them. Whether to protect them or to protect others from them, Eddred wasn't sure. He suspected the latter.

For the first two blocks, they might have been in any city on the continent. Stone buildings with tile roofs predominated. There were the usual mix of businesses, taverns, and inns. The people they passed dressed in typical tunics of various colors along with a mix of leathers and canvas.

When they rounded the third block, it became instantly clear they weren't at home anymore. A wagon was being pulled down the street by a horse made of steel. A blue gem glowed in the construct's chest. Two blocks after that, they passed a building site where human-shaped constructs were lifting beams like they were twigs.

"Thirty or forty of those would make short work of Wolfric's army," Uther said.

Eddred could only agree, though how effective they'd be against wizards was another question. It would be an awful thing to send the constructs into battle only to have the enemy wizards turn them against their masters. He shuddered to think what would happen if Otto Shenk got his hands on them. His grip on the continent would be so tight they'd have no hope of victory.

At last they reached a fortress within the city. While it had no outer walls, the keep was built of heavy gray stone and the main gate had iron-bound doors that looked strong enough to withstand a battering ram. Even more impressive were the four suits of giant armor patrolling the area. They looked suspiciously like the armor used by Garenland's army. Only the color of the gem on their chest differed.

Paxton hurried ahead and spoke to one of the guards in the armor. Soon enough the gates were opened and Eddred and Uther ushered inside. The first chamber held a table and six chairs.

"You can have a seat," Paxton said. "I'll let the council know you've arrived."

The harbormaster went through a door to the right and Eddred settled into a surprisingly comfortable leather chair. Uther seemed happier pacing. The guards watched him, but didn't insist he sit.

Five minutes passed and the clunking of Uther's boots began to grate on Eddred's nerves. "Could you possibly relax? Your anxiety is going to infect me."

"I hate waiting." Nonetheless Uther dropped into a chair facing Eddred. He chose one without arms so as not to get his sword tangled. "How long do you think this is going to take?"

Eddred shrugged. "Until they're ready to talk to us. It's all a game to establish their position at the top of the hierarchy. I'd tell them they didn't need to since we're the ones who came looking for help, but some habits are hard to break."

"This is why I spent as little time in the other kingdoms' courts as possible. I hate stupid political games. Whatever they want, they should just do it."

Eddred leaned back and closed his eyes. He might not know magic or combat, but when it came to court matters, he felt in his element. Granted this was a court unlike any he had ever encountered, but people were people at the end of the day.

Their wait ended faster than Eddred had expected. After a mere half an hour or so, a young, female servant in a simple blue dress came into the waiting room from the same door Paxton left by, bowed, and said, "The council will see you now."

Eddred stood and Uther joined him. The nine soldiers that had been watching them since they left the ship remained behind. Eddred took that as a good sign. If the powers that be trusted them enough to leave them to the care of a woman barely in her twenties, they must have decided they didn't represent a dire threat. Either that or there were magical protections in place he couldn't see or sense. A distinct possibility given how much magic they'd seen since arriving.

Eddred and Uther followed their guide through the second door, down a long, curving corridor that ended with an open door. The girl stopped and motioned them through. Eddred marched through without hesitation. If the council meant them ill, they were dead already.

Inside, a round table filled most of the space. Eleven people, seven men and four women, all of different ages, from a woman old enough to be Uther's grandmother to a man that looked like he'd just started shaving the week before. And while their ages varied, their dress was uniformly rich—lots of silk, velvet, and gold. Eddred guessed that if they killed the councilors and looted their bodies, they'd have enough wealth to hire Naja and her assassins.

The eldest woman stood, the wrinkles of her face deepening as she smiled. "Welcome to Bandon City, King Eddred. My name is Helena and I have the honor of serving as the lord governor of this city-state. Paxton has told us a bit of your story and that you seek our help against your enemy. Before this council calls a meeting with the diplomatic corps, we need you to convince us that there is a threat to our nation. While it is unfortunate that you've met with difficulty at home, the war is far from here."

Eddred bowed. "Lord Governor, councilors, I understand your desire not to involve yourselves in matters that you think don't concern your nation. Markane used to take a similar path with regards to the continent. That choice came back to haunt us. Please allow me to tell you the tale from the beginning."

For the next fifteen minutes, Eddred recounted everything that had happened from the moment the nations voted to kick Garenland out of the compact until they set sail from the tomb that was Markane City. When he finished he said, "So you see, despite our best attempt to remain neutral, Markane still ended up fighting and losing a great deal in the process."

"You say that, yet it seems to me that if you hadn't gotten involved at the end, your city would have remained unharmed," Helena said. "I feel your mistake was sticking your nose into matters that didn't directly concern you. A mistake you're trying to convince us to make as well."

There were murmurs of agreement from the other councilors. This was the moment he'd feared. The lord governor wasn't wrong, but that didn't mean inaction held no risk.

"There's no guarantee that Garenland won't turn its sights on Colt's Land," Eddred said. "If you strike first, before they gain any more strength, you can end the threat now."

"At what cost?" one of the men asked. "We're thousands of miles away and our portals remain deactivated, so they can't slip an army across the ocean without us noticing. I think you overstate the risks to bring us around to your way of thinking. I, for one, am not inclined to go along."

That brought even louder murmurs of agreement.

The lord governor raised her hands. "Thank you for speaking with us, King Eddred. We will consider your words carefully. In the meantime, please enjoy your stay in Bandon. A few areas of the city are off-limits, but you and your crew are welcome to enjoy our taverns and shops. When we have made a decision, we will let you know."

Eddred bowed and led Uther out of the chamber. Their guide was waiting outside and showed them out of the building. Of the guards that had escorted them, there was no sign. At the very least they seemed to have convinced the council that they posed no threat to the city.

"They won't help," Uther said. "This trip was a waste of time."

Eddred turned back toward the docks. "You're probably right. This was always a long shot, but we needed to try. If they don't help us, I fear we have no hope of retaking the continent."

"What about the Celestial Empire?" Uther asked. "Might we not try them?"

"The empire was known to be insular even during the time of the Arcane Lords. I can't imagine that has changed since their passing."

"So what do we do now?"

"We wait."

✧

E ddred sat alone at a table in a tavern not far from the docks. A day had passed since his visit with the ruling council and still no word. That gave him just the faintest hope that they might offer some sort of help. He didn't dare get too excited. Nothing they did or said during the interview seemed especially sympathetic to his cause.

At least they let the men off the ship to blow off steam. The journey across the ocean had been a long one and everyone was happy for a day at least of shore leave. All the sailors knew to be on their best behavior. Nothing could be allowed to reduce their already slim odds of success.

He took a sip of his wine and sighed. Waiting and hoping was absolutely the worst. Part of him wished the council had ordered his ship to set sail immediately if they weren't going to help.

"Excuse me."

Eddred looked up to find a slim, nondescript man of about thirty years dressed in gray standing next to the chair opposite him. Since the tavern wasn't even half full, he assumed the stranger wanted to speak with him specifically.

"Can I help you?" Eddred asked.

"May I join you?" the man asked. Eddred nodded toward the chair and he slipped into it. "Thank you. When I saw you drinking alone, I couldn't help but come over. It's not often we get visitors from across the ocean."

"How do you know where I'm from?"

"Rumors abound if you know where to listen. The reason for your visit has been a bit more difficult to ascertain."

There was a meaningful pause while the stranger waited for Eddred to offer an answer. Instead he offered a question. "Which embassy are you from?"

"Figured that out, did you? I'd just as soon not say."

Eddred nodded and took another sip. If the council hadn't shared the purpose of his visit, Eddred doubted his doing so would win him any favors. On the other hand, if they weren't going to help, what could it hurt?

"We came looking for help. Our homeland is at war and we're losing, badly." Technically they had already lost, but no sense being quite that negative.

The stranger nodded as if Eddred had confirmed something he already knew. "I fear you will find no help here or in any of the city-states."

"The council indicated as much after we spoke. We're simply awaiting their formal response. Since I've shared a bit with you, perhaps you'd share something with me." When the man indicated he should proceed Eddred asked, "Why are things so tense between Bandon and its neighbors?"

"I guess it couldn't hurt to tell you. Lord Colt, in his great wisdom, kept the balance between the city-states. None of us received more resources than any other. Should any city attack its neighbor, it risked losing resources and inviting an attack in turn. Aside from a skirmish here and there, we're at peace. Of course, should any city be stupid enough to weaken themselves by helping you, they would soon find themselves destroyed and their lands divided between the remaining cities."

Eddred stroked his chin. He'd suspected something like that. Helping Markane would be in essence destroying themselves. No sane ruler would risk that by aiding a complete stranger. Just as he feared, his cause was a hopeless one. No doubt the order to leave would be coming soon enough.

The stranger stood and bowed. "Thank you for speaking with me. My master will be pleased that I gathered the information she sought. I wish you luck in convincing the council as my lord governor would be delighted to take a piece of Bandon should it fall."

Eddred watched him make his way out of the tavern. Life, it seemed, was no simpler on this side of the ocean.

CHAPTER 5

Otto shifted in his hammock, trying to find a comfortable position while not losing his place in the book he was reading. After nearly two months at sea he still hadn't gotten used to the bloody thing. The only good thing about it was that lying in the hammock was more comfortable than sitting on the trunk that held his gear. Along with a small writing table, that was the extent of his cabin's furnishings.

When they got home with the chamber, he was going to have the ship refitted with an actual bed and a comfortable chair before his next journey. After everything he'd done for the empire, Wolfric could spare him the coin to pay for it. And if he couldn't, Edwyn would.

At least the book's subject matter was interesting enough to distract him from the crudeness of his surroundings. Everything he brought on the journey held details about Lord Colt, the nation he built, and most importantly how he liked to use magic. Unlike most of the Arcane Lords, Colt preferred enchanting items to casting spells directly. Not that he wasn't tremendously powerful in battle, all the lords were basically armies unto themselves.

He used crystals, like those that powered the magical armor, as conduits to connect constructs to the ether. Some of his devices required pilots and others would obey simple voice commands. Otto envisioned an army of steel soldiers, totally obedient and utterly fearless. With a force like that, the empire would stand forever.

Someone knocked on his door.

"Come in."

Corina poked her head in. "Ship approaching, Master."

"Are we within sight of land?"

"The lookout hasn't said anything and I can't see anything from the deck. But we must be getting close if they sent ships out to meet us."

Otto wasn't so certain of that. He marked his place and rolled out of the hammock. "Let's have a look."

Up on deck, Hans and his men were gathered at the rail. They had put on hard leather breastplates and belted on their swords. Six soldiers against an entire ship's crew wasn't the best odds. Lucky for them, they had a pair of wizards as backup.

"Hans?" Otto said. "What are we looking at?"

"Not sure, my lord. That little ship is headed right for us."

"Have they made any attempt to signal their intentions?"

"Not that we've seen." Hans turned his way. "I don't like the feel of this."

"Nor do I. Best to just ask what they plan."

Otto closed his eyes and extended his sight toward the approaching ship. Quick as thought he found himself amidst a collection of ragged men armed with bows and cutlasses. He sensed no wizards and saw no sign that they were in any way connected to Bandon, the city Otto assumed they were nearing.

A stout man with a beard and missing left hand stood at the helm. Given his position and slightly better clothes, Otto assumed he was the captain.

Extending his voice and hearing Otto said, "Identify yourself."

The captain jumped and looked around for whoever spoke.

"I'm a wizard on the ship you're approaching. Identify yourself and turn aside or I will assume you're an enemy and send you to the bottom of the ocean."

"Wait! We are the Bandon City Coast Guard. We've come to inspect your ship and guide you in."

"Please, spare me such an obvious lie. You fly no flag, wear no uniforms, and appear not to have bathed in a month. Even if you were who you say you are, I wouldn't let stinking thugs like you on my ship. You have ten seconds to change course before I incinerate the lot of you."

Otto began a loud countdown.

He reached six before the captain began to turn.

"Tell your crew to drop their weapons and prepare to be boarded. You and I are going to have a face-to-face conversation."

When he didn't obey instantly, Otto rubbed his fingers together and sent a stream of flames streaking into the rigging of what he'd decided was a pirate ship. The canvas and rope caught quickly and soon flaming debris was raining down among the shouting crew. In seconds they were too busy trying to avoid catching on fire themselves to worry about anything else.

Otto returned his senses to his body. "Captain Wainwright! When that fire has burned itself out, bring us alongside."

From his place at the helm, Captain Wainwright waved his understanding.

"Orders, Lord Shenk?" Hans asked.

"I want to talk to the captain. Anyone else makes a move or gets in the way, kill them."

"And if they behave themselves?" Hans asked.

"Depending on his answers, maybe we take them prisoner or maybe I sink their ship with them still aboard."

9

Half an hour passed before the pirate ship's sails burned themselves out. It helped that the crew cut some away so they ended up in the ocean. As soon as it was safe, Captain Wainwright brought them right up alongside the other vessel and Hans tossed grappling hooks across to bind the ships together.

Hans and the men hopped across. When Corina went to join them Otto said, "You stay here. Make sure none of them try and sneak across. You don't have to hurt anyone, just bind them like I taught you."

"I can fight," she said. "I'm not scared like I was with King Villares. I won't hesitate this time, I promise."

Otto smiled and patted her shoulder. She talked tough despite her faint trembling. Corina had been wanting to prove herself after what she saw as a failure in Rolan last spring. Otto understood that, but now wasn't the time. He needed his full focus.

"I know you can fight. That's why I want you to protect the ship. There's no one else I trust to do it."

Corina shook her head but smiled. "You're a terrible liar, Master."

Otto considered himself an excellent liar when he actually wanted to deceive someone. He followed Hans across to the pirate ship. The singed crew glared at them, but no one went for their weapons. Otto led the way toward the helm, stepping over charred debris along the way.

The ship's captain stood facing him, his face contorted with rage and his hand resting on the hilt of his cutlass. Perhaps he was hoping to get himself killed before he could be questioned. Otto wasn't about to let that happen. He flicked his iron ring and bound the pirate in his tracks from the neck down.

"Okay, here's how this works," Otto said, planting his fists on his hips as he faced the captain. "I ask questions. You answer them. Lie to me and one of your men goes over the side, bound exactly as you are now. We can listen to him scream before he drowns. Understand?"

"Perfectly."

"Excellent. Were you hunting us or did we have the ill luck to run into you?" Otto watched the ether swirl around in the man's skull as he considered his answer.

Finally he settled on the truth. "We were hunting you. Well, not you specifically, but any ship that might be coming from the east. I figured if one came from that way, maybe another would."

So Eddred had arrived ahead of them. No great surprise there.

"When did this other ship arrive?"

"About a week ago."

That wasn't so bad. Eddred couldn't have done too much damage in such a short time.

"Are we in danger from any other ships in the area?"

"No, we work alone and we certainly didn't tell anyone that another prize might be arriving at any moment."

"I assume the actual coast guard will be along eventually?"

"Yeah, another hour west and you'll run into them. I've been pretty obliging here. How about you let us go?"

"You would have murdered us and taken all that we have and now you ask for mercy? I don't think so. We'll take you into custody and turn you over to the coast guard, a gift to show our good intentions. Hans, find rope so we can tie them up."

"Yes, my lord."

Hans and his men got to work and soon enough they were back aboard the *Sea Star* with twenty prisoners. They cut the pirate ship loose and continued on their way.

Corina looked over their dirty captives and shook her head. "They didn't put up much of a fight. I've read books about pirates and they're always bloodthirsty, fight-to-the-death types."

Otto shrugged. He was happy to have come through the encounter with no one on his side hurt. "Life is often full of disappointments."

"What are we going to do when we finally arrive?" she asked.

"I don't know. We're guests here, so it will be largely up to our hosts how we proceed. My hope is for a prompt, friendly meeting that ends with a new trade deal at best and a peace deal at worst. Convincing them to give me access to Colt's Workshop will be the really hard part."

Otto went to join Captain Wainwright near the helm. They sailed west for most of an hour before the lookout said, "Two sails on the horizon headed this way. They're flying pennants."

Otto sent his vision out over the water. He kept his distance in case they had wizards, but flew close enough for a good look.

This lot was certainly better equipped. Both their gear and ship were clean and well maintained. The sailors wore leather armor and white trousers. One woman in a blue and white robe glowed with ethereal energy. Otto couldn't tell how powerful she was, but until he knew otherwise would assume the worst.

"Those are the proper authorities. Lower our sails and prepare to welcome them aboard."

Wainwright bellowed orders and soon the *Sea Star* had come to a virtual stop. The coast guard ships joined them ten minutes later. Since they had no ladder, ropes were tossed over the rail. Two at a time sailors came over the side and took up defensive positions. They didn't draw their cutlasses, but they did keep a close watch on Otto and the crew.

The last man over the rail was older than the rest though still spry enough to climb aboard. He wore blue and white with a gold insignia. He looked the ship over, his gaze finally settling on the captured pirates.

"Looks like we weren't your first visitors."

"No," Otto said. "These bunch claimed to be you, but it wasn't hard to determine they were lying. We took them into custody as a welcome gift. My name is Otto Shenk, chief advisor to Emperor Wolfric Von Garen."

Otto held out his hand and after a moment's hesitation the older man gripped his wrist and they shook.

"Captain Kendy of the Bandon City Coast Guard. I must admit given the way your enemy described you, I expected a fire-breathing monster."

Otto chuckled. "Eddred of Markane has a reputation as a less-than-effective ruler. In truth, he's a fool that rules only because Lord Valtan doesn't want the job. Naturally he would make us out to be monsters. The truth is, all we've ever wanted is peace. That our neighbors refused to give it to us can hardly be considered our fault."

"Sorting that out is beyond my area of expertise. My job is to guide you in and turn you over to the harbormaster. From there, it's up to the council and lord governor. Having spoken to your foe, I'm sure they'll want to hear your side of the story."

"Thank you, Captain. We put ourselves entirely in your hands." Otto indicated the pirates. "What would you like to do with them?"

"Unless you object, I'd like to leave them where they are then turn them over to the harbor patrol when we reach port."

"That would be perfectly satisfactory."

Captain Kendy shook his head and offered a rueful smile. "I was sure we'd have all kinds of trouble with you, but it seems the king of Markane has led me astray. I hope your visit to Bandon is a pleasant one."

"As do I, Captain. As do I."

When they finally tied up at the Bandon City docks and the slob of a pilot had taken his leave Corina turned to Otto and said, "You've been very polite and deferential. Like more than I've ever seen."

"I'm not in charge here," Otto said. "Never forget the goal. We need to convince them we're not a threat. If we accomplish nothing beyond showing them that helping Eddred isn't in their best interest, we're already halfway to the finish line. My father, while not much of a diplomat himself, did teach me and my brothers the basics of diplomacy. It's an essential skill for the nobility. Knowing where you are in the pecking order at all times is the key. Back home, I'm right near the top. Here, just the opposite."

"But you're just as strong here as you are at home," Corina said.

"Magically, certainly, but at home I have access to armies, wizards, magical armor and weapons, and the emperor's ear. I have none of that here. My army is you and six very skilled soldiers."

"This is all very complicated, Master."

Otto laughed. "Yes. It's a big world and the more of it you see, the less you realize you know. Just be on your best behavior and everything will be fine."

"Lord Shenk," Hans said from his place at the ship's rail. "We have people approaching."

"That will be the harbormaster and a patrol." Otto joined him just as an older man with a white beard approached along with nine soldiers in mail and armed with cutlasses. "Are you here to collect the pirates littering my deck?"

The harbormaster laughed. "They are. I'm here to collect whoever's in charge. The lord governor wants to hear your story as soon as possible."

"Well, I'm Otto Shenk and I'll be happy to speak with the lord governor right now. Or at least as soon as the pirates are safely taken off our hands."

The harbor patrol quickly gathered up the prisoners and led them off down the boardwalk. Once those pests were dealt with Otto strode down the gangplank with Hans and his men directly behind him.

The harbormaster raised a hand. "Only one person may speak for you. The rest will remain on your ship until you receive permission to leave. A second patrol will be keeping an eye on you, so don't do anything stupid."

Hans turned to Otto. "Lord Shenk?"

"You heard the man, back on board. This is, I assume, some sort of preliminary hearing so I hopefully won't be too long."

"Yes, my lord." Hans led the men back on board.

Corina waved and Otto set out behind the harbormaster. As they walked through the neighborhood near the docks, his gaze kept darting to the city's portal. The rune markings were identical to the ones at home, but the positions, aside from the master rune at the top, were different. Power still flowed to it, so reactivating and slaving it to the portal in Garen would be simple enough. But best not to put the cart before the horse.

Deeper into the city, they began to pass some examples of the constructs he'd read about. A steel horse with a crystal in its chest caught his eye. Fine veins of mithril ran from the gem, along its frame, and down to its limbs. Ether flowed through the mithril like blood through veins. Lord Colt had to have been a genius beyond compare to devise such things. It was an absolute pity he'd never meet the man.

"You're very quiet," the harbormaster said. "I figured you'd have all kinds of questions about the council and such."

"Can you tell me anything?" Otto asked.

"Not much beyond 'be honest and to the point.'"

"That was precisely my plan. I'm sure Eddred painted Garenland in a bad light. I hope I can give our side of the story and in so doing show we aren't Bandon's or anyone in Colt's Land's enemy."

They stopped in front of a tall stone building that looked a bit like a fortress. Four suits of armor like those he took from Lord Karonin's armory marched back and forth on either side of the entrance. They must have either been faster than the ones Otto used or they were there more for intimidation than combat.

The harbormaster went through the front door first and deposited Otto in a simple waiting room. There were no guards either inside the room or in front of the building. Two doors led deeper into the building and they both had ethereal locks on them. They were strong spells, but if he really wanted to, Otto could have blown them apart without expending a great deal of effort.

The wards at least explained the lack of guards. Unless you had the power to deal with the magical locks, you were stuck in this room anyway.

"Someone will be along to fetch you shortly," the harbormaster said. "I'd wish you luck, but from what Eddred said, I'm not sure I should."

"I appreciate your honesty."

The harbormaster left and Otto settled into one of the leather chairs. It was quite comfortable and he was happy to be somewhere that wasn't swaying. He allowed his body to relax a fraction, but his magical awareness never wavered. No one would be sneaking up on him today.

Happily no one tried anything and after a ten-minute wait, a young woman perhaps two years Otto's senior appeared through one of the locked doors. She wore a plain copper ring that glowed in the ether and allowed her to bypass the locks. Determining how the magic interwove would have been an interesting experiment, but now was not the time.

"They'll see you now," she said.

Otto stood and waved her forward. He followed his guide down an unadorned corridor that branched neither left nor right and ended at a second, open door. Beyond it waited a round table around which a varied group of men and women sat. The eldest of the group, a gray-haired woman that looked to be in her seventies, stood when he entered.

The servant closed the door behind him with an ominous thud. Otto scanned the room as the old woman facing him rose out of her chair. He sensed no hidden wizards or guards. The council members themselves were nothing special, at least magically speaking. Two of them had weak ethereal barriers that wouldn't stop him any more than the locks would have. Of course, he had no doubt that if he killed them all, a massive force would be waiting outside to repay him in kind.

Lucky for everyone then that he had no desire to start a second war.

Otto bowed. "Thank you for seeing me so quickly. Though I fear the long journey has left me not looking my best. My name is Otto Shenk, chief advisor to the emperor."

"I'm Helena, lord governor of Bandon." The old woman nodded a polite greeting. "You are younger than I would have expected for a chief advisor."

Otto offered a thin, humorless smile. "You're not the first to say so. I'm sure you have questions. Shall we begin?"

Helena sat back down. There were no chairs for guests so it appeared Otto would have to stand for his interview. A petty power play, but hardly surprising. He'd done similar things when interviewing the palace guards.

"Very well. Eddred of Markane has asked for our help in defeating your empire and restoring the former kingdoms to their rightful rulers. He claims you've committed horrible acts, slaughtering thousands, and wiping out any who dare stand against you. How do you answer his claims?"

"I plead guilty on all counts." The councilors all gasped at his reply. "My father taught me that if you fight, fight to win. Garenland didn't start the war. We were betrayed and attacked, surrounded by enemies on all sides. We used every weapon at our disposal to end the war quickly and with as few deaths on our side as possible."

There was a good deal of muttering now. The councilors were looking back and forth at each other, clearly at a loss.

"That is the point of a war, ladies and gentlemen. You fight to win. You kill as many of your enemies as possible as quickly as you can with the minimal number of losses to your own forces. I won't apologize for winning."

"Then you admit to wiping out the capital of Markane?" the lord governor asked.

"Yes. It was unfortunate that I was driven to such an extreme action, but Lord Valtan refused to see reason. Drastic measures were needed or we would've had nothing but endless attacks and interference. I offered him a peace treaty that left Markane unharmed and under Eddred's continued rule. Valtan refused. So I did what I had to do."

"You seem unfazed by wiping out an entire city," one of the councilors said, drawing a hard look from the lord governor.

"The loss of one city in exchange for the peace and safety of an entire continent. A simple, if unpleasant, calculation. Is there any other supposed crime I need to answer for or can we move on to other proposals?"

"What sort of proposals?" Helena asked. "I had assumed you came here to refute Eddred's claims and prevent us offering him aid."

"Eddred's claims are those of a loser desperate to be saved. Our nations are an ocean apart. We're not your enemies but there's no reason we can't be allies. Colt's Land and Etheria used to trade back in the days of the Arcane Lords. Why can't we do so again?"

"Only Valtan can reactivate the portals and won't do so

unless we agree to the terms of his compact," Helena said. "And that, all the city-states have agreed, we will not do."

"The situation has changed," Otto said. "I can reactivate your portals and add you to the regular rotation. All Garenland asks in return is—"

Helena raised her hand. "I will stop you there. This is not a matter our council can decide on its own. We must bring the issue before a gathering of the other cities through their representatives. Please return to your ship and await our summons."

"And the matter of Eddred and his military aid?" Otto asked.

"We never intended to provide any. Fighting another nation's war, in the absence of an immediate threat, isn't in Bandon's best interest. I wished to hear your words before telling you. I must admit, for one so young, you speak with wisdom befitting someone far older."

"The nobles of Garenland prepare their children for the real world, not the world as they might wish it to be." Otto didn't actually know if that was true, having met the late King Von Garen, but Otto's father had certainly made a point of beating reality into *his* head. "I will await your summons."

The door opened behind him and the servant girl guided him back outside. Instead of the harbormaster, a younger man in a blue and white uniform waited. He had the same gold insignia as the harbormaster only on the opposite shoulder.

"I'm to guide you back to your ship, my lord," the young man said. "My superior was called away on an urgent matter."

Otto didn't especially care who guided him back to the ship. In fact, his so-called guide was probably only there to make sure he didn't wander off without permission.

"After you then," Otto said.

The walk back followed exactly the same route and passed

with an equal lack of conversation. That suited Otto fine as he had a great deal to consider. Whatever pitch he made would have to be perfect if he wanted to convince all the cities to accept his offer to form a trade alliance and thus give him an excuse to come and go as he pleased while he searched for Lord Colt's workshop.

Back at the ship, his guide bowed again and hurried off. Otto climbed the gangplank and was greeted by an eager Corina and relieved Hans.

"They didn't clap you in irons," Hans said. "That's a good sign."

"How did it go?" Corina asked.

"Good, better than I feared certainly. The threat of them aiding Markane is gone. They're calling a meeting with the other cities' representatives where I'll have a chance to make my case for a trade arrangement. We're halfway to our destination."

Otto just needed to get them the rest of the way home.

CHAPTER 6

Paxton could hardly believe what he'd heard during the outlander's meeting with the city council. Not only did they have no intention of helping King Eddred, they were even considering making a deal with a murderer.

He stalked away from the small gallery that allowed high-ranking members of the city service to listen in on council meeting and made his way around to the front of the council building. One of his underlings, Lieutenant Gordon, stood waiting as instructed.

He saluted and asked, "You had a task for me, sir?"

"Yes. I need you to escort the outlander back to his ship. A matter has come to my attention and I won't be able to do it myself."

"No problem, sir." Gordon looked around then asked, "What do you think of them, sir? Two ships from across the ocean arriving within days of each other. I never imagined something so exciting happening in my lifetime."

"Ours is not to question, Lieutenant, but to follow the will of the council. Personally, I think they're all nothing but trouble." Paxton hated lying to the youthful officer, but if he gave any hint of his true feelings, they might betray his plans.

Paxton took his leave and hurried via a more direct route to the docks. To be safe, the harbor patrol had tied the foreign ships as far from each other as possible. He made his way directly to Eddred's vessel but when he arrived he saw no sign of the king.

"Can I be of help, Harbormaster?" Captain Carter asked from his position on the foredeck.

"I had news for King Eddred. Is he aboard?"

"I'm sorry, no. His Majesty is drowning his sorrows at a tavern called The Gull. I'd offer directions, but I'm sure you know the area better than I."

In fact Paxton knew exactly where to find the tavern. "Thank you for your help."

He waved and turned back the way he'd come. The Gull was only a block inland from the boardwalk and two minutes after he set out, Paxton arrived. He stepped inside and quickly spotted Eddred sitting by himself at a corner table. His ever-present bodyguards kept a watchful eye on him from another table twenty feet away. Two empty mugs sat on the table in front of Eddred and he held a third in his hand.

Paxton took a deep breath. What he was about to do would end his career and maybe his life. He owed Eddred nothing, yet his story of death and loss tugged at Paxton's heart. Steeling himself, he strode over to the king's table.

Eddred looked up with bleary eyes. "Paxton? What brings you here? Another summons from the council?"

"No, though I do have news. May I join you?"

Eddred indicated the seat opposite him with a disinterested wave. "They're not going to help me, are they?"

Paxton settled into his chair. "No. The council never had

any intention of sending soldiers to die on shores thousands of miles away. It's not in Bandon's best interest, they say."

"Of course it's not." Eddred took a long pull on his mug. "It was always a long shot. Thank you for coming to tell me."

"That's not the only reason I've come to speak with you. While I can't offer you an army, I can get you revenge." Paxton leaned forward. "What do you think about assassinating Otto Shenk?"

"I like the idea very much, but he's a powerful wizard. To have any hope of success, we'd need at least four to help Lilly and Adam. Can you round up that many wizards willing to kill a foreign dignitary?"

"No. In fact I can't muster a single wizard, though I can arrange for a squad of men loyal to me to lend a hand. I can also manage three guardian constructs assigned to the harbor patrol. Powerful or not, he's no match for steel men immune to fire, lightning, and just about any other sort of magic."

Eddred stared at him as if afraid to believe what he was hearing. "Why would you do this for me?"

"I lost my own wife some time ago so I understand your pain. If she had been killed the way yours was, I can't imagine how I would stand it. If I can do something to help you, I feel it is my duty to do so."

"Succeed or fail," Eddred said. "There will be no place for you or your men in Bandon. But there is a place for you on my ship if you want it."

Paxton held out his hand. "I accept, Your Majesty."

Eddred grasped his wrist in the Bandon way. "On the way home, we will drink to the death of Otto Shenk."

Otto sat in a cafe within sight of the ship and sipped a glass of white wine. A slight, salty breeze kept the worst of the summer heat at bay. They had received permission this morning to explore the city, bar a few sensitive locations. The harbormaster had delivered the news, along with the usual warnings that would only be needed by fools and children, with a sour grimace.

Clearly the old man had bought into Eddred's rhetoric and looked at the Garenlanders as the enemy. It was just lucky for Otto and his crew that the people actually in charge of the city didn't feel the same way. While the sailors wandered about the city, enjoying their shore leave, Otto preferred to keep close to the ship in case someone came with a summons. The sooner he completed his business with the council the better.

"When do you think they'll summon you?" Corina asked. She sat across from him, a glass of chilled tea in her hand.

"I hope within the next day or two. Once I say my piece, the various diplomats will have to contact their leaders, hopefully by magical means. Heaven help us if we need to wait for them to travel to and from their home cities. That will take months."

"Is there a rush?" she asked. "I mean, it's quite nice here. Other than the fact that I feel like everyone's watching every move I make."

"They are watching every move we make." Otto darted a quick look to his right and caught one of the harbor patrolmen assigned to them staring. The young man quickly looked away. "Bandon might not be an enemy, but that doesn't make them a friend. Whenever you're off the ship, watch what you say."

Corina stared over his left shoulder seemingly not paying attention. Annoyed, Otto was about to chastise her when she said, "Company coming, Master. Eddred and two wizards."

Otto craned his head enough to see a furious Eddred of Markane and his two bodyguards. The wizards didn't concern him. There was no way a wizard trained by Valtan would have broken through their personal barrier which meant they probably couldn't handle over a dozen threads each, not nearly enough to threaten him.

"I'll need a minute, Corina."

She favored him with a worried look then went to sit at a nearby empty table. Eddred and his companions stopped directly in front of Otto who looked up at them with bland disinterest.

"Give me one good reason not to kill you where you sit," Eddred said.

"Because if you tried, I'd have all the justification I need to defend myself and ship your severed head back to Wolfric for public display?"

Eddred's jaw bunched and his wizards tensed, the ether gathering around them as they prepared to defend their king. Otto didn't so much as lift a finger, though he did increase the power to the barrier that constantly surrounded him.

He refused to believe Eddred would be stupid enough to strike first in an effort he had to know would be futile. It would be wonderful if he did. Removing another irritant was always welcome.

Finally Eddred relaxed, just as Otto knew he would.

"Another time," Eddred said.

"Any time you like. And don't think these two weaklings will be enough to protect you."

Eddred glared down at him. "What do you want here? Isn't the continent enough for you?"

"My business in Colt's Land is largely commercial.

Convincing them not to help you was easy enough. Negotiating a trade deal will be considerably harder."

Eddred stared, aghast. "The council told you they didn't intend to help me? What did you offer them to convince them to stay out of the war?"

Otto laughed. "Nothing. They'd already decided not to help you before I showed up. Now, if you wish to talk more, sit down. I'm getting a crick in my neck from looking up at you. Otherwise, leave me alone. You're ruining my morning."

The look of pure rage and frustration on Eddred's face warmed Otto's heart. After a final glare, Eddred stalked off with his bodyguards in tow.

As soon as they were gone, Corina hurried back to join him. "Wow. You handled that really well. Weren't you afraid they'd attack?"

"In the middle of the city with the harbor patrol watching right over there? Not a chance. Eddred just wanted to bluster and blow off steam. Maybe now he'll go home, settle on one of the barrier islands, and lead a quiet life far from me."

"What do you think the odds of that are?"

Otto just shook his head and took another sip of his wine. The odds were so terrible they didn't bear consideration.

♋

"Lord Shenk?" Hans's voice calling from the entrance of his cabin woke Otto from a dead sleep. He'd been up late the night before speaking to Wolfric and Draken. Matters in the empire remained quiet, thank heaven, so there was no need to risk a trip back through the ether.

"What?" Otto asked.

"The harbormaster is here. He says the council is ready to hear your proposal."

"What time is it?" Otto rolled out of his hammock, conjured a light, and rubbed his eyes.

"Barely sunup, my lord."

Otto grumbled as he dressed. Whoever heard of anything happening this early in the government? Perhaps it was some sort of test to find out how he reacted to getting woken up and forced to speak without much preparation. No, that was ridiculous. More likely they figured it was going to be a long day so they might as well start early.

Dressed and with his sword belted on, Otto went up on deck. Corina and Hans's squad were ready to go.

The harbormaster, still scowling as he glared at everyone, locked gazes with Otto. "They only want you."

Hans was about to protest, more as a matter of professional annoyance than because he could have thought it would do any good. After all, as a bodyguard, it was hard for him to do his job if he was always getting left behind.

Otto raised a hand to stop him. "It's fine. I'm sure I don't need any protection walking from here to the council building."

"Even with him going along?" Corina pointed past the harbormaster and Otto finally noticed Eddred standing alone on the boardwalk.

"Yes, even with him going along. Why he's going along is another question."

"He's going along to try and convince the council not to go into business with a snake like you," the harbormaster said.

Hans went for his sword but Otto waved him off again.

"How, exactly, have I offended you?" Otto asked. "I don't

believe we've spoken more than a dozen words since I arrived, yet you seem to hate me."

"Eddred told me what you did and you didn't deny it when asked by the lord governor. As far as I'm concerned that makes you a mass murderer who should be hung from the nearest gallows."

Otto shook his head at the simplistic response. "Bad things happen in war. Innocents die. These truths are unfortunate, but undeniable. If you can't understand this simple fact, then you've clearly never been in a real war. You have my envy for that. I hope you never find yourself in a position where you have to make the choices I have. Now, let's not keep the council waiting."

At the base of the gangplank, Eddred fell in beside the harbormaster and both of them walked ahead of Otto toward the council building. The dawn light cast long shadows and made it impossible to see what hid in the alleys between buildings.

Otto considered the two men ahead of him and how much they both seemed to despise him. The possibility of an ambush, no matter how remote, couldn't be ruled out.

When they made a turn that wasn't on the familiar route, he loosed his mithril sword in its scabbard. Hopefully he was just being paranoid, but if he wasn't, they wouldn't find him an easy target.

A couple more minutes of walking brought them to a small, empty park cloaked in shadows. Eddred and the harbormaster broke off and hurried away from him. A trio of glowing blue eyes appeared and what he'd first taken to be decorative boulders straightened into humanoid constructs with blue crystals set in their chests. They carried no weapons but given that they were made from steel, their fists probably served as admirable maces.

"I'm assuming the lord governor and her council don't know about this," Otto said.

"No," Eddred said. "The leaders of Bandon refused to help me get justice for my people, but Paxton has proven a true friend, both to me and Markane. These devices are immune to most kinds of magic. Fire, lightning, poison, disease—your tricks will avail you nothing against them."

"And you think this will help you?" Otto asked. "Even if I die, the empire will endure. And I can't imagine your superiors will thank you for trying to kill someone they wanted to do business with."

The harbormaster shook his head. "They won't. But Eddred has kindly offered me a place at his side. Even at my age, the chance to do some good in the world is welcome. But enough talk. Kill him!"

The constructs took a step toward Otto.

He reached into the ether and sent streams of it out, wrapping their crystals and trying to cut them off from the ether. Ten threads each slowed them, but they kept coming.

Cursing Eddred and the universe in general, Otto shifted all his focus to the rightmost construct.

It stopped at once, but the other two picked up speed. Of course speed was relative and he had no trouble staying away from them.

Otto backed away from the approaching steel men, counting slowly in his head to five.

When he reached it, he released the magic and the construct he'd targeted went still.

Instantly he sent threads to wrap up the other two crystals.

Fifteen each did the trick and they stopped dead. This time

Otto counted to ten and released the spell. The constructs were all disconnected to the ether and wouldn't be functional until a wizard reactivated them.

Otto drew his mithril sword and turned to face Eddred and Paxton. "I spent the voyage studying your magic. Now, how would you two like to try and do your own dirty work?"

"Patrol!" Paxton shouted.

Ten men dressed in the familiar leather breastplates and carrying cutlasses came running from further up the street. Uther stood in the lead, his mail coat gleaming in the slowly brightening sunshine.

"Lord Shenk!" Hans, Corina, and the rest of the squad came sprinting from the other direction.

The soldiers formed a semicircle in front of him while Corina stood at his side.

"I sensed your magic from the ship," she said. "Only serious trouble would make you use that much ether."

"You were quite right." Otto gave her a reassuring pat on the head.

"This is getting out of hand," Paxton said. "Soldiers that don't answer to me will be coming soon. We have little time."

For his part, Otto was content to wait them out. Slaughtering patrolmen, even in self-defense, would do nothing to endear him to the powers that be.

"We need to end this now," Eddred said. "If the city-states ally with them, we'll have no hope of stopping Garenland."

"You'll have no hope of stopping them from a Bandon prison either. Alright, men, that's it. Anyone that wants to come with me, now's your chance. Anyone that wants to stay will have to take their chances with the council."

To a man, the patrolmen fell in behind Paxton. Uther held

his ground, glaring and gripping his hilt so tight his knuckles turned white.

"Uther! Enough," Eddred said. "They've won this round. If you stay and fight, you do it alone. We're leaving."

"Another time." Uther stalked off behind Eddred as the group made their way back toward the docks.

Otto followed them with his extended vision for six blocks with his magical sight before feeling satisfied that they didn't intend to come back.

"Fine timing, Hans. I doubt I could have ended that confrontation without violence had you not shown up when you did."

"Glad we made it in time, my lord." Hans sheathed his sword and the rest of the squad followed suit. "What now?"

"Now we continue on to the council building and see what they have to say about their harbormaster going rogue, assuming anyone is actually there at this unholy hour."

The rest of the walk was happily uneventful until they arrived. The appearance of an armed band got the attention of the soldiers manning the magical armor and they quickly moved to block the entrance.

"We received no word of your impending arrival," the guard on the right said, his voice echoing oddly from the armor's interior.

"I'm not surprised." Otto moved out from behind Hans and his men. "Your harbormaster came to summon me half an hour ago only to lead me into a trap. He's currently fleeing aboard Eddred of Markane's ship. If you hurry you might stop them."

The magical armor shifted as the two guards looked at each other. A moment later the one on the left took a knee and the rear of the armor opened up. A man not much older than Otto climbed down and ran inside.

Out of curiosity, Otto closed his eyes and sent his sight flying back toward the harbor. On Eddred's ship, some of the sailors were frantically getting the sails ready while others rushed to untie them from the dock. The wizards wove the ether and used a pair of heavy tentacles to push them away from the dock. Even if they hurried, there was no chance of the harbor patrol catching them. Assuming the commanders would even try given that the harbormaster was on board.

"Lord Shenk," Hans muttered.

Otto returned to his body just in time to see the guard emerging with the lord governor behind him.

"I was in early today, preparing for the conclave," she said. "A good thing I was. Paxton argued strongly against having anything to do with you, but I never imagined he'd go so far as to attempt an assassination on his own authority."

Otto shrugged. "Eddred can be surprisingly persuasive. He talked a former queen into betraying us and getting herself killed. I suppose it's not unreasonable to imagine him talking your harbormaster around. I assume the man has no family."

"No. I remember two years ago his wife died. There were no children as I recall."

The pieces suddenly fell into place for Otto. Eddred had lost his wife to the enchanted curse. No doubt the man played on Paxton's sympathies. A more clever and, one might even say, evil ploy than Otto would have credited him with.

"How long until the meeting?" Otto asked.

"I had it planned for noon. Given what happened, I'll allow you to keep your guards with you. There's a tavern not far from here if you'd like to wait there or you're free to return to your ship." The lord governor turned to the right-hand guard.

"When they return, give our guest no trouble about entering. Paxton has already made us look bad enough."

"Yes, ma'am." The guard raised his hand to his forehead, palm out.

"Until later then." She turned on her heel and marched inside. No doubt to give a chewing out to whoever Paxton answered to.

"What do you think, Hans, tavern or ship?"

"I don't know about you, my lord, but I could use a drink."

Otto nodded. "Tavern it is then."

○

Noon arrived and Otto found himself back in a now much more crowded council chamber. In addition to the lord governor and the Bandon city council, nine others had been jammed in around the table. Each of the new arrivals wore the finest silks and jewelry.

Despite the abundance of gold, silver, and gemstones, the one decoration missing and one Otto would have expected the rich and powerful to flaunt, was mithril. In a society founded by an Arcane Lord and one that had things as wondrous as the magical constructs that had tried to kill him that morning, it seemed impossible that no one wore mithril as a decoration. Yet there wasn't a bit of it to be found save for his sword.

The door closed behind him and the lord governor stood. "I would like to begin the conclave by apologizing for the behavior of my subordinate. Our former harbormaster was acting on his own initiative and without the knowledge of this council."

Otto offered a shallow bow. "That was my belief, but I

thank you for the apology. For myself, I'm content to put the matter behind us."

"That suits us as well. I've already provided the representatives a basic explanation of your offer, but why don't you make your pitch directly?"

"As you wish. The New Garen Empire's offer is simple, we will reactivate your portals and integrate you into the daily rotation so that you can travel between our cities and each other's instantly. We require free access to your markets and a one-gold-piece portal tax when you travel to one of our cities. All merchants on our side pay it as well so you will be at no competitive disadvantage. This covers our cost of maintaining the portals and paying the soldiers that guard them."

"And the restrictions on wizards Valtan demanded?" asked one of the diplomats, a middle-aged man with a scruff of white hair running around the base of his skull.

"Already done away with on our side, so they certainly won't be imposed on you. Our empire encourages wizards to become the best they can be to better contribute to our nation. Some may even want to travel here to learn from you."

That brought a few mutters, whether of surprise or concern he wasn't sure.

"Colt's Land is fully self sufficient," a shrewish-looking woman in black with a voice to match said. "What could you offer us that we don't already have?"

"That would be for the merchants to decide. Certainly it would be more efficient for you to trade amongst yourselves via portal rather than over land or by sea."

"Humor me," the shrew said. "You must have some specialties."

"Well..." Otto scratched his chin. "Garenland makes the finest steel weapons and armor. We also control the most productive mithril mines. Rolan produces quality grain and meat."

She raised a faintly trembling hand. "That's enough, thank you."

Otto looked around to see if there were more questions, but the diplomats were already talking amongst themselves. "Are there no other questions? I can return home and begin forging the patches to reactivate your portals as soon as you agree to our terms."

The lord governor stood. "We'll need some time to discuss your offer. Please return to your ship and await our reply."

Otto nodded. "Of course. I look forward to hearing good news."

The door opened behind him and he was guided out. Hans, Corina, and the others were waiting near the entrance where he'd left them.

Corina brightened as he approached. "Did they accept? When do we get started?"

"They're in discussions, but I'm not hopeful."

Her good mood dimmed. "Why? You're not really asking for much."

When they'd moved a little further away from the council building Otto said, "It's something to do with mithril. I saw it in their faces when I mentioned controlling the mine. They wear none of it for decoration and I saw none in their weapons. As far as I can tell, the people here only use it in their constructs."

"What does that mean?" Hans asked.

"It means they have a limited supply, probably carefully managed, and the idea of getting a large influx worries them." Otto shook his head in frustration. "What I thought would be my trump card may end up being what costs me the deal."

CHAPTER 7

Twenty-four hours after his meeting with the conclave of city-states, Otto was summoned back to the council building. Such a quick decision couldn't mean anything good for him. Still, he kept his face blank as he followed the same servant girl back to the council room.

The entire group was once more jammed in around the table and all of them were watching Otto as he entered. He looked back at them, trying to get a read on their position. As his gaze drifted over the assembly one person caught his eye. She had bronze skin, long black hair, and dark, sparkling eyes. Otto guessed her age at midtwenties. Not exactly a grizzled veteran of diplomacy.

It wasn't just her beauty that drew his attention. No, he felt certain she hadn't been here last time. One of the diplomats he'd spoken to must not have even cared enough to return to deliver their verdict. That pretty much told him all he needed to know about the results of the meeting.

When his gaze had lingered on her for a few seconds she

offered a faint grin and winked. Otto forced himself not to respond and shifted his attention back to the lord governor.

"You have your decision?" Otto asked.

"We do," the lord governor said. "While we have no quarrel with you or your new empire, we've decided not to accept your offer to activate the portals."

Otto nodded, not at all surprised. "May I ask why?"

"I prefer not to offer any details, but suffice it to say that such a decision can only be made by unanimous vote and some of the city-states had objections. Even one refusal would have been sufficient."

"Fair enough." Otto kept himself under perfect control. No hint of the rage and frustration boiling just under the surface reached his face. These fools could never know just how much self-control it took to stop him from killing them all. "What now?"

"We grant you three days to buy whatever supplies you need to make the journey home. Also, as a token of goodwill, I have rented you the finest suite at the best inn in the city. A small taste of comfort before you have to make the long trip across the ocean. The inn is called The Pearl and it's two blocks from the dock. You'll have no trouble finding it and they're expecting you." The lord governor stood. "I trust there are no hard feelings."

Otto forced himself to smile and bow. "None at all. Should you ever change your mind, please feel free to send a ship east. We would be delighted to host your delegation."

They looked at each other across the table and Otto felt certain each knew exactly what the other was thinking. She was relieved to see her problems sail away and he was disappointed but resigned. At least that's the feeling he was trying to convey with his expression.

"I'll take my leave then," Otto said. "We have a great deal of preparations to make for our departure."

The door opened behind him and he made the silent journey outside. Corina, Hans, and the others fell in around him as they made their way back to the ship. When they'd put three blocks between themselves and the council building and Otto was certain they weren't being followed he said, "We have three days to purchase whatever supplies we require before they kick us out. Before those three days are up, I need to figure out a way to return without being noticed."

"What about leaving one of your rune-marked coins outside the city?" Hans asked.

"I doubt they'll let us outside. There are a lot of wizards in this city and someone is bound to notice if I leave a mark in one of the inn's rooms." Otto shook his head. "I don't know."

"You'll think of something, Master." Corina spoke with such confidence she nearly convinced Otto himself.

Not only did he need to succeed to complete his mission, but he couldn't disappoint his apprentice as well.

♭

Eddred couldn't believe how badly he'd failed. In the distance, Bandon appeared as little more than the outline of a city. The ship had made good time escaping the harbor, with a little magical help from his bodyguards. As he'd hoped, the harbor patrol didn't want to do anything that might harm their former leader.

Speaking of Paxton, the ex-harbormaster sat slumped in the shade of the main mast. He looked as defeated as Eddred felt.

He went over and crouched beside Paxton. Eddred had

changed the course of the man's life forever. He had at least some responsibility to him now.

"Are you alright?" Eddred asked.

Paxton finally looked up at him, his expression bleak. "I gave up everything to right a wrong and failed miserably. I can never return to my home, and for what? Otto Shenk remains unharmed and free to do whatever he wants."

"Otto will answer for his many crimes. He escaped justice this time. He may escape it next time. But eventually, the evil men do catches up to them. His enemies only multiply. Difficult as it may be, we must stay patient and dedicated to the fight. I didn't offer you a place at my side only in gratitude. I think your help will make a difference in the war."

Paxton straightened a little. "Thank you, Your Majesty. I'll be ready when the time comes."

Eddred clapped him on the back. "Good man. Why don't you go downstairs and sleep? The journey home is a long one."

They rose and Eddred led the way belowdecks. He dropped Paxton off at the crew quarters. He could find himself a hammock. Right now, Eddred needed to contact Lord Valtan and let him know about this most recent failure.

In his cabin, Eddred retrieved the magic mirror Valtan had given him before they left. It was enchanted to allow Eddred to activate it without the help of a wizard. Not because they didn't trust Lilly and Adam, but in case he ever needed to make contact when no one was around to help him. The poor exhausted wizards had used up all their strength getting them out of the harbor and were both sound asleep in their bunks.

Eddred placed his finger on the mirror frame and soon a familiar warmth seeped into the metal. Most of five minutes passed before Valtan's grim face replaced Eddred's reflection.

"You failed," the wizard said without preamble.

"Yes. The people of Bandon have no desire to help us, nor do the rulers of the other city-states. If you can believe it, Otto Shenk is attempting to forge a trading compact with them."

Valtan's scowl deepened. "He probably wants to activate their portals to weaken me even more. We shall have to hope he fails."

"Hope is in very short supply here. What's our next move?"

"For now, return home. I will think more on our options."

"What about the assassins?" Eddred knew how Valtan felt about hired killers, but he had to ask at least once more.

"No. We risk becoming as evil as our enemies if we go down that path. I've seen too many once-honorable men fall to the darkness. There must be other options and I will find them."

Valtan severed the connection and Eddred sighed as he removed his finger. The Arcane Lord worried about doing evil, but Eddred worried that greater evil may be done if they refused to take drastic measures.

In the end, he had to accept that it was out of his control. Without Valtan's support, he had no way to gather the gold he needed. Eddred would just have to trust in the wisdom of a man far more experienced than him.

Hopefully Valtan would succeed. For the sake of the world, he'd better.

⟲

After a long afternoon of making arrangements with Captain Wainwright to ensure they would have all the food and supplies they'd need for the trip home, Otto was delighted at the prospect of a night sleeping on a real bed.

The Pearl was indeed easy to find. Painted off-white and

with a giant clam shell over the door, the inn was the only building on the block that stood three stories. The front doors were gilded and the windows clear and clean.

"Nice place," Corina said.

She, Hans, and his squad had escorted Otto to the hotel despite his reassurances that he would be fine. After the ambush, they seemed to have decided not to let him out of their collective sight. While he appreciated their concern, if they got too demanding, he'd have to remind everyone who was master here.

Inside, the common room was nearly full of people dressed in fine gowns and slick formal wear. They glanced at Otto's group and quickly looked away in disdain. Otto didn't blame them. A day of running around on the dock had done nothing for their appearance. They all needed baths in the worst way. Hopefully this fine place would be able to accommodate them.

They angled across the room toward the bar. Halfway there a skinny runt of a man intercepted them, waving his hands in distress.

"Who are you? Who are you?" he demanded. "Not just anyone can come in here, you know."

Hans moved to stop him, but Otto caught his arm before he could level the unlucky servant.

"My name is Otto Shenk. I believe the lord governor has arranged a room for me."

The little man's eyes nearly leapt out of his head. "Of course, I didn't recognize you at first. Follow me, follow me. All the arrangements have been made. Yes, they have. Our finest suite for the lord governor's guests. And two smaller rooms for his companions. Yes, yes, just as I was told. Everything's ready for you all. This way, this way."

The servant led them to an impressive, curved staircase. Up

they went to the third floor. It seemed the lord governor had rented the entire floor for their use. Otto's suite was in the center and the smaller rooms flanked it.

The servant pushed the central door open. The inside was mostly dark save for the light from a single window. When their guide turned away, Otto saw a flash of movement and the young woman from the council meeting that caught his eye walked through the light.

"I'll have hot water brought up for the bath, indeed I will. Hot water for everyone. That's just the thing."

"That will be fine, thank you." Otto nudged the servant back toward the stairs.

He took the hint and hurried away.

"We'll sweep the room," Hans said.

"I already checked it magically," Otto said. "And if anyone's hiding, I'll make them wish they weren't. Now, you lot sort out the other two rooms. Unless you hear screams, I want to be left alone until morning. Understood?"

Hans scowled but nodded. "As you wish, my lord."

Otto stepped inside and closed the door behind him. Next magical defenses settled around him and a sound barrier formed around the room.

"You can come out now," he said.

The young woman stepped into the light again. She had traded her formal diplomatic wear for a gown that would have made a two-copper whore blush. Slit up to the hip on both sides and cut so low that her considerable cleavage nearly spilled out, the red dress revealed more than it hid.

"I thought we might have a private conversation," she said, her voice a deep, throaty purr.

"Did you?" Otto conjured a light, revealing the entire room in all its nautical-themed glory.

She sat on the sea-foam-blue blankets, crossed her legs, flashing an expanse of smooth thigh, and patted the bed beside her. Whoever sent her must have thought he was the sort of fool that went empty-headed at the sight of a beautiful woman. Little did they know just how much experience Otto had dealing with pretty poison.

"I'm fine here, thank you. I assume your master sent you with a message. Let's hear it before the servants show up with a tub and hot water."

She stuck a bright red lower lip out in a charming pout. "You're going to hurt my feelings."

"I'll hurt more than that if you keep wasting my time. Now out with it."

"Fine, business it is." All signs of the playful sex kitten vanished in an instant, her face freezing in a hard, expressionless mask. "My master, as you put it, is the chief diplomat for the city-state of Audin. The conclave may have turned down your offer, but we would be interested in a private arrangement."

"Oh? I thought the conclave's decisions were final. After all, I'm to leave in two days. I doubt the powers that be in Bandon will have any interest in letting me go somewhere with you."

"You're quite right. If the conclave learned that I was here, I'd likely lose my head in short order." A hint of the playful smile returned. "My life is in your hands."

Otto didn't want to play. "Your life was in my hands the moment you snuck into my room. What's your offer?"

"I have none. A negotiation this dangerous is well above my level. If you wish to discuss the matter further, I will arrange for a ship to leave the city tomorrow. It will sail approximately three hundred miles due east. Well beyond the range of the coast guard patrols. You can transfer aboard and the captain will bring you to Audin. Our lord governor will then discuss an arrangement with you personally."

"Just me?" Otto asked.

"You may bring two others, your apprentice and one guard. That's all. Bring too many and one of the diplomats in Audin will be likely to spot you, and if that happens, well, let's just say it will be bad for my city."

Otto nodded. If they were willing to risk defying the will of the conclave, the lord governor of Audin must be serious. Given Otto's complete lack of other ideas, he was inclined to accept.

"Agreed. With one condition."

"Anything within reason."

"I want you on the ship."

Her sultry smile returned full force. "I'm flattered. It is a long journey and I don't blame you for wanting some entertainment."

"You misunderstand. I want you aboard because if this is a trap, you'll be the first one I kill." That murdered her smile permanently.

∽

The next day, as barrels and bundles of various supplies were being loaded onto the *Sea Star*, Otto couldn't help watching every ship that left port and wondering if that would be the one he was to meet. He had informed Hans and Corina that they would be making a side trip and after a bit of complaining, they had accepted his decision.

Not that they had much of a choice. He was going and they certainly weren't going to stop him. This might be his last chance to get access to Colt's Workshop and no way was he going to miss it. And the truth was Otto would have preferred to go alone. If things went sideways, he could always escape into the ether. With Corina and Hans along, if he fled, he'd be leaving them to almost certain death. That wasn't a result he considered acceptable.

Corina joined him at his place by the rail. She watched a schooner sail out of the harbor in silence then asked, "What do you think the other city will be like?"

Otto glanced down at her. She'd been very patient about not demanding lessons since they arrived. He hadn't had time and was grateful she understood what he needed.

"Much like this one I assume. Hotter, I suspect. When we got back this morning I checked the atlas in my room. Audin is several thousand miles to the southwest. The trip will take at least a month. Maybe during that time I can teach you the Far Seer spell."

Her smile nearly split her face. "Really? I didn't think I was strong enough yet."

"You won't be able to extend your vision very far, but I think practicing the basics wouldn't be a bad idea. If nothing else, such a complex spell will build up your stamina. Just be sure not to exhaust yourself. Our position is going to be a tricky one and if we have to move quickly, you'll need to be able."

"I won't overdo it, I promise."

"Good. Be sure to pack only necessities. Nothing you're not willing to leave behind if we need to escape."

"I'm already set."

Otto nodded and turned away from the dock. There was no way of knowing which ship they'd meet and guessing would do him no good. Better not to worry about it.

The next two days passed in a haze of activity. The lord

governor never called for a final word and if a new harbor-master had been assigned, Otto saw no sign of them. When the time came to leave, Jameson came aboard once more and guided them out of the harbor with the same coast guard ship shadowing them.

Twenty miles out, Jameson transferred over to his ship and they were on their own.

Otto joined Captain Wainwright at the helm. "Keep a course dead east of the city. It'll probably take most of a day if not more to reach our rendezvous."

"As you say." The captain cleared his throat and asked, "Any orders for us after you depart?"

"I left the charts with you. Head back to Lux and tie up at the dock. You're free to enjoy yourselves in port until I'm ready for the next leg of the journey."

"May I ask where we're going next?"

Otto couldn't see any harm in telling him. He'd done a thorough study of the man's thoughts and found no sign of betrayal. The good captain was exactly what he appeared, a sailor trying to make a living. Working for the Crown was certainly the best way to assure that.

"The Celestial Empire," Otto said at last.

"Heaven above! No one's made that trip in centuries, even longer than the last journey to Colt's Land. Are there even charts mapping out the route?"

"There are. I found a logbook from a captain that made the trip a decade after the portals were shut down. It sounded quite arduous, but he survived and made it back to Markane, so it is possible. Unfortunately, he was turned away at the border, but that's a problem for after we arrive."

"If I make that journey, I'll be a legend among the captains."

Wainwright wore a broad smile and Otto felt even more confident that he'd do nothing to upset the plan.

"I'm glad you're excited. If you make it back to Lux before we return, be sure and send a message to Garen and let the emperor know we're making progress."

Wainwright frowned. "You think you might reach the continent before us?"

"If this works out the way I hope, we should be returning by portal, so there's every possibility. Don't worry about it either way. Just send the message. Even if we're back it will do no harm."

Otto left the captain to his seamanship and retreated below deck. He needed to decide what to take and what to leave. Several of the magical items he brought from home were quite valuable and risking them on what might be a trap seemed unwise. He just had to decide whether having no way to check in on Wolfric was even less wise.

⌒

The next day seemed to drag on forever. Otto stood on the forecastle and stared out over the ocean. He didn't know what it was about waiting that made time seem to slow, but it never failed. It was the same when the cook baked the first apple pie of the year back in Shenk Barony. He could almost smell the sweet treat as he thought back.

"Sail on the horizon!" the lookout called. "Three points off the starboard bow."

Finally.

Just to be sure it wasn't another pirate trying their luck, Otto extended his sight for a closer look. The caravel had three masts and most of its sails furled. He swooped down closer to the deck and quickly spotted the woman that had contacted him back at the inn. She stood out like a rose amid the weeds. Almost literally since she'd changed into a practical red blouse and tan pants.

None of the sailors around her showed any sign of preparing for a fight. He spotted a wizard standing near the center of the ship, but she didn't appear to be preparing any magic.

Satisfied that he wasn't sailing into a battle, Otto blinked and turned toward the helm. "That's them. Bring us alongside. Hans! Get our luggage up on deck."

Hans saluted and hurried down the stairs. Otto had settled on the very minimum he thought he'd need. That didn't include the communication mirror. He'd alerted Wolfric the night before that he would be out of contact for a while. The emperor had simply waved a hand and smiled, assuring Otto that he had every confidence that he'd manage on his own. Hopefully the run of peace wouldn't destroy everyone's focus.

Otto shook his head. The empire would have to manage without him. Acquiring the chamber was all that mattered for the moment.

An hour, along with some careful maneuvering, saw them tied up with the Audin ship. The diplomat stood at the rail, a bright smile revealing perfect teeth. "Welcome. You had no trouble finding us?"

"We just sailed east as you said." Otto frowned. "You know, you never gave your name when we last spoke."

"So I didn't. I'm Renna, assistant diplomat for the city-state of Audin. Please come aboard. We have a long way to go and my lord is eager to meet you."

Otto introduced Hans and Corina and the three of them

crossed over to the Audin ship. Ten minutes after that, the two ships went their separate ways.

As the Audin ship unfurled its sails and turned south Renna said, "I'm afraid this is an actual merchant ship with a load of cargo bound for Audin, so the quarters will be tight. You'll be bunking with the crew who have strict instructions to ask no questions about you or your business. In fact it would be best if you didn't talk to them at all. The less they know the better for everyone."

"Do you fear a spy?" Otto asked.

"Not especially, but what we're doing could well start a war if we're found out. Audin would as soon avoid that, at least until we're ready."

Renna guided them toward the stairs that led below deck. She walked with the easy rolling gait of a sailor. Clearly this wasn't her first trip by boat.

At the bottom of the stairs, they went toward the front of the boat where a cramped room filled with swaying hammocks waited. Beneath each hammock sat an iron strongbox.

"I warned you it would be tight. Any hammock with an unlocked box is yours for the taking. May as well get comfortable. The trip usually takes three weeks with favorable winds."

She left them to settle in.

"This isn't nice at all," Corina said as she looked around in distaste.

"It's better than my first post." Hans set about searching for three hammocks close together.

"We'll sleep in shifts just to be safe. I'll take the early morning hours." Otto scowled but made no complaints. After all, no one said the path to immortality would be a comfortable one.

CHAPTER 8

Otto stood at the ship's rail watching Audin City grow larger in the distance. It took them twenty-two days to make the trip, a tedious and uncomfortable but otherwise tolerable journey. Otto had no complaints save for the heat. This far south, even on the water, the heat felt oppressive, especially for a northerner like Otto.

He'd gained very little new information during the journey. During his occasional conversations with Renna, the woman talked a lot while saying almost nothing of importance. The one time he'd asked her straight out what Audin wanted, she had said it wasn't her place to discuss such matters. He hadn't asked again. Most likely she simply didn't know anything.

Soon they were close enough that Otto could make out the city's portal along with several towers that nearly rivaled it in height. Most of the buildings looked taller than those in Bandon. Did the city have a larger population or did they simply prefer to build up rather than out?

In the end, Otto couldn't have cared less. He'd been so bored, any little question to occupy his mind was welcome.

A soft cough from behind him prompted Otto to turn around. Renna had snuck up on him. His focus must really be out of whack if that happened. She'd changed from her practical sailor outfit to a fine, pale-blue dress, cut in a far more conservative style than the one she'd worn to his room when they first met.

"Is there a problem?" he asked.

"There is. You're on deck. You need to stay below until tonight. Someone from the other city-states is always watching the harbor. We really don't want them to learn you're here instead of a quarter of the way home."

Otto grunted. He wasn't anxious to return to the close, stale confines of the hold. But like it or not she had a point. Secrecy was truly necessary, so he'd play along. He was breaking the council's decree by coming here after all.

"Fine, I'll await your summons below."

Otto made his way back to the crew quarters and found Hans and Corina engrossed in a game of cards. They'd been playing a lot, anything to help pass the time. The crew had made it clear they didn't appreciate amateurs trying to help so this was what they'd settled on.

"We're almost there," he said, drawing a startled look from Corina. He couldn't chastise her for her lack of awareness since he'd just been snuck up on as well. "Renna says we need to remain here until nightfall."

"What time is it?" Hans asked.

"Midmorning."

"Want to sit in for a hand?" Hans asked.

"No, thank you. And try not to hook Corina on the game. Bad enough your squad mates can't help starting a match whenever we stay still for ten minutes."

"But they're always ready to fight when the time comes," Hans countered.

Otto wouldn't argue that. He'd never met a finer group of soldiers. He didn't even care all that much about the cards. He was just in a foul mood and felt like complaining. Noble prerogative and all that. Rather than pestering the only two people he fully trusted on this ship, he settled into his hammock and closed his eyes. Maybe a quick nap would soothe his sour disposition.

He hadn't actually expected to fall asleep, but the next thing he knew was the sound of the hull hitting the dock with a dull thunk. Hans and Corina had quit their game and taken up position near the door. An ethereal glow surrounded Corina's eyes.

"Release that spell, now!"

She gave a shake and the glow vanished. "Master?"

"We don't want anyone knowing there are wizards aboard. If any of the spies can see the ether, they'll realize something's up." Otto rolled out of his hammock and popped his back. "It's not your fault. I should have warned you not to use magic, at least not until we're off the ship and somewhere safe. Speaking of which, how long ago did we arrive?"

"Not long," Hans said. "They just finished tying up and are beginning to unload."

Otto nodded. They probably had another ten hours of waiting. Fantastic.

He drew his sword, checked the edge, and found it as perfect as the day Edwyn gave it to him. He couldn't even kill time sharpening it. All he'd do was wear down the whetstone.

Hours passed like days until finally a knock sounded on the door.

"It's clear," Renna said, her voice muffled by the wood.

"Thank heaven." Otto opened the door and found the diplomat dressed in a black cloak with a deep cowl, currently lowered. She held three more just like it out for them.

Otto and his companions shrugged the bulky cloaks on and shouldered their packs. They followed Renna up on deck and when she pulled her hood up they followed suit.

"Now for the tricky part," Renna said.

"Do you fear more spies?" Otto looked left and right as if he might find them hiding nearby.

"No, the spies left an hour ago. Our agents followed them back to their various embassies. I'm more worried about wizards."

How did an assistant diplomat assigned to a distant city-state know about Audin's agents?

That was a question for anther time.

"Don't be," Otto said. "Anyone trying to watch us magically will quickly regret it. I know a trick or two to dissuade that sort of behavior, some that leave the watcher alive, others that don't. Do you have a preference?"

"If you have to strike, leave no one alive to report it."

Otto nodded, swallowing a smile. After three weeks on that miserable ship, he really hoped someone gave him an excuse to lash out. Nothing like killing a spy to make you feel better.

◯

The journey across Audin took less than half an hour. Otto kept all his magical senses focused, but he sensed no watchers peering through the ether. Nor did he sense anyone extending their sight, which would have done them little good anyway given the darkness and the hoods he and his companions wore. On a more mundane level, no thieves or other opportunists presented themselves for slaughter.

As soon as they reached a large, fortress-looking building surrounded by a high wall, Renna took a small object from inside her cloak and flashed a bright blue light twice. A moment later the sally port in the gate opened and they hurried inside.

Once they cleared the door she threw back her hood and grinned. "We made it. For the moment at least we're safe. I'm sure the three of you are looking forward to a good night's sleep on a real bed after nothing but hammocks for most of a month, but the lord governor requested I bring you to meet him the moment we arrived. I pray you'll indulge me."

Otto debated with himself about how much diplomacy he had in him given his current exhausted state, but in the end he couldn't exactly start a new alliance by offending his potential partner. Hopefully it would be a quick hello then off to bed.

"Of course. I'm at the lord governor's service."

"Excellent, this way please." Renna led them to the keep.

When they were fifteen feet out, the heavy double doors swung open on their own. The interior was lit by blue crystals that could have been made in Lux. A long hall ran straight into the heart of the fortress. They passed a handful of closed doors before reaching an intersection and taking a right. That quickly brought them to a flight of stairs.

At the fourth-floor landing, Renna opened a door that led to a sprawling office. A single person waited inside behind a desk so big that it might have doubled as a bed. The man, Otto assumed he was the lord governor, had a thick mustache that connected to mutton-chop sideburns, a bald head, and a vast stomach covered by a blue silk robe.

He rose and moved to stand in front of his desk on legs that looked far too small to hold up his bulk. Otto led the way over and held out his hand. They shook, grasping at the wrist as seemed to be the habit in Colt's Land.

"Welcome, welcome. I'm Lord Governor August Audin. Terribly happy to have you here. Renna and her superiors tell me good things about you and what you can offer my city."

"Otto Shenk and the pleasure is mine. I'm sure we'll be able to come up with a deal that will benefit us both."

"Excellent! That's what I like to hear. But I'm sure you and your friends are tired. Please, rest and refresh yourselves. We can begin proper negotiations tomorrow, perhaps starting with lunch?"

"I look forward to it, Governor Audin." Otto bowed.

"No need for all that. Please, call me August. And may I call you Otto?"

It seemed the governor wanted to go the "new best friends" route. Otto could play along with that. "Certainly. I've never been overly interested in formality, only results."

"A man after my own heart. Renna, show them to the guest suite we prepared, the one without windows. Mustn't have anyone catching a glimpse of our guest."

"As you say, Lord Governor." Renna gestured toward the door and led them back to the staircase.

At the third level, they entered another hall lit by blue crystals. Unlike the one downstairs, this hall had portraits of men that very much resembled August hanging at regular intervals. Renna stopped at the third door in from the landing.

"Here we are." She opened it and waved them through.

Their suite consisted of five rooms, all lit by more of the crystals. There was the main sitting room, three bedrooms, and a garderobe. All the furniture was of the finest quality, fine enough that it wouldn't have looked out of place in Franken Manor.

"Wow," Corina said, her eyes wide.

"Servants will bring hot water shortly," Renna said. "They have no idea who you really are so please don't tell them. I'll fetch you at noon for lunch."

She started to leave and Otto followed her to the door. "I couldn't help noticing that the lord governor has the same name as the city. I assume that's not a coincidence."

"You don't miss a thing. He's actually a direct descendant of the founder chosen by Lord Colt himself to rule the city. We also have no city council. All decisions are made by the lord governor."

"That will simplify negotiations anyway. See you in the morning."

Renna left and when the door had closed Hans asked, "Do we set a guard or do we trust them?"

"We're in a city surrounded by thousands of potential enemies. If we don't trust them, it's far too late to do anything about it now."

○

The lunch spread put out by the lord governor would have satisfied Edwyn and that was saying something. Ten different dishes crowded a round table set up in a room of August's office. Four different kinds of meat prepared in various fashions filled the air with a savory aroma. Having eaten little beyond ship's rations, Otto was happy to indulge himself.

Otto and August were the only ones present. It was an act of good faith on both their sides to meet one on one. Hans and

Corina had gone with one of the servants to get a meal somewhere else. Otto was confident they'd be fine, for the time
being at least.

When he'd finished a bowl of spicy red stew Otto sighed
and said, "That was delicious, thank you."

"Not at all," August said. "Just a sample of local favorites. If
you're ready, we can begin preliminary discussions."

"By all means. I assume my suggestion of activating your
portal and trading with our empire is why I'm here, correct?"

"Not exactly."

Otto cocked his head, surprised. "Oh?"

"I'm only interested in mithril. We have everything else we
need. Is there something else we can offer you in exchange for
a supply of the metal?"

This was it. Time to put his cards on the table. "There is
something I want. Do you know where I can find Colt's
Workshop?"

"Yes, but it's taboo. No one goes there."

Otto smiled. "Surely you don't believe in curses and ghosts.
I've seen plenty of magical things, but never either of those."

"It's not taboo because of a curse, but because anyone that's
ever entered the place hasn't returned. After Lord Colt's death,
scores of expeditions were launched as different city-states
sought to gather the Arcane Lord's secrets and increase their
power. Audin sent three teams of highly skilled magical engineers backed up by squads of our best soldiers. All lost. We
ended up worse off than when we started, the same as
everyone else."

"Be that as it may, I need to go there." Otto leaned across
the table to make sure August understood he was serious. "I'm
not asking for help, only access. Your people can remain
outside while I collect what I came for. I will need something I

can use to transport it back to the portal. In exchange, I'll give you a wagonload of mithril ore. You'll have to process it yourself."

"How many pounds?" August asked.

"I don't know exactly. At least a ton of raw ore, probably two hundred pounds of pure mithril."

August whistled. "Unbelievable. With that much mithril our arcane engineers could nearly double our force of knights."

Otto's confusion must have shown on his face because August asked, "Would you like to visit the armory?"

"I'd love to."

↶

What August called the armory was housed in a huge stone building attached to the government fortress. Three stories tall and a hundred yards long, built from massive stone blocks two feet thick, the armory would have made a fine castle in its own right. The only entrance was a pair of double doors twenty paces wide and thirty feet tall. Luckily the right-hand door had a human-sized sally port that allowed easy access to the interior.

When August knocked, a slit opened, snapped shut, and the door instantly opened.

"Lord Governor." A young man in a crimson tunic, armed with a short, wide-bladed sword offered a hasty salute. "We weren't informed you were paying a visit."

"Are you implying I need to alert you if I wish to tour my own armory?" August's tone was hard and unforgiving. Otto hadn't heard him use it before. It certainly made him sound more like a ruler than the jovial tone he'd used with Otto.

"No, sir." The guard hastened to add, "I just meant we could have had the head engineer ready to answer any questions you might have."

August grunted. "Where is she, anyway? I want to introduce Otto to our esteemed head of magical engineering."

The guard smiled, seeming relieved to have evaded punishment. "Where else? She's tinkering with one of the Mark Vs."

"Has she gotten it working?"

The young man's smile turned glum. "Not yet. Though she's assured anyone that will listen that she's close."

"She's told everyone that for a year and a half and still nothing. My new friend may have the solution to her problem."

August led the way inside and Otto followed. He didn't fully understand the magical discipline Lord Colt had named magical engineering. He did grasp the fundamentals. Basically it involved combining magic and mechanical objects like the armor Hans and his men had used to such good effect during the war. Beyond that, the details escaped him. Certainly the idea that he would be able to solve anyone's problems was laughable. Perhaps the chief engineer could offer some clarity.

Beyond the door was a long line of slots that reached from floor to ceiling. Ten of them held magical armor of the same size as those Otto found. Twelve more held smaller units that would barely encase a man like plate armor. Six beyond them held armor that towered nearly three times the height of the ones he found. Each of those massive suits looked like it was capable of bringing down a castle on its own. And the final two suits were bigger yet, but also sleeker and less bulky, like a race horse compared to a draft horse. All of the large units were positioned on one knee to allow access to the interior.

Four teams of three wizards worked on different units along with non-wizard assistants. Everyone that noticed them passing paused and saluted. August ignored them and kept going to the sleek units. They stopped in front of the left-hand suit. The chest was open and a pair of legs was sticking out.

"Illsa!" August said. "Get out here, there's someone I want you to meet."

The legs wiggled around until a surprisingly young woman with some black substance covering her forehead and slicking back her hair fell out and landed with a thud on her ass in front of them. She peered at them through glasses that made her eyes look ten times their normal size.

"Lord Governor?" Illsa asked as though not entirely sure who she was looking at.

"Illsa. Still at it I see."

"I'm close, I swear. If you'd just let me scrap one of the Mark IVs I'd have all the mithril I need to complete the connections."

"For the last time, no. If anything happens on the frontier and we need to replace a damaged suit, we can't be caught short."

"Fine." She turned her magnified gaze on Otto. "Who are you again?"

"Otto Shenk. Your magical armor is very impressive. All we have back home are the medium-sized units and for some reason ours use purple crystals, not blue."

"Wow! That's a really old style. We haven't used life crystals in centuries." She belatedly noticed Otto's frown and hurried to add, "Not that they don't work just fine, it's just, you know, you have to kill a bunch of people to make them activate. We've learned to connect the blue ones directly to the ether, bypassing the use of mortal life force. We can also recharge them in an emergency so you're not limited to eight hours of runtime."

"Interesting," Otto said and he meant it. "How do you connect the crystal to the ether directly?"

"Basically you charge it with streams of ether until the crystal matrix is fully charged, then you create a link to the ether itself." She spun her finger around. "Like a constant loop pulling power in. The life crystals are designed to create the connection automatically so a wizard not trained in magical engineering can use them."

"It seems like that would be a long process," Otto said.

"Oh, it would take days for a single wizard to empower a crystal, that's why we work in teams of six, each wizard perfectly matching the ethereal flow to the others. That sort of control takes years to develop and not all wizards can do it."

"If that's the case, you seem rather young to be the head magical engineer."

"Illsa is a genius," August said. "She was only fifteen when she developed the basic concepts for the Mark V units. Unfortunately, we lack the mithril to bring her designs to life. You see, Otto, there are no mithril mines in Colt's Land. None of the metal exists on the entire continent."

Otto glanced around the armory. "Then where did all this come from?"

"Lord Colt, of course. Every year he would bring each city-state twenty pounds of pure mithril mined in Etheria. Every city got the same amount so the balance was always maintained. Since his death, the lord governors have been obsessed with maintaining that balance. That's why your generous offer was declined. Free trade with your empire would be an invitation to upsetting the balance."

"You don't seem concerned about upsetting the balance," Otto pointed out.

"I'm sick of being one among ten." August spat the words

out with surprising venom. "I want to be first among ten. We have the finest magical engineers in Colt's Land. If we had the resources we needed, every other city would have to acknowledge our greatness."

So August was ambitious. Otto respected that and even better, he could use it. "Clearly you have more courage than the other lord governors. No one else even reached out to me for a private meeting. The people of Garenland are warriors and we respect courage. We also respect talent, which you and your people clearly have in excess. I'd be honored to provide you with the mithril you need."

Illsa perked up at this. "You have mithril? How much and what purity? I need at least ten pounds at 98.5% purity to make the Mark V work. How soon can you have it here?"

Otto turned to August who said, "We're still working out the details, Illsa. You can go back to work. Rest assured, as soon as Otto brings us the mithril, you'll have first choice."

She clapped her hands like a little kid offered a favorite sweet and clambered back into the suit.

August led the way back toward the entrance. As they walked he said, "You must forgive Illsa. She's very passionate about her work, but somewhat lacking in social skills."

"There's nothing to forgive," Otto said. "I have the utmost respect for anyone that feels that strongly about their work. People like her drive our understanding of what's possible forward. I'd be delighted to talk with her again sometime, not that I imagine I'd understand half of what she said."

When they reached the door Otto snapped around. He would have sworn he felt an unfriendly gaze on his back. All the magical engineers and their helpers were busy at their posts and not paying the least attention to Otto or August.

"Is everything alright?" August asked.

Otto finally turned back. "Yes. Just my overactive paranoia. I guess I've spent too much time hunting assassins and other rogues."

"No need to worry." August led the way through the sally port. "You have nothing to fear here."

The walk back to August's office took only a few minutes and they were soon seated in their respective places at the huge desk.

"Your armory was very impressive," Otto said. "I can see why you want access to more mithril. I can't imagine what Illsa will dream up with two hundred pounds to work with."

"So you're willing to trade with us?"

"Of course, assuming you're willing to guide me to Colt's Workshop and help transport the artifact back to Audin so I can send it through the portal."

"If you're determined, I can lend a patrol to guide you, but my people won't set foot inside the workshop."

"Agreed. The only question now is, how will we hide the portal's activation? Assuming you want to keep our business secret from your fellow lord governors."

For a change August was the one confused. "I'm not sure I understand."

"The portal gives off magical bursts like lightning when activated. At night it would be visible from anywhere in the city. There's no way the diplomats won't notice."

"That is a problem. If anyone learns we have more mithril than them, it could encourage an invasion from multiple enemy forces. If that happens before we're ready..." August shook his head and smiled. "Why are these things always so complicated? I'll arrange for my most trusted magical engineers to work on the problem. How soon can you activate the portal?"

THE CHAMBER OF ETERNITY

"I need to return to my own workshop and prepare a patch. That shouldn't take more than two weeks. When I return, I'll activate the portal and give you, say, half the raw mithril as a sign of good faith. Once I have the artifact I seek and have returned safely home with it, you can have the other half. Deal?"

August thrust his hand out, they grasped wrists, and shook. "Deal. When will you leave?"

"I need to speak with my companions then I'll depart."

"Once we complete our business, deactivating the portal again will pose no difficulty?"

"None. As far as anyone looking will know, the portal will appear exactly the same as before." Otto took a breath and let it out slowly. Time to take another risk. "I feel the city of Audin and the New Garen Empire would benefit greatly from continued trade. I understand your desire not to have a magical backdoor into your city, but if you're willing, I think setting up a way for you to contact me in the event you desire further exchanges might not be a bad idea."

August nodded. "I'll consider it. Good enough?"

"Good enough." Otto had baited the hook, whether August bit or not was out of his hands. "I have preparations to make. If you'll excuse me."

Otto stood, offered a polite bow, and took his leave. It would be a relief to return home and sleep in his own bed. Hans and Corina could keep an eye on things here. Since they all wanted the same thing, the danger should be minimal.

Renna left her small office and made her way back to the lord governor's office. She'd been eavesdropping on their conversation and now her lord sought her opinion of their new ally. She found him seated behind his sprawling desk, a tumbler of amber liquid in his hand. He looked at her over the rim of the glass, his dark eyes hard and narrow.

"What do you think?" he asked. "Will he keep his word?"

"I believe so, my lord," she said. "Otto has done nothing to indicate an ulterior motive. At least nothing I've seen. I suspect he wants exactly what he claims and is willing to pay for it."

The lord governor took a sip of his drink. "Anyone willing to part with a huge quantity of mithril just for access to Colt's Workshop must know something we don't. Given the fate of our expeditions, I can't imagine them succeeding. But if they do…"

"They may bring out something amazing," Renna finished for him. Hunger and greed gleamed in his eyes. That was the danger with Lord Audin. If there was anything of value to be had, he wanted it for himself regardless of the danger.

"We need more information," he said. "Earn Otto's trust and find out exactly what he's after. That is supposed to be your specialty."

Renna swallowed. Information gathering was her primary talent, but from what she'd seen, Otto wouldn't succumb to her usual tricks. On the trip here, he made no effort to take her to bed despite her making it clear that she was perfectly willing to join him. If she couldn't use sex to influence him, that would make her job far more difficult.

"I'll do my best, of course, but I suspect he may be a tough nut to crack."

"Then get a bigger hammer. We need to know more so we

can make plans to claim whatever treasure he finds, assuming his group even survives whatever dangers lurk in the workshop."

Renna bowed. There was no arguing with him when he was in a mood like this. "If there's nothing else, my lord."

He waved her away and Renna took her leave. As she made her way back to her own much more modest quarters, she tried to think how best to acquire the information Lord Audin wanted without angering the volatile young wizard.

Loyal as she was to Audin, she had no intention of getting herself killed for his greed.

CHAPTER 9

Otto inscribed a rune mark on the floor of his bedroom in the guest suite they'd been provided and gave Hans and Corina instructions to follow during his absence. Basically don't do anything stupid and generally mind their manners until he got back.

They were largely unnecessary, but he felt a certain responsibility for the companions he was leaving behind. Even if the risks were minimal, they weren't zero. The most important thing was to avoid giving away any information on his true plans and the artifact he wanted from Colt's Workshop. Not that either of them knew anything beyond his ultimate destination. Still, why take chances?

When he'd done all he could, Otto became one with the ether and willed himself back to Franken Manor. Over such a long distance, sensing the energy from his rune took a moment, but soon enough he found what he sought and an instant later he emerged from the walk-in closet. A quick look around made it clear his arrival had gone unnoticed. Not surprising given that it was pitch black out. By his calculations, it was after midnight here.

Otto stretched and yawned. The stress of the past few months had left him exhausted. A good night's sleep would see him ready to begin forging the patch. Luckily he had ten spare sheets of mithril in his basement workshop.

He stripped off his sword and clothes and climbed into bed.

It seemed no time had passed and the sun was stabbing him in the eyes and urging him to wake up. A quick washup and change of clothes had him feeling like a new man. Sword firmly back at his side, he set out.

Barely a step from his door, a piercing wail filled the air. He grimaced. Not having to listen to the squalling brat was one of the only good things about the past four months. Whatever, he wouldn't be able to hear it downstairs anyway.

Otto marched on, rounded a corner toward the stairs, and froze. His mother was pacing in the hall, a screeching Abby held in her arms. She was dressed in a simple gray housecoat and facing away from him.

After recovering from his surprise Otto said, "Mother? What are you doing here?"

She turned and frowned at him. "I came to help look after your daughter, which is more than you seem willing or able to do. What are you thinking, leaving Annamaria on her own to raise Abby? Don't you want to be a better father than Arnwolf?"

Otto swallowed a retort. If he simply avoided beating Abby on a regular basis he'd already be better than his father. "Annamaria has whatever help she needs. There are dozens of servants around here and if she needs more Edwyn has more than enough money to hire them. I have more important things to do than worry about Abby's feeding and fussing."

His mother shook her head and Abby finally quieted. "I'm ashamed of you, Otto. Of all my sons, I thought you would be the best father. Granted, being a better father than Stephan wouldn't be much of a challenge and Axel appears married to the army, but the point stands. You need to do better."

He spotted Mimi approaching from behind his mother. "Mimi, come here and take Abby. Mother and I need to have a talk."

She paled, no doubt understanding exactly what that discussion would be about. Luckily for her, she didn't hesitate to obey his order. His mother reluctantly handed Abby over and they started toward the stairs.

"Have you eaten?" she asked. "You look awfully thin. And when did you arrive? Annamaria said you were on a long journey for the emperor."

"I returned via magic last night. There's something I need to do before I return to Colt's Land."

Her eyes went wide. "You crossed the ocean? What's it like?"

"The ocean? Wet and boring. Or did you mean Colt's Land? That is a tangle of city-states, politics, and maneuvering. They have no desire to trade with us long term, so my primary objective failed. Happily I've made a deal to complete the second half of my mission, which is why I'm back for the moment. But that's not what I wanted to talk to you about."

They reached the bottom of the stairs and turned toward the dining room. A single girl in a black servant's uniform stood waiting.

"Eggs, bacon, toast, and wine," Otto said.

She hurried out the door to the kitchen. That should give them enough time alone. Just to be sure, when they'd sat side by side, Otto wove a spell of silence around them.

"The truth, Mother, is that Abby isn't my daughter."

His mother opened her mouth to speak and he raised a hand.

"Let me tell you the whole story then you can ask me what you will. Okay?"

She nodded and Otto proceeded to relate everything that had happened since he met Annamaria for the first time. He did edit out the part where he and Wolfric arranged the king's assassination, but other than that he told her every detail.

When he finished Otto said, "Annamaria is an old friend of the emperor's and heaven only knows what would happen to her father should he learn the truth. For now, it's best that we keep playing along. I couldn't care less what happens to Annamaria or the child, but I very much want to keep things in the empire on an even keel. If I have to swallow my pride to do that, so be it."

For a moment Mother stared up at the second floor then she sighed. "I had grown quite fond of Abby over the past few weeks. Having a granddaughter to fuss over was lovely. I'm so sorry she put you through this, Otto."

He shrugged. "No one ever said an arranged marriage would be easy. Frankly, I have better things to do than waste my time worrying about her. As for Abby, feel free to fuss all you like. You playing the doting grandmother will help sell the lie."

She smiled, a thin, humorless expression. "I see your father's cynicism has taken a firm grasp on you. Very well, I'll play along rather than denouncing her for the whore she is. I'm not keen to return to Shenk Barony before I have to anyway."

"What's happening?"

His mother's answer was cut off by the return of a pair of

servants laden with platters piled high with the items he'd ordered. Even with Edwyn still asleep, the cook clearly had no idea how to cook a normal-sized portion of food. There were a dozen fried eggs, half a loaf of toast, and a full side of fried bacon. The servants poured them wine and resumed their place at the wall in case he needed anything else, like a priest to heal him after eating so much food.

They fixed their plates and Otto took a sip of wine before turning back to his mother. "You were saying about trouble at home?"

"Oh, it's nothing important, just your father and Stephan arguing about what to do with your wedding gift. Stephan wants to fancy up the keep and Arnwolf wants to save for a rainy day. The continuous shouting matches were giving me headaches, so I decided to visit the capital."

Otto relaxed and set to eating. If it was only Father and Stephan fighting, he had nothing to worry about. They argued often enough when there wasn't a huge chest of double eagles to spur them on.

When they finished breakfast Otto stood. "It was wonderful talking with you, Mother, but I really do have work that requires my attention. If you'll excuse me."

"Of course, dear. Just be sure to say goodbye before you leave again."

Otto smiled, maybe the first genuine smile he'd shown in months. "Promise."

With that he headed for his workshop. He had a lot to do and the sooner he finished, the better.

"This is so boring." Corina tilted her head back over the side of the couch until she could see Hans. "I feel like a prisoner, not a guest."

Hans grunted and turned away from the game of solitaire he had laid out on the dinner table. "Patience is a soldier's best virtue. As long as no one is trying to kill you, it's a good day. Try and relax. Didn't Lord Shenk leave some exercises to do while he was gone?"

"Yes, but I can only do them for fifteen minutes at a time then I have to rest three hours. And it's not exactly challenging. I just infuse as much ether into my body as possible and hold it until I feel like I'm going to burst. He said it was like lifting weights for fighters."

Hans nodded and returned to his game.

Corina frowned, rolled off the couch, and bounced to her feet. She adjusted her black and gold war wizard's robe and marched over to Hans. "Do you even know what he's planning? He wouldn't give me any details."

"All I know is we're supposed to fetch some magical thing. Apparently he needs the locals' help to get it. That's all I know and I had to piece that together on my own." He put the cards down and looked up at her. "The thing with nobles and Lord Shenk in particular, is that they expect you to do what they say. If they decide to explain things, it's a bonus. He's actually pretty good compared to some of the nobility I've dealt with."

"But I'm his apprentice for heaven's sake. How can I help if I don't know what's going on?"

"Maybe there's nothing for you to do anyway. Come on, take a seat and we'll play a few hands."

"Fine." She dropped into the chair opposite him.

Before the first card could fly, someone knocked.

"Saved!" Corina leapt to her feet and hurried over. Outside, Renna stood waiting in a lovely, light-blue dress. She was so pretty Corina could hardly compare with her scrawny figure. "Hi. You know my master's gone, right?"

"I do," Renna said. "I thought perhaps the two of you would like a tour of the city."

Hans tossed down his cards and joined them by the door. "I thought us being here was real hush-hush. Walking around the city doesn't seem like a good idea."

"We can arrange disguises, like the cloaks you wore from the ship."

"We were seen by the lord governor and her guards," Hans pointed out. "The local diplomats from Bandon might have our descriptions. I admit the odds of trouble are small if we're disguised, but Lord Shenk wouldn't want us doing anything that might risk the mission."

Corina slumped. Hans was right, curse him. Her master would be most upset if he found out she'd put his project, whatever it really was, in jeopardy. "He's right. Thanks anyway."

"Your loyalty is admirable," Renna said. "Perhaps a compromise. There's a training yard between the armory and administrative buildings. A little fresh air and exercise might help with the boredom."

Corina snapped an eager look at Hans who shrugged, smiled, and said, "I guess it couldn't hurt."

Renna led them out a side door into a tramped-down dirt clearing with six archery targets fixed to hay bales on one side and a training circle in the center. No soldiers were currently practicing which explained why they'd been brought here. The practice ground was well hidden by the compound's wall so there was no chance of them being seen.

"Where are the bows?" Corina asked. "I haven't shot one in ages."

"You good with a bow?" Hans asked.

"Better than you I bet." Corina grinned and stretched her fingers. Finally something fun. "What do you say, old man, best out of ten wins?"

"What does the winner get?" Hans asked.

"Bragging rights."

"And the loser?"

"The loser has to ask Lord Shenk what we're really doing here." Corina couldn't believe she'd just suggested that. The truth was, she doubted either of them had nerve enough to ask her master that particular question.

"We'll see." Hans took a bow and quiver from Renna who had retrieved them from a storage building while they talked. "You can have the first shot."

"Ha!" Corina bent her bow, strung it, and nocked an arrow. "You'll regret that."

༄

Hans yawned and looked up at the ceiling. Corina had surprised him with her archery skill. He'd beaten her, but only by two points. He'd never live that one down when she told the guys. At the very least it was good to see the girl smiling. Lord Shenk might be a good teacher, but he could be distant and hard. It was probably a noble thing. Most of them held others at arm's length. Easier to keep secrets that way.

And he had no doubt that Lord Shenk kept more secrets than most. It was unavoidable considering he was both a wizard and chief advisor to the emperor. Hans suspected he'd never get used to thinking of Wolfric as emperor. He remembered when Wolfric was a boy barely big enough to sit on a pony and now he ruled an entire continent. Strange times indeed.

He was about to pull the covers up and go to sleep when he noticed smoke coming from under the door. Didn't smell like smoke. In fact he couldn't smell it at all.

Hans leapt out of bed and ran to the door in nothing but his nightclothes. He snatched up his sword, paused, checked the door handle, and found it cool.

Definitely not a fire then.

The room wavered around him and his vision blurred at the edges as he pushed the bedroom door open. In the main room, three figures dressed in black and wearing masks stood holding wooden clubs. A fourth emerged from Corina's room with the girl over his shoulder.

Hans took a step toward them and tried to shout.

No sound emerged and his knees buckled, his strength gone.

Through the haze he barely saw two shapes come to stand over him.

"What do you want to do with the bodyguard?" one of the intruders asked.

"Leave him," the other said. "Two prisoners is one more than we need."

That was the last thing Hans heard before the room went black.

༄

Corina woke to the worst headache she'd ever experienced. It felt like her brain was trying to smash its way out of her skull with a hammer. The blows came in time with her pulse which was racing. She took slow, deep breaths until she'd calmed a bit then opened her eyes a crack.

Everything was blurry, but what little she could make out didn't resemble her room and the pain in her back, which she only noticed since the headache had faded a fraction, indicated she was sitting on something much harder than her feather bed.

She tried to rub her eyes, but her arm refused to move. In her fuzzy mental state, it took a moment for her to realize she was manacled to the chair and not paralyzed. That was actually a relief, though she couldn't help wondering why she was bound to a hard chair and how she ended up here.

There was movement to her right as an indistinct figure approached. Corina blinked a few times and that helped her see better. Of course all she saw was a person in black wearing a mask that resembled images she'd seen in Lord Shenk's books of the Reaper.

Her stomach dropped and her heart sped up again.

Stop!

She couldn't panic. Whatever was going on, she'd have a better chance of getting out of it alive if she kept her head.

"Awake at last," the figure in black said.

She groaned, trying to buy time and make him think she was in worse shape than she really was. Corina tried to reach for the ether but found her mind too muddled to focus.

"The knock-out powder we used on you and your friend has some unpleasant aftereffects, but rest assured they are temporary. That said, you may notice that you can't work magic at the moment. That's because we've dosed you with an experimental alchemical substance that blocks the portion of the mind that controls the ether. We're reasonably certain that the effects of that are temporary as well."

Corina hardly noticed when he moved closer, looming over her. All she could think was that she might never wield magic again, never feel the Bliss again. It was too horrible to contemplate.

"Hey!"

She flinched at his shout.

"I need you to focus on me. See, one thing I can guarantee is that if you refuse to tell us what we want to know, your death won't be temporary."

She sneered at him. As if death was a worse threat than never touching the ether again. "When my master finds out you've taken me, your death will be permanent and not at all quick."

"Interesting. Your master is exactly what we want to talk about. You will tell us everything he's planning with that arrogant pile of filth August. All we know for certain is that he's planning to trade some mithril for something. How much mithril is he bringing and what does he want in exchange?"

Corina laughed. What were the odds she'd be questioned on the exact subject she and Hans had been debating the day before.

"You find some humor in your situation?" the masked interrogator asked.

"No, it's just I have no idea what the answer to either of your questions is. My master only tells me and Hans what we need to know when he thinks we need to know it. I'd be surprised if even Emperor Wolfric knows the full extent of his plans."

Hard, narrow eyes stared at her through slits in the mask. At last he said, "You really don't know, do you? Your master is certainly not a very trusting fellow. He must have little faith in you."

Corina sighed and looked away. "I think he has little faith in humanity in general. After all, what I don't know I can't reveal, no matter what you do to me."

"No, I suppose you can't, can you. That is unfortunate. We can't allow Audin to gain access to a source of mithril. It would ruin the balance between the city-states and invite chaos. I fear we'll have to eliminate your master before he can bring the mithril here. I assume he'll transport it through the portal, so at least we know where to set our trap."

Corina shook her head. "You wouldn't be the first to try and kill him. Everyone else that has is either dead or on the run. Lord Shenk is the most powerful wizard in the world right now and the least willing to show restraint to anyone that dares challenge him. If you want to die, I recommend leaping from the city wall, it will be less painful than what he'll do to you."

"You have great confidence in your master. Appropriate for an apprentice." The masked man stared at her until she grew uncomfortable. "Maybe we don't need to set a trap at the portal. We already have the perfect bait right here."

"I suggest you release me and pray to whatever angel or demon you favor that I can convince him to let the matter drop."

Corina didn't care where they set their trap or what they used as bait, Lord Shenk would kill them all and if she didn't survive the encounter, well, there were other wizards for him to train. She did like to imagine he would at least feel bad about losing her.

enna left her room and made her way back to the guest suite where her current assignment had been placed. With Otto gone home to prepare whatever magic he needed to reactivate the portal, Renna figured her best bet would be to work on his companions. Subtlety, obviously, would be key. Coming right out and asking would only increase their suspicion. Hans especially seemed the cautious sort.

He'd quickly shot down her suggestion of seeing the city yesterday for fear of risking his master's plans. She couldn't imagine what Otto had done to secure such loyalty. The girl might be a better target. Young, bored, and eager to impress, she might let something slip just to show off how much she knew.

Renna froze the instant she came within sight of the suite's door. The two guards she'd left outside were unconscious or dead, slumped on the floor outside. The door was wide open.

The dagger she kept hidden at the small of her back was in her hand before she was conscious of drawing it. On silent feet she made her way to the door. A quick peek inside revealed Hans lying unconscious on the floor dressed in nothing but his smallclothes, a sword lying on the floor beside him.

She bent and checked the pulse of her guards. Both were alive. Hopefully Hans and Corina were as well. If Otto came back and found his retainers dead, he'd never trust them.

Inside, she checked Hans and let out a breath of relief. He was alive, thank heaven. When she shook him, he didn't so much as twitch. Whatever had been done put him out cold. Leaving him where he lay, she went to Corina's room.

There was no sign of the girl.

Renna shook her head in disbelief. This couldn't be happening. The administrative building was the most secure place in the city. The gates were sealed at night and no one could enter from the outside.

She frowned, sheathed her dagger, and swept out of the room. No one could get in from the outside, but maybe someone from the inside had opened the way. She didn't like to think any of the employees would betray Audin, but it was impossible to deny reality. Nothing else made sense.

At a near run she made her way down to the front gate. Even as she strode across the grounds she saw that they were open. A group had gathered as if uncertain what they should be doing. The magical armor towered over them, huge, intimidating, and useless now that the damage was done.

Everyone turned as she approached. "What happened?"

They parted to reveal the night watchmen. Both men were sitting in the dirt, heads in their hands.

"Look at me!" When the watchmen finally craned their necks up to face her she repeated her question.

"Last thing I remember was Miles coming to the gate in a panic. He said he forgot something important in the armory and couldn't we let him in. He said he'd only be a minute. When we looked away, he threw some kind of powder in our faces and the next thing I know the morning shift is shaking me awake and the gate is unlocked."

"Who's Miles?"

"One of the assistants at the armory. Nice guy. Always chats on his way out at night. Whatever he needed, he must have needed it badly."

Renna ignored the fool and ran for the main building. They kept records on everyone that worked here. Miles would have a folder with all his contact information. Her people would have vetted it as well, so at least the address should be accurate.

If she didn't want to lose what little trust she'd gained with

Otto's team, she needed to have information as soon as Hans woke up. Anything less would be an invitation to disaster.

☽

Hans came slowly awake. Someone was shaking his shoulder and it felt like he was lying on the floor. How did he end up here? Like a flash of lightning the previous night's events came back to him. The intruders and…

"Corina!" He sat up and found himself face to face with Renna. "Where?"

"She's gone," Renna said. "As best we can tell, one of the assistants in the armory was a spy. He opened the gate for them after knocking out the guards."

Hans staggered to his feet and put a hand to his throbbing head. "Have to find her. If anything happens, Lord Shenk will kill me."

"He can't hold you responsible for the actions of others."

Hans snorted. He only had one job while Lord Shenk was gone: keep Corina out of trouble. Now she'd been kidnapped and taken heaven only knew where to have heaven only knew what done to her. The worst part was she didn't know anything.

"We know where the spy was living. If you want to join me and the guards when we go hunting, you're welcome. Though I recommend putting on pants."

Hans finally remembered that he'd gone out in his night-clothes. Horrified, he hurried back to his bedroom, washed some of the grogginess from his eyes, dressed, and returned to the living area. It was only when he emerged with a clear head that he noticed Renna had dressed in tight-fitting trousers and top and that she had a short sword at her waist and daggers sticking out of the tops of both boots.

"I thought you were a diplomat."

"I wasn't entirely honest with you when we first met. I was attached to the ambassador corps in Bandon because there were some questions about the ambassador's loyalty. I'm actually a member of Audin's secret police. I was assigned to keep you and your companions safe. The lord governor wasn't pleased when I brought him the news."

"So both our necks are on the line." Hans followed her out of the administrative building and into the street where a squad of ten guards waited.

It was later in the day than he'd expected. The drug must have really knocked him for a loop. One of the guards held an extra cloak which he handed to Hans.

When he'd slung it over his shoulders Renna nodded and said, "Good, you look like just another guardsman. Luckily the suspect's flat isn't far from here."

"I assume he lives alone," Hans said as the group set out down the street.

"No, according to the logbook he has a wife. Whether he has an actual wife or an accomplice, we'll find out soon enough."

The streets were quiet considering the late hour. Most people had probably already arrived at their workplaces. That was ideal since it would make it impossible for the spy to escape in a crowd. It had been a long time since Hans had gone on a mission without Lord Shenk's magic to rely on. Hopefully he remembered how to work as a normal soldier.

"Did you bring any wizards?" Hans asked.

Renna shook her head. "We're trying to keep this quiet. If

word got out that some of our magical engineers had been reassigned, it would only alert anyone paying attention."

She had a point, but he still would've liked to bring at least one wizard for backup. He'd discovered that if you wanted to take a prisoner, magic made that much easier.

Ten minutes after setting out, they stopped in front of a three-story stone rooming house. It had a slate roof, white shutters, and appeared well taken care of.

"Sergeant, take five men and circle the building," Renna said. It took Hans a second to realize she wasn't talking to him. "The rest of us will go inside."

The oldest man in the group, his chin whiskers shot through with gray, saluted in the odd, palm-out, fingertips-to-forehead style and led his chosen guards away. Renna took the rest of them right through the front door.

Inside was a common room with a nook that held a napping old woman. Behind her was a wall covered with boxes, some with keys dangling below them and others holding rolled-up scrolls. Renna stalked up to the counter and slammed her fist down.

The old woman sat up, snorted, and looked around as if not certain where she was. Hans could sympathize. His head had only now stopped throbbing in time to his pulse.

Finally the old woman focused on Renna. "How can I help, Guardswoman?"

"We're looking for one of your tenants, Miles Stand. Is he or his wife home? If not, we'll need access to their flat."

The proprietress blinked at them then shrugged. "I have no idea if he or his wife are home." She reached under the counter then handed them an iron key. "That's the master key. It'll open any door in the place. Miles lives on the second floor, unit three. It's on your right at the top of the steps.

When you're finished, please put the key back on the counter."

With that pronouncement, she leaned back in her chair and was soon snoring again. It would seem she wasn't overly concerned about her tenant's privacy. Then again, when armed guardsmen showed up at your boarding house, arguing with them was a good way to end up in trouble.

They found the staircase and hurried up to the second floor. The door to unit three was closed and Hans heard nothing from behind it. Renna gave Hans a pointed look. "Weapons ready. But remember, we want him alive."

Hans drew his sword and the rest of the guards followed his lead. Renna used the key then eased the door open. The hinges shrieked horribly. Clearly maintenance on the inside wasn't as big a focus as taking care of the outside. Unless he'd intentionally let the hinges rust so they'd make noise.

There were no shouts or other signs of movement.

Hans lunged through the door and found the living area devoid of occupants. There was a single bed, a chest of drawers, a night stand, and a four-panel privacy barrier. The entire room measured around twenty yards square. There were no other rooms.

"Looks like we struck out." Hans sheathed his sword.

"Finding anyone home was a long shot," Renna said. "My hope is that Miles wasn't as thorough hiding his plans as he was escaping. Tear this place apart."

The group went to work. Hans took the bed, pulling the cover and sheets off before flipping the mattress.

Nothing.

The chest of drawers turned out to be totally empty as was the single drawer on the nightstand. From behind the privacy screen, one of the guards said, "I found something."

He came out with a garbage bin in one hand and a small, brown pouch in the other. The pouch had a symbol on it that looked like a pipe with smoke coming out in the shape of a dragon.

Renna took the pouch, sniffed it, and grimaced. "Pipe weed, a nasty variety as well. It would seem our man is a smoker. Interesting, but it doesn't help us find him."

"Ma'am?" one of the guards said. "That's a dragon weed pouch. My cousin smokes and is always complaining that it's expensive since only one shop in the city sells it. If we keep watch…"

"Then eventually he'll show up for a refill." Renna grinned. "Good work. Clean this mess up and let's go."

Relief at finding a lead warred with concern in Hans's mind. It could take days to catch the spy and that was if they were lucky. Heaven only knew what would happen to Corina in the meantime.

CHAPTER 10

I t took three days of watching, but finally Miles put in an appearance to feed his pipe weed habit. Those three days of waiting were among the longest of Hans's life. He dearly hoped Corina was okay. Much as he liked the girl, he really worried about what Lord Shenk might do if he returned and found a body instead of an apprentice waiting for him.

Hans was watching the shop from the common room of a tavern across the way along with a team of five guardsmen dressed in civilian clothes. Renna and another five were watching the rear of the shop which had a small door that allowed for deliveries. It was doubtful that anyone would show up there looking to buy, but they weren't taking any chances.

"Get in position," Hans said. "I'll go out the back and let the second team know."

The guardsmen pushed away from the table they shared, tossed four silver coins to cover the tab, and went outside. Hans crossed the common room and went out the rear. The men had orders to follow Miles back to wherever the spy was holed up. They'd take turns, switching on and off in the hope that he didn't notice and make a run for it.

It was a risk and, frankly, Hans would have preferred to snatch him off the street, take him to a dark room somewhere, and beat the information out of him. But this wasn't his city or his call. He had to trust that Renna and her people knew their business. His even being involved in the mission was a courtesy. They'd order him back to the government building the moment he caused trouble.

He stepped out into an alley and double-timed it around the block to the shopping area where Renna and her team were waiting. He spotted her quickly at an antique dealer's table and angled that way. At the very least, the beautiful woman stood out in a crowd.

She spotted him coming and smiled as though meeting an old friend. "How good to see you again."

When she kissed his cheek Hans whispered, "He showed. The others are in position."

"Excellent." She caught the eye of one of her people and made two subtle hand gestures. "Now all we have to do is let him lead us to our lost lamb."

Hans dearly hoped it would be that simple. The second group left the open-air shopping district and made their way to a street one block over from the tobacco shop. As planned, one of the first group was waiting.

The guardsman nodded in lieu of a salute. "He emerged a few seconds ago and turned north giving no sign that he was aware of our pursuit."

"Good. Return to your team. We'll trail you from this side. Remind them I expect regular reports."

Another nod and the guardsman left them to follow on their own.

"I don't like this," Hans said. "If Miles gets a whiff of us on his trail or we lose him—"

"You've made your feelings on this matter perfectly clear," Renna said. "It's my decision and it's the right one. Have faith. My people are the best at this sort of mission."

Hans swallowed his concerns and they set out to the north. Every five minutes a different guardsman would show up with an update and they'd shift direction, moving two streets east at one point then back to the west two streets. There seemed to be no rhyme or reason to his course.

After fifteen minutes Renna said, "He's trying to figure out if someone's following him. I'd hoped we were dealing with someone good at infiltration only, but it seems evasion was part of his training as well."

"So what do we do?" Hans asked. Everything was falling apart. If the spy escaped and knew they were on to him, his fellows were apt to kill Corina and dump her body in the harbor.

"We do what we've been doing. Miles can only circle the blocks so many times. Unless my people make a mistake, which they won't, he'll take us where we want to go eventually."

Hans ground his teeth in frustration. Making a conscious effort to relax, he took a deep breath and slowly released it. The game continued for another half an hour, but finally a guardsman came and said, "He just went into a dry goods shop. We have it surrounded."

Renna grinned. "Finally. Lead the way. When the full team is assembled we'll swoop in and grab them."

Hans felt some of the tension go out of him. The stupid spy games were over. Now it was time to fight. And if he knew how to do one thing, it was fight.

Hold on kid, we're coming.

Corina's head was killing her. First they'd force-fed her some nasty concoction they said was a truth potion. Under its effects she told them exactly what she knew about her master and his plans, which was basically nothing beyond the fact that he wanted access to some place called Colt's Workshop and an artifact therein. Next they tried slapping her around and trying to beat the information out of her. Since it wasn't there, that did them no good either. They seemed to know that and were mostly taking their frustrations out on her.

Now she found herself with her hands tied behind her back, sitting in a hard-backed chair in the dark waiting for whatever they planned to do with her next. In the dark room time meant nothing. She could have been there for hours or days for all she knew. Even worse, they kept her dosed with some other stuff that kept her from focusing on her magic. She felt helpless and useless and it made her angry.

The door to her cell opened and the light nearly blinded her. A masked man, the same one that questioned her she assumed, entered with a plate of bread and water, the second of her twice-daily meals.

He seldom said a word outside of questioning her. Silently he walked over and held out the bread. She took a small bite then a sip of water. So it went, bite, sip, bite, sip until the food was gone.

"Do you need the bucket?" he asked.

"Yes, badly."

He grabbed her arm and guided her over to the room's only

other piece of furniture, a two-gallon wooden bucket. Corina hovered over it and sighed with relief.

She was almost done when a second person appeared in the doorway. "Miles is back at the secondary location."

"Did he catch any hounds?" her captor asked.

Corina was done, but she kept quiet, hoping to learn something useful.

"We don't know yet. At the very least, no one obvious was following him."

"Any activity at the portal yet?"

"Nothing. How are we going to set a trap when we don't know when he's coming?" the second man asked.

"Hopefully he'll come after our bait and we won't have to." Her captor jerked her away from the bucket and half dragged her back to the chair. "Anything you'd like to tell us that would convince us to let you go?"

Corina just shook her head. Even if she knew anything, she wouldn't betray her master.

"Fine. Sit here in the dark and keep quiet then."

The two men left and closed the door, plunging her into absolute darkness. She hoped when Lord Shenk finished with them, at least one was still alive so she could show them what it felt like to live in the dark.

ᴑ

Hans said he was going in with the first group and no one even tried to argue with him. Just as well since it wouldn't have done any good. His duty was clear and short of tying him up, nothing would stop him from saving Corina.

Three guardsmen joined him and they snuck closer to the front door of the dry goods store. There was no business and nothing moved either inside the building or within sight of it. To the left of the entrance was a stack of burlap sacks labeled "beans." He leaned down and picked up two that had fallen out. The red outer shell crumbled between his fingers. If this was a business, it hadn't been operating in a long time.

His gut twisted with familiar fear and anticipation. They were certainly walking into a trap. Hans might have wished for mail and a shield, but he wasn't going to get either.

A quick glance at the man behind him drew a nod.

They were as ready as they'd ever be.

Hans took two steps to the right and kicked the door open.

The flimsy board smashed to pieces. He was through before the last chunk of shattered wood hit the ground.

Inside, the shelves were empty and there was no sign of Miles.

The team fanned out in a sweep from front to back. At the rear of the main room was a door that probably led to storage.

Hans kicked that one open as well.

It was pitch black. One of the guards pulled out a glowing crystal that revealed an open trapdoor and a ladder that descended into a tunnel.

"Son of a bitch!" Hans wanted to scream but he kept the curse to a hoarse whisper. "It was a setup. He led us here to see if he was being followed."

"Do we chase after him?" a guard asked.

"Of course we do."

Hans put one foot on the ladder and it collapsed into the shaft. Only strong hands grabbing him by the arm and shoulder kept him from ending up in a heap with the broken wood.

"Then again, maybe not." Hans dusted himself off and blew out a breath. "We're done here. Let's join up with the others."

It was a short walk to the rear of the building where they found Renna and her team with Miles in custody.

Hans stared, drawing a laugh from Renna. "I spread my men out and what should pop up but a little mole. We're going to have a long talk with this little mole."

She smiled down at Miles, who cowered.

"Tell us where she is," Hans said. "And save yourself some pain."

"I don't know, I swear. As soon as I left, they moved her."

Hans watched his face and as soon as he stopped talking punched him in the gut. "Liar. I'm going to ask you once more and if you lie again, I'm going to show you all the interrogation techniques I've learned over the last twenty years. Don't worry, none of them will kill you, just leave you wishing you were dead. My favorite is driving sharpened needles of wood under your fingernails then prying them off one by one."

Miles was practically whimpering now. "If I tell you, you have to promise to protect me. There's no way I can go back home."

"Of course we'll protect you," Renna said, swooping in front of Hans as if to shield the spy. "There's a nice, quiet country estate where people that help the government spend the rest of their lives in comfort. It's very peaceful, I swear."

She was good. Hans actually believed every word she said. Maybe it was true. Hell, he didn't care one way or the other as long as they got the kid back in one piece. What Lord Shenk might do when he returned was another matter altogether.

"Okay, they're holding her in a basement room under an iron foundry called The Works."

Renna nodded. "I know it. How many people?"

"Just three. We can call on more at the embassy if we need

them, but the ambassador wants to keep this mission small and quiet."

"Bandon?" Hans guessed.

Miles nodded.

"Get him out of my sight." Renna thrust the spy at one of her men who hustled him off toward the administrative building. "The Works is halfway across town. We'll need to hurry if we want to find them before word of Miles's capture reaches the enemy."

Hans wasn't about to argue. The sooner they found Corina the better.

○

Corina spent more time in the dark, the only bit of light she saw was during her twice-daily feedings. She had come to both despise and yearn for those moments when the door opened and the sweet light reached her watering eyes. Her mind was still too fuzzy to work magic and the meager rations had left her weak while the uncomfortable chair made it nearly impossible to sleep. If she could have seen herself, she had no doubt she would have looked a mess.

Not that her looks were of paramount concern.

A thump from outside heralded the arrival of her meal. Supper, breakfast, she had no idea. The door opened and the familiar light lanced in, piercing her eyes.

Her captor was little more than a silhouette as he approached, tray held in his right hand.

"Feeding time," he said as though she were a prize hound. Though likely a hound would have eaten better.

He stopped in front of her but didn't have a chance to lift

the bland bread to her lips before a second set of steps came running.

"What is it?" he asked.

"The guard captured Miles," the second man said. "You know what a weakling he is. They won't need long to break him."

Her captor muttered something she couldn't make out. Curses aimed at Miles no doubt.

"Tell Kent we're moving to the third safe house. Leave nothing behind." He turned back to Corina. "You're still valuable, but not that valuable. Cause me a moment of grief and I'll cut your throat and dump your body. Understand?"

She managed a nod.

"Good." He jerked her to her feet.

Corina's legs wobbled but held her up. How far she'd be able to walk was another matter.

He didn't bother blindfolding her. Instead she was half shoved, half carried through a series of stone corridors devoid of decoration. The faint, acrid smell of molten metal reached her along with the distant sounds of pounding steel on steel carried through the floor. She'd gotten used to that sound back in Garen. They were under some kind of metal working factory. The familiar setting helped calm her nerves and she found her head had cleared a little.

Not enough, not yet, but she could almost reach the ether. She could even see it again, right there, but still just a fraction out of her grasp.

At the end of the tunnel an open door waited. Beyond it was a wagon hitched to a team of steel horses. Under different circumstances she would have been fascinated to learn how they worked. Right now all she wanted was for them to turn into regular statues that wouldn't move or haul her somewhere Hans couldn't find her.

Her third captor stood in the wagonbed and the first handed her up to him.

"Halt!"

Corina turned to see a force of guards come racing around the right side of the building.

"Stay where you are!" Another group was coming from the left, a furious Hans in the lead.

Corina's heart raced, clearing the last of the fog from her mind. A moment later the second man in the driver's position snapped the reins and the wagon lurched forward.

She reached for the ether and remembered what her master told her about the magical constructs. There was a crystal power source in them somewhere.

Focus on that.

Find it and cut it off from the ether.

Everything else faded away as she sought the left-hand horse's crystal.

Time slowed and she barely noticed as she was bounced around in the back of the wagon.

There!

She wrapped the blue crystal with every drop of ether she could summon. Her limited strength quickly faded, but the horse slowed and got out of sync with its partner.

It was enough to send the wagon spilling over sideways.

Corina went flying, bumped her head, and the world went dark.

೧

The Works was a smallish foundry by Garen standards. Hans eyed the place as they approached. Two chimneys belched black smoke into the clear sky. The main building covered a full block and had only a single story. Even so that was a lot of area to cover. Corina might be anywhere in the basement. He wished they had time to collect more guards, but neither he or Renna wanted to risk word getting to the kidnappers.

They stopped directly across the street from the main entrance and Hans asked, "How do you want to handle this?"

"We'll encircle the building then go in from all entrances at the same time," Renna said. "We converge on the center, clearing every room as we go."

"How many entrances are there?"

"I don't know. We'll have to check the perimeter before we go in."

Hans nodded. It was a good plan given their lack of time and knowledge of the foundry's layout. They broke up into the same groups as last time and approached the building from opposite directions. Hans took the front while Renna led her team toward the rear.

The main entrance was obvious and he left three men to cover it. The rest of the team circled left. That side had a pair of windows but no door. A quick glance made it clear the windows didn't open. Nothing to worry about there.

A shout rang out. "Halt!"

It came from the rear where Renna was searching.

Hans didn't need to think twice. "Come on!"

He sprinted toward the back of the building just in time to see a wagon pulled by a pair of steel horses emerging from a delivery entrance. One man in black wearing a hood sat on the wagon's bench and held the reins while two more rode in the back.

"Stay where you are!" Hans shouted as he raced toward the wagon.

The kidnappers paid his command no attention. But something happened. As the steel horses started to gather speed, one of them slowed and ruined their timing. The wagon lost its balance and seemed to move in slow motion. It fell on its side. Corina came flying out, her hands bound behind her.

She bounced twice and didn't move. If she was dead...

He didn't finish the thought. The kidnappers were pulling themselves from the remains of the wrecked wagon. The men looked left and right at the guards coming toward them. One of them shifted his gaze to Corina's unmoving form then shook his head.

One of the others pulled something from his pocket and threw it to the ground. A blinding light exploded out and when Hans's vision cleared the kidnappers were gone.

He sheathed his sword and rushed to Corina's side. Please, please be okay. On his knees, Hans touched the side of her neck. When he found her pulse strong and steady he let out a breath. Thank heaven she was okay. Her face was a mass of bruises and she looked even skinnier than before, but otherwise appeared unhurt. He cut the ropes binding her wrists and lifted her.

"Let's get her back to your suite," Renna said. "I'll have a healer look her over. Then I'll place an extra guard on your door, some of my people, ones I trust completely."

Hans very much liked the sound of that.

CHAPTER 11

Otto wiped sweat from his brow and scrutinized the mithril patch he'd forged for Audin's portal. The thin, smooth metal had taken the rune mark and ethereal charge exactly as he wanted. It was flawless and he'd only needed a week to make everything just right. That was a month faster than when he created the original patches. The old saying that practice makes perfect really was true.

Not that he was eager to create more of the patches than he had to. He had plenty of other ways to practice using his magic after all.

He sniffed and found the air in his workshop rank. A moment later he realized the source of the stench was his sweaty body. Eager as he was to go to Straken and retrieve the mithril he needed to pay off August, showing up looking and smelling like he'd just worked a shift in one of the foundries wouldn't do his reputation any good. While he didn't especially care what anyone thought about him, it made life more diffi-cult if those in power didn't respect him. Fear could still get the job done, but constant threats became exhausting after a while.

Otto used the same leather case that had held the original patches to hide this one and headed upstairs. The mansion was quiet, even Abby had decided to enjoy a moment of peace. It was still daytime, wasn't it?

After days of working virtually nonstop he'd completely lost track of the time. Sun shone through the windows when he reached the dining hall. So it was still daylight out. That was good.

As usual a single servant stood waiting for orders. Otto asked, "What's the hour?"

"Two bells past noon, Lord Shenk," the young woman replied.

Perfect. He had plenty of time to wash up and collect the mithril before dark. His stomach snarled that it was also time for a meal. "Would you fix me a sandwich? I'm going to clean up."

"What would you like, my lord?" she asked.

"I don't care as long as there's plenty of meat. You can just leave it on the table for me."

She curtsied and slipped out the door into the kitchen.

An hour later, clean, fed, and refreshed, Otto set out for the portal. He'd used so much magic over the last week he doubted anything less than a life-or-death threat could force him to become one with the ether.

As he walked through the streets of Gold Ward he took in the familiar scents and sounds. While he harbored no particularly warm feelings for the place, it was good to be home. In Colt's Land he constantly felt under threat.

He garnered a few looks as he passed the people out for an afternoon stroll. He'd been Wolfric's chief advisor long enough that people now recognized him more often than not.

When he reached the portal fort, the guards hurried to open the gate for him. Otto was pleased to see they hadn't lost their focus during his months-long absence.

Just inside, the fort commander stood, fist to heart. "Welcome, Lord Shenk. It's been awhile."

"Indeed, Commander. In fact I'm glad to find you here. I have a job for you."

"Anything, my lord."

That was exactly the answer Otto liked. "I'll be returning from Straken with a valuable cargo as well as some extra guards. How are you fixed for space?"

"The barracks has a handful of extra beds, but not many. How many soldiers are you bringing back?"

"Ten scouts, plus a squad of wizards to beef up security while the cargo is here. Fourteen total."

"No way can we fit that many in the barracks. I might be able to cobble something together in the storage building."

Otto nodded. "See to it. I'll be back before dark."

With that he pulled out the control rod, charged it with ether, and touched the rune for Straken. A single stride carried him from one fort to the next. As usual he was greeted with a flurry of salutes. One of the advantages to being the only one capable of activating the portal off schedule was everyone always knew who was arriving.

He spotted the unit commander hurrying over but Otto waved him off. He didn't want to delay retrieving Axel and the mithril.

The walk to Castle Straken took about ten minutes. He reached into the ether and quickly found his connection to Axel which he followed to the same barracks that had housed the scouts last time he visited. There was no one on guard outside so he knocked.

The door slammed open. "What?!"

Otto found himself nose to nose with Axel's surly second-in-command, Cobb. "Is my brother awake? I have a matter to discuss with him."

Cobb swallowed audibly. Having seen what Otto did with the lightning, most of Axel's scouts reacted that way when they met him. "Ah, Lord Shenk. Sorry, I thought you were one of Governor Varchi's stupid messengers. Come on in. The commander's just reading."

Otto stepped inside and immediately drew the nervous attention of every scout in the building. Axel sat beside a glowing Lux crystal, an open book in his hand. He looked up at Otto and actually smiled.

Axel stood, marked his place, and strode over. "Little brother, this is a surprise. Please tell me you have a mission for us."

They shook hands and Otto said, "Of sorts. I'm taking a wagonload of mithril back to Garen and I need guards I can trust. That's you, a squad of your men, and four war wizards I'll collect later."

Axel's smile faded. "You don't need the whole company?"

"No, just you and a squad of your best men." Otto cocked his head. "What's going on? I got the impression from your second that you weren't terribly happy with the new governor."

"Nothing's going on," Axel said. "That's the problem. With no enemy to fight, the general is becoming more and more like a noble and less like a soldier by the day. He holds court, has meetings even though there's nothing to talk about. It's a huge waste of time and even worse he expects me to attend these meetings. Some of the other sons of the nobility are summoned as well but most of them have a gift for sucking up."

Otto frowned. He'd assumed the peace would be less trouble than the war. Maybe he was wrong, but at least no one was getting killed. "So he's not actually doing anything harmful to the empire, just acting like a jackass. Does that about sum it up?"

"Pretty much. Can't you find something useful for us to do?" Axel was almost pleading which told Otto all he needed to know about the situation.

"You know what, I believe I can help you. Right now, I've only got Hans and his squad as my personal guard. They're great soldiers, but the numbers are limiting. How would you like to be reassigned to the capital where you'll serve as my combat troops? But before you agree, please understand that there will be considerable danger from time to time. Other times it will be as boring as here, but you won't have to worry about answering to anyone but me and the emperor."

"What kind of danger?" Axel asked.

"Who cares," Cobb said. "Anything's better than rotting here."

There were murmurs of agreement from the other scouts. Clearly peacetime didn't agree with everyone.

"Right now I'm making arrangements to access the work-shop of Arcane Lord Colt," Otto said. "No one has ever entered there and returned to tell the tale. I assume there will be magical traps along with constructs of various sorts. If you agree, you'll need to visit the royal armory to upgrade your equipment. I'll write you a letter of introduction."

Axel hesitated then shrugged. "Hell with it. Better to die

fighting than to sit around here until I get so fed up I cut the governor's throat. When do we leave?"

"Do you have paper, pen, and ink?" Otto asked.

They were quickly produced and Otto wrote a note to Governor Varchi informing him that Axel's scouts had been reassigned to the capital and that Otto was taking a wagonload of mithril as well.

He signed it and said, "Prepare your men and meet me at the portal. I also need someone good at driving a wagon."

"Take Cobb," Axel said. "He's good with a team."

Cobb shot his commander a black look before saying, "At your service, my lord."

"Excellent." Otto handed his brother the note. "Nail that to the barracks's door when you leave. The next person that comes to get you can take it back to the governor."

Axel grinned. "With pleasure."

With Cobb in tow, Otto left the castle grounds and returned to the city proper. Specifically, to the warehouse where the wagons of mithril were stored. A pair of soldiers in black and gold uniforms and armed with spears stood guard in front of the double doors.

They both snapped to attention at Otto's approach. The man on the right, who had corporal's chevrons on his shoulder said, "Can I help you, my lord?"

"I'm taking one of the wagons. Where can I find a team of horses?"

"Do you have a letter from the governor?" the corporal asked. "We have orders not to allow anyone in without one."

Otto just stared at the man until he started to squirm.

"Right," the corporal said at last. "There's a stable two blocks up and one to the right. We'll open the door for you."

"Very good." Otto was pleased that he hadn't had to resort

to a threat. It was important for the soldiers to remember that the governor wasn't the top of the food chain. "Cobb, you get the horses. I'll pick out a wagon."

Cobb saluted and trotted off to the stables. Otto went into the warehouse and conjured a light. Unless he was mistaken, another wagon had been added to the collection. That was excellent. The mines must have hit a good vein. He was starting to realize that the mithril was more valuable as a potential trade good with the other nations than it was for simply making weapons.

"Um, my lord, what should we tell Governor Varchi?" the corporal asked.

"Tell him Lord Shenk took a wagon of mithril. If he has a problem with that, he can take it up with the emperor." Otto made a mental note to visit Wolfric before he left and let him know a complaint might be headed his way.

A few minutes later Cobb returned with a team of horses and with the soldiers' help hitched them to the fullest wagon. Otto climbed up beside him and glanced back at the heap of stone in the wagon bed. He couldn't say exactly how many double eagles the load was worth, but he suspected more than the dowry Edwyn paid Father before the wedding.

After a quick stop to collect four war wizards nearly as eager to leave as Axel, they continued on to the fort. When they arrived, Axel and the scouts were waiting. They had loaded packs on their backs and big smiles. Otto hoped those smiles remained when they reached Colt's Workshop. While he didn't know exactly what to expect, he doubted it would be good.

Otto climbed down and activated the portal. A stride later and they were in Garen. When the fortress commander saw how many soldiers emerged with him he gaped with wide eyes. "There's no way I can house this many men, my lord."

"You don't have to. I'll take most of them to Franken Manor with me. We have an empty barracks now that the war wizards have completed their training. Axel, pick ten men for guard duty and we'll head out."

While his brother shouted orders, Otto saw to moving the wagon out of the way and getting the ore covered with a tarp. When it was secure he led Axel and the remaining scouts out the gate deeper into Gold Ward. All the wizards would remain behind. This time he definitely drew the gaze of every person they passed. After all, it wasn't every day a full company of soldiers marched through the streets.

Even the guards at the manor gates stared for a moment before hastening to open them. When the group reached the barracks Otto asked, "Axel, would you join me in the mansion for a few minutes?"

"Sure. Cobb, get everyone settled."

They went in through the side door and after it closed Axel asked, "So what's the big secret? Something horrible that's liable to kill us all?"

"Not at all." As they neared the dining room Abby's wailing reached them. Couldn't the brat stay quiet for more than five minutes at a time?

When they arrived he called the servant on duty over and whispered, "Fetch my mother, but don't mention I've brought a guest. It's a surprise."

"Yes, my lord," she whispered back then hurried upstairs.

"What's going on, Otto?" Axel asked. "Sneaking around has never been your style."

"Humor me, brother. I promise you'll enjoy the surprise."

A minute later Mother said, "Otto? Did you need some—"

She froze at the top of the stairs and stared at Axel who was also struck dumb.

The spell was broken a moment later when she rushed down the stairs and wrapped her arms around Axel. "My dear boy."

Otto smiled in genuine pleasure as his mother and brother held each other in silence. When Axel opened his eyes Otto would have sworn they were damp, not that he would dare point this out.

"I'm glad you both enjoyed my surprise. I need to pay a visit to Wolfric, but after that I thought we might have dinner as a family before I return to Colt's Land."

"That sounds lovely, Otto," his mother said. "I'll make the arrangements. How long will you be?"

"Better give me three hours."

"I need to make sure the guys have settled in," Axel said. "But I'll be back shortly."

They walked out together and at the door Axel stopped and put his hand on Otto's shoulder. "Thank you for this, little brother. I doubted I'd ever have a chance to spend an evening with Mother again."

Otto smiled. "We have some time before matters in Colt's Land come to a head. Cobb seems competent enough. Why don't you let him handle security while you enjoy your time together?"

"I may just do that."

CHAPTER 12

After a brief conversation with a distracted Wolfric, a wonderfully peaceful dinner with Mother and Axel, and a blissful night's sleep in his own bed, Otto was ready to return to Audin. He had the patch in his satchel and the mithril was ready. Everything else should be just details. Though if he'd learned anything from his marriage, the demon was in the details.

Since the sun had barely touched the horizon, he didn't bother to say goodbye to his mother. They'd taken care of that the night before. She asked for no details of his mission, only hugged him and told him to be careful. Otto doubted that was an option given where he planned to go, but he could at least keep a close watch.

He took a deep breath and focused his mind before becoming one with the ether. Reaching for the farthest marker, he found the one he left behind in Audin a second later. Quick as thought he shot through the ether and appeared in his room in Audin.

Everything looked exactly as he left it. Good, his instructions had been obeyed. By his rough calculations it should be approaching noon here. Hopefully August would see him at once and they could conclude their business.

There was a knock on the door and Hans said, "Lord Shenk?"

Otto walked over and opened the door. "How did you know I was here?"

"There's a sound when you appear and I was listening for it. Something happened while you were gone."

Otto's stomach clenched. He'd never heard such trepidation in Hans's voice before. Hopefully whatever it was wouldn't ruin his agreement.

"Tell me."

"Corina was kidnapped. It seems one of the workers in their armory was a spy. They used some kind of alchemy bomb that put us to sleep and made off with her. Renna and I got her back, but she wasn't treated kindly."

"Where is she?" Otto asked, his jaw tight with controlled fury.

"In bed. The healers say she'll be okay, but she hasn't actually woken up since we brought her back yesterday."

Otto brushed past Hans and went directly to Corina's room. She was swaddled in blankets; only her bruised, thin face showed above them. It looked like someone had used his apprentice as a punching bag. Whoever it was would soon wish they had never been born.

Ether flowed between Otto and Corina. He didn't have much skill in healing, but at least he confirmed that the damage wasn't serious. After a moment of checking he found no broken bones or other injury beyond superficial bruising that would heal quickly. He let out a sigh of relief. Otto had become fond of Corina and had no desire to replace her.

"Master?" Her eyes fluttered open.

"I'm here. Just rest, you're safe now."

"They wanted to know what you were planning. A trap when you open the portal." Her hand shot out and grabbed his arm. "Be careful, they have alchemy, some kind of gas that keeps you from using magic."

Otto patted her hand. The iron ring he'd given her was gone. "You did very well, Corina. I couldn't be more proud. Focus on healing. I have a few things I need to take care of."

"Yes, Master." She closed her eyes and was soon sleeping again.

Otto eased out of the room and found Renna had joined them.

"Otto, both August and I wish to offer our most sincere apologies for what happened to your apprentice."

"I was given assurances that we would be secure here," Otto said. "Had I known what your promise was worth, I would have made my own arrangements. Who took her?"

"Agents working for Bandon," Renna said. "We haven't been able to track them down, but my people are working on it."

Otto swallowed his anger. Much as he would have liked to kill her and the lord governor, that was impossible. Instead he turned to Hans. "Do you have her rings?"

His face scrunched up. "No. Things have been so crazy I didn't even realize she wasn't wearing them. I'm sorry, my lord."

"Don't be. If you don't have them, then the kidnappers still do. That will make it easy to find them. When I finish with them, I'll need to speak with August. The mithril is waiting for his inspection once we activate your portal."

"I'll let him know." Renna cleared her throat. "If you can

find the spies, you should let the guards know their location. We can—"

Otto rounded on her. "*I* will deal with them. No one harms my people and gets away with it. Do you understand? No one!"

She flinched back. "I understand perfectly. The guards won't interfere."

"It will be well for them if they don't. Now go away. I have to get ready."

Renna bowed and fled the room.

When she'd gone Hans asked, "Is there anything I can do to help, my lord?"

Otto settled on the floor in preparation for his search. "Yes. Find me a pillowcase big enough to hold three heads."

↻

Renna raced up the stairs to Lord Audin's office. Her heart beat so fast she feared it must burst out of her chest at any moment. Never, never in all the years she'd served Audin had she been as terrified as when Otto turned on her with those cold, dead eyes. Eyes that would look at her corpse with no more feeling than she might a dead insect.

How could someone so young have those eyes? She shuddered to think what he must have done to earn them. Of course, she'd read the report their embassy made about his meetings with the council in Bandon. But it was one thing to read a report and another to look into the eyes of the one that did it and know without a doubt that not only had he done what he claimed but that he would kill you just as easily.

When she reached the door to the office, Renna took a moment to steady herself. Somehow she had to convince the lord governor that betraying Otto would be unwise. Heaven only knew what the young wizard might do if they failed to keep their word.

Her pulse slowed to a regular rhythm and she knocked on the door.

"Enter!"

She pushed the door open and slipped inside. Lord Audin looked at her and frowned. "Are you well? Your face is rather pale."

"I'm fine, my lord. Otto has returned and was most displeased to see the state of his apprentice."

Lord Audin grimaced. "How displeased?"

"He's currently searching for the spies with the intention of killing them all. I'm not one to worry about our enemies, but I pity those three."

"I'll have to thank him for doing our security force's job. Is he still willing to proceed with the deal?"

"Yes. Otto said all preparations for reactivating the portal are ready." Renna tried to work up some spit in her dry mouth. "I feel it may be best to rethink our plan to double-cross them. We should just take the mithril and consider ourselves fortunate."

Lord Audin stood and came around his desk to stand directly in front of her. "He's shaken you that badly? A stripling of a wizard who will most likely end up dead in Colt's Workshop? I thought you were made of sterner stuff. Perhaps I need to find someone else to lead my secret police. Someone with the stomach to do what needs to be done."

She bristled at the insult, but couldn't deny the truth of his assessment. Otto had shaken her. Deep down in her gut she knew if they didn't play straight with the young wizard, Audin would regret it. That said, if the lord governor commanded her to betray Otto, then she would obey. Replacing her with someone who didn't appreciate how dangerous he was would only reduce the chances of success.

Maybe they'd all get lucky and he would die in the workshop. That meant no more mithril, but it also meant no more danger. That was an outcome she could live with.

"No, my lord. I will carry out my orders. I simply wished to offer a warning. Assessing threats is one of my duties after all."

"I appreciate your honesty," he said. "But the potential gains outweigh almost any risk. In fact, I want you to go with them, oversee the operation personally. Show me you're not too scared to do your job."

That was the last thing she wanted, but Renna just nodded. "As you wish. If I'm to travel north with them, I'll need to pack. Is there anything else?"

"Only a final warning." He grabbed her by the chin and pulled her face down so their lips almost touched. "Otto Shenk isn't the one you need to fear. I am."

Lord Audin shoved her back. Renna bowed and hurried out of the office.

Now she had a furious wizard on one side and a lord governor that didn't trust her on the other. Marvelous. How much worse could things get?

Otto's sight soared above Audin as he peered through the ether looking for the unique glow of the runes he'd inscribed inside Corina's ring. When he put them there, he never imagined he'd be using them this way. Whoever kidnapped her wasn't a wizard and must not have access to one. Even a cursory examination would reveal the ring's glow, even if they didn't immediately realize its purpose.

Oh well, it was good luck for Otto and bad luck for the kidnappers.

He found what he was looking for halfway across the city from the administrative building. The faint spark led him to a basement room under an inn. Three men dressed in black were gathered there. One was pacing while the other two sat on wooden crates. The one pacing carried the ring in his pocket.

Otto sent his hearing to join his eyes.

"What are we going to do?" one of the seated men asked.

"Nothing's changed," the pacing man said. "We still need to stop him from delivering the mithril. Losing the girl was a blow, I don't deny it, she would have made a useful bargaining chip despite her ignorance. But done is done. Now we focus on planning the ambush. Whatever the cost, we have to succeed. The consequences for failure don't bear consideration."

The others mumbled their agreement.

Otto had heard enough. He left a thread to mark a spot in the left rear corner of the basement and returned his senses to his body. Hans stood to one side and held a large silk pillow-case that looked just big enough for his needs.

"I found them." Otto stood, took the case, and tucked it into his satchel. "This won't take long."

He became one with the ether and followed the thread he left back to the basement hideout. All three kidnappers were staring at him when he stepped out of the shadows.

Otto flicked his ring and bound them all in place. A moment later a dome of silence surrounded the room. "I assume you all know me. You have considerable courage, kidnapping a drugged girl in the middle of the night. It is unfortunate that you chose my apprentice as your target. That's not the sort of thing I can just let slide."

Otto drew his sword and snapped his wrist, slicing open the leader's pocket. Corina's iron ring fell out. He collected it and straightened. "Where's the mithril ring?"

Otto released the binding on the leader's head so he could answer. "Help! Someone, help!"

The sword flicked out again, this time slicing the leader's forearm to the bone.

He howled in pain.

"Answer my question or I'll take your other hand off at the wrist," Otto said.

"Stop, please. I gave it to the ambassador as proof that we had the right girl. Our people made detailed notes on you and your party during your time in Bandon. A mithril ring was kind of hard to miss."

Otto couldn't deny that. "How many people are aware of your plan to ambush me at the portal?"

"Just us and the ambassador. If you let us go I promise we'll leave Audin tonight and never interfere with you again."

"Surely you weren't planning to attack with only three men. You don't strike me as stupid, despite kidnapping my apprentice."

"We were going to use constructs. Half a dozen armored warriors are nearly unstoppable when they attack humans, even wizards."

"And where are these constructs now?" Otto asked.

"In a ship that docked two days ago. We haven't smuggled them into the city yet. She's called the Bandon Bird. Now please, let us go. I've told you everything I know."

Otto examined the kidnapper through the ether and as far as he could tell the man wasn't lying. His hand tightened on the hilt of his sword. Much as he wanted to send these three fools' heads to the ambassador as a message, that wouldn't serve his plans. Better by far if no one ever knew they existed.

"You've been very helpful. Unfortunately, I can't allow anyone to harm those under my protection without consequences. Rest assured that had you lied to me or been less forthcoming, your deaths would have been far more painful."

Before the lead kidnapper could make another sound, Otto lashed out, slicing his head off. He repeated the process with the other two. A quick look around revealed nothing that might betray his presence.

Now he just needed to speak to the ambassador.

9

Otto found the Bandon ambassador alone in her modest office reading a page from a huge stack on the center of her desk. Middle-aged, forty pounds overweight, and wearing a conservative dress of deep blue, the woman clearly didn't get her job based on her looks. Probably political connections then or, heaven forbid, actual competence.

No magical wards protected the embassy, which indicated that Renna was right about them not having wizards among their staff. That certainly made Otto's job easier. Forcing his way in would have alerted any magic user within ten blocks who was paying attention.

He marked the office with a thread and traveled through the ether. Before she could even look up from her reading he bound her in place and wove a ward of silence around the office. There was no time to mess around. Otto took a step toward the desk, paused, and went to the office door instead. It had a simple lock which he secured. Satisfied that he wouldn't be interrupted, he moved to stand beside the ambassador.

"Whatever you're going to do, please don't," she said the moment he released the binding on her head.

"Don't worry, I'm not going to kill you." Otto glanced down at her hand and found Corina's ring shining on her little finger. He wrenched it off. "That doesn't belong to you. Now, I have a couple questions. Please understand that your answers will determine whether I simply erase your memories of me or if I lop your head off like I did those of your kidnappers."

"My agents are dead?" Her calm expression gave way to fear.

"Oh, yes. What did you think was going to happen when I returned and learned what you'd done? Wait, let me guess. You thought those idiots would kill me when I showed up to rescue Corina. I'm almost insulted. Now, have you sent any reports about your plans back to Bandon?"

Otto drove threads of ether into her brain when a section lit up and ripped the truth out of her mouth. "No. I wanted to wait until the task was complete. My hope was that my superiors would be impressed and give me a promotion out of this wretched city."

She stared at him, clearly aghast at what she just said.

"I know, for someone used to lying, this spell can be disconcerting. On the other hand, it is considerably less painful than the other techniques I know for extracting information. Lucky for you, the answer you gave is the one I was hoping for. Now, just try and relax and stare straight ahead."

Otto conjured a wheel of spinning light and with no magic to protect her, the ambassador was quickly under. Next, threads of ether shot out into her brain.

"Otto Shenk." When a portion of her brain lit up he used his threads to scrub it away. The process continued until her brain no longer lit up when he said his name.

Next he erased all knowledge of the mission she'd given her agents. Finally, he eliminated Corina and Hans. A thin line of drool now extended from the ambassador's mouth to her chin and he hoped he hadn't done too much damage. He needed the woman functional, at least for the near future.

He released the spell and she slumped forward, head resting on the table. Satisfied with his work, Otto unlocked the door, removed the silence ward, and vanished into the ether.

When he appeared in his room back at the government building, his knees nearly buckled. Using that much magic over such a short time had left him exhausted and weak. He needed to rest, but first he had something important to do.

Otto opened the bedroom door and Hans sprang out of the chair he'd been sitting in. "Is all well, my lord?"

"I believe so." Otto tossed him the pillowcase. "Is Corina awake?"

"If she is, she's been quiet." Hans held up the pillowcase. "This is awfully clean for having three heads in it."

Otto offered a thin smile. "I had a better idea. Not nearly as satisfying as lining her minions heads' up in a row on her bed, but more useful to the mission. Find Renna and tell her that I'll be happy to join the lord governor for a late dinner. Right now I need sleep. Just as soon as I return something."

Hans saluted and went out into the hall. Otto eased the door to Corina's room open and peeked inside. Her eyes were open and she smiled when she saw him.

"I heard you talking," Corina said. "Sorry if I made trouble for you, Master."

Otto stepped inside. "You didn't and those that hurt you will never hurt anyone else. How are you feeling?"

"I'm okay. My head's still a little fuzzy, but that's all."

"Good. I'll be counting on you when we set out for Colt's Workshop."

He held out his hand and she gasped. "You got my rings. Thank you, Master."

She took them and slipped them on with a sigh of relief.

"Make sure not to lose them again." Otto offered a gentle smile and returned to his own room. The overstuffed bed looked like the sweetest thing he'd ever seen.

He dropped into it and was soon fast asleep.

CHAPTER 13

After a four-hour nap and a delicious meal, Otto felt nearly back to normal. Across the table from him, August seemed calm and at ease. Considering his failure to protect Corina, that confidence seemed ill placed. Otto had remained largely quiet during the meal, letting the lord governor muse on what he might be thinking. He was still annoyed at the terrible quality of their security, but in the end, nothing had really changed. They each still wanted something from the other, and neither had another way of getting it.

Otto took a last sip of his wine and said, "The patch is ready and I've brought your mithril to the portal. Have you devised a way to activate it that won't draw the attention of every spy in the city?"

August brightened a bit now that they were back to business. "No. The problem is I can't think of a good way to distract everyone. It would have to be something major to draw every embassy's attention."

"How about kicking the Bandon ambassador out of Audin. Would that do it?"

"Certainly, but I'd have to give a reason and we don't want to advertise your presence."

"Did I not mention they were smuggling a number of animated soldiers into the city? They're on a ship in the harbor right now. I assume that goes against whatever agreement you all have with each other."

August's expression darkened. "It certainly does. We can even claim the traitor that told us where to find your apprentice told us about the weapons. I'll make a big show of grabbing them and announcing the embassy's expulsion from the city. While I'm doing that, you can activate the portal. Illsa will go with you to examine the mithril and bring back our first half for processing. Agreed?"

"Agreed. I'll be bringing some reinforcements back to help me search the workshop."

August frowned. "How many? Remember, we have to keep this quiet."

"I thought a scout company. That's a hundred men."

August immediately shook his head, just as Otto expected. "That won't do at all. Not only couldn't we hide them, but I can't have such a large foreign force in my city. Heaven only knows what they might get up to."

"Ten then," Otto said, naming the number he actually wanted. "If the workshop is as dangerous as you say, I'll need at least that many."

"Fair enough. Considering how badly we bungled your security, I can't blame you for wanting backup. When should I make the announcement?"

"Noon would be ideal since that's the brightest part of the day and will hide the portal's activation best."

"Very well, noon tomorrow."

They shook, grasping wrists, all the tension that had been

building between them long gone, and grinning like two kids up to a prank. Only this was a prank that would change the world.

⌒

At a little before noon, Otto, Hans, Corina, and Illsa were gathered across the street from the portal. Three squads of guards had been dispersed to keep anyone in the area away. Luckily, for some reason, the locals considered the portal bad luck and the area around it was largely abandoned. Beside Illsa a floating cart, for lack of a better description, hovered a foot off the ground. It was about four feet square and had high sides. She called it a load carrier and planned to use it to transport their mithril back.

Otto watched as the shadows grew ever shorter. Not much longer.

"What's it like traveling through the portal?" Illsa asked. "I've always wondered."

"It's like taking a step through a tunnel of light," Corina said. "I've never seen anything so pretty."

"It can also leave you dizzy and a little sick," Hans added, eyeing the portal with clear distaste.

"They're both right," Otto said. "I've done it so many times I don't even think about how remarkable the whole process is. The power of the Arcane Lords never ceases to amaze me."

"We tried to process the portal, you know," Illsa said. "Nothing we used even scratched the mithril."

"Garenland tried that as well with equal success." Otto shook his head. "The power required to destroy a portal boggles the mind. I doubt a single Arcane Lord could do it."

150

The shadows reached their shortest point and a minute later a messenger came running around the corner.

"The lord governor has moved on Bandon's embassy."

"Fingers crossed that everyone's looking where they should be." Otto took the patch out of his satchel and tossed it at the master rune.

The ether flared like lightning and dragged the patch into place. It only took seconds, but anyone watching would have been treated to quite a light show.

As soon as the ether settled Otto pulled out the control rod, charged it, and touched the rune for Garen. The instant the connection was established he motioned the others through. A single step brought Otto to the portal fort.

"We have little time." He guided Illsa toward the covered wagon and motioned the scout on duty to pull the tarp back. "Where's my brother?"

"At the Franken barracks, my lord."

"Send a messenger for him and his chosen men. Make sure they have their new equipment and make it clear they need to hurry."

The scout saluted and ran off at a dead sprint.

Illsa had her full attention on the rubble in the back of the wagon. Ether flowed from her fingers and wove through the stone.

"Is there anything we should do, my lord?" Hans asked.

"Watch the portal. I don't want any surprises coming up behind us."

Otto doubted August would do anything so stupid as attacking Garen, but then again you never knew. He'd seen smarter people do dumber things.

At last the ether faded and Illsa said, "It's amazing! There's nearly as much mithril in this wagon as we have in all our armor combined. I'll do wondrous things with this metal."

"So you're satisfied?"

"Perfectly. Let's begin loading." She gestured and the carrier floated over and stopped directly below the wagon's gate.

Otto pointed at the four nearest soldiers. "Half the ore needs to be transferred over to her cart. Double time."

They saluted, leapt into the back of the wagon, and soon the crash of stone landing in a metal box filled the fort. Illsa watched every stone fly through the air with the same hunger a starving cat looks at a mouse.

The carrier was nearly full when Axel, Cobb, and eight other scouts came trotting through the fort's gate. They all carried mithril weapons and the archers had mithril-tipped arrows. Whatever they encountered in Colt's Workshop, those weapons would give them the best chance of winning.

"Axel," Otto said when his brother stopped in front of him. "I see you had no trouble getting the weapons."

"None at all. Your name opens all kinds of doors." Axel took out a spare sword and handed it to Hans who looked at Otto.

"An upgrade, just in case. You can leave your old sword here. Don't worry, no one will make off with it."

Hans unbuckled his worn blade, laid it down as gently as a newborn and belted on the mithril weapon. "The weight feels off."

"It takes a little getting used to," Otto agreed. "The effectiveness more than makes up for it."

"I'm ready," Illsa said.

"Good. Everyone back through the portal." The whole process had taken at most fifteen minutes, but even that might have been too long. If the wrong pair of eyes saw them going or returning, it might mean the ruin of all Otto's careful plans.

Otto was the last one through and as soon as he cleared the portal he used his control rod to deactivate it. No one could come or go until he let them.

Illsa led the way back to the government compound. Axel and his men would be garrisoned overnight in an old barracks scheduled for demolition in preparation for hopefully an early morning departure. Assuming the ancient building didn't collapse on them during the night.

Otto started to ask a question but Illsa was already hurrying off toward the armory with her treasure. Left to his own devices Otto turned to Axel. "You might as well get comfortable. I need to find the lord governor and arrange the details for our journey."

Axel waved him off. "We'll be fine. I've camped in worse places than this."

"When?" Cobb asked.

Axel shot him a look. Before an argument broke out Otto cut in. "Don't mingle or do anything to draw attention. The fewer people that know you're here the better."

"I'm not an idiot, little brother. Go do what you need to."

Otto restrained himself from shooting Axel a dubious look and set out for the main building with Hans and Corina behind him. Renna met them at the entrance with a warm smile.

"I take it things went well?" Otto said.

"Very. We found the autonomous soldiers exactly where you said they'd be. The Bandon ambassador sputtered out some stupid explanations but the evidence of her breaking the law couldn't be denied. She made no mention of you or the portal."

"I should think not given how much time I spent erasing her memories. I am pleased to hear her brain is still functioning properly. Is August ready to discuss your end of the deal?"

"He's put me in charge of making the arrangements. We have a border fort two days south of Colt's Workshop. We'll mingle you and your team in amongst a rotation of soldiers headed to relieve those on duty. From there you can make the rest of the journey on foot. The commander of the fort's magical engineers will slave a load carrier to your will so you can transport whatever it is you're after back out. When you return, you'll make the journey back with the soldiers going on leave."

Otto nodded. "Sounds like you have everything sorted out. When do we go?"

"August thought it best not to delay any longer than necessary. You set out at first light tomorrow."

"That suits me very well. If you'll excuse us, we need to pack our gear and rest up for the journey."

Renna bowed. "I wish you the best of luck."

She withdrew and Otto led the way back to their suite. As soon as Hans closed the door, Corina opened her mouth to speak.

Otto touched a finger to his lips. She fell silent and he sent streams of ether out into the rooms. In each one he found a small crystal hidden amidst the decorations. Otto collected them all and dropped them down the hole of the garderobe. Let whoever planted them fish them out of there. He closed the door and sealed it with a silence spell.

"There, now we can talk freely."

"How did you know those were there, Master?" Corina asked.

"I didn't, but I suspected August would try and learn more about what we sought in Colt's Workshop. I searched the suite when we first arrived and have checked it again every time I return. It's just a good habit when you're in a space you don't fully control. Anyway, the real problem won't arrive until we return with the artifact."

"Do you think they'll try and seize it?" Hans asked.

"I wouldn't be surprised. August is a greedy man, at least that's how I read him. He'll probably try and take it then negotiate for more mithril."

"Will you renegotiate?" Hans asked.

"No. If August betrays us, I'm going to drain his melted brain out his eye sockets. But first I need to run an errand. If anyone comes looking for me, tell them I exhausted myself activating the portal and need to sleep."

Otto extended his senses and checked the hall. Two men on duty as always. A thread of ether into each of their brains activated the section that controlled sleep. Overwhelming exhaustion soon sent them both slumping to the floor.

Satisfied, he wrapped himself in invisibility and slipped out. He needed to talk to a woman about some mithril.

◯

When he reached the courtyard, Otto let his invisibility fade and marched toward the armory. Illsa didn't strike him as especially loyal to August. With any luck the prospect of unlimited mithril would bring her around to working for him. Of course if her loyalty ran deeper than he thought, she might run straight to August and tell him everything Otto said. He needed to make this look like an offer to come work for him, not a threat against the city.

He didn't see another soul as he crossed the courtyard. At the armory's sally port, he knocked. A moment later the door opened and one of the guards stared at him as if he'd never seen another person.

"Can I help you?" the guard asked.

"I need to speak to Illsa," Otto said. "I assume she's still here trying to refine the mithril. I have some expertise in that and thought I might be able to help."

"Angels bless you," the second guard said. "She's been on about purifying that stuff since she got back. Anything you can do to help would be welcome."

That wasn't the reaction Otto expected. He had a whole bunch of threats all lined up. Simply getting invited in seemed anticlimactic.

"Wait a minute," the first guard said. "We're not supposed to let anyone in without an escort."

"Idiot!" the second man said. "This gentleman is the lord governor's guest and has toured the armory. He's already seen any secrets that might be lying about. Now move aside so he can silence that madwoman and we can get some quiet."

The hesitant guard finally moved aside and Otto slipped past with a nod to the second man. "Where can I find Illsa?"

"She has one of her contraptions set up near the back. Just follow the pillar of black smoke and curses, you can't miss her."

"Thanks."

Sure enough the moment he took a closer look, black smoke was indeed billowing up toward the ceiling. She must have set up a smelter inside the armory. A quick glance at the ceiling made it clear they had little in the way of ventilation. If she wasn't careful, Illsa might end up suffocating everyone in the place.

Not that there was actually that many people. In fact, there wasn't a single person, wizard or assistant, to be seen. That worked in Otto's favor so he wasn't about to complain.

He found Illsa scowling at a cube that glowed bright red and had smoke coming out the gaps around the door.

She looked up as he approached. "I can't make it melt! I have the smelter at maximum output and the mithril just sits there in ugly little lumps laughing at me."

"How much heat can that box take?" Otto asked.

"I don't really know. The crystal that powers it has reached its full output so it doesn't really matter."

Otto gathered the ether and wrapped it around the small pile of mithril ore. Enhancement magic was one of the first things he learned and soon enough the heat doubled, then doubled again. The ore wavered then finally liquefied, draining through the floor of the box into a crucible underneath.

Illsa darted in, grabbed it with a pair of tongs, and dumped the liquid metal into a form. She wiped the sweat from her face and smiled.

"That was amazing. You used the ether directly to increase the heat in a localized area. I've never seen that done before."

"Really? This sort of magic is among the first things all wizards learn where I'm from. Many of those without the power to join the war wizards make their living working in the forges and foundries of Garen."

"Interesting. Here we learn how to enchant crystals and use them to power mechanical objects."

"That sort of magic is unheard of back home." Now for the bait. "If you're interested, I'd love to have you come back to Garen and continue your work. I can promise you a large supply of mithril and wizards eager to learn your style of magic. I'd also be happy to teach you our style."

"I'd love to, but Lord Audin would never let me." She looked away then back. "Can you show me that spell again? If I'm going to process all this mithril, I'll need to get it right."

He obliged, showing her twice more how to use the ether to make the heat increase. It wasn't all that different from using air in a forge, only because it was magic, you didn't use a ton of extra fuel.

When she'd at least gotten the basics down he said, "With a little more practice you'll be an expert."

She smiled, reminding him of Corina for a moment. "Thank you for helping. If I show the others tomorrow we should be able to process the ore in two weeks or so."

Otto smiled back in what he hoped was a friendly, nonthreatening way. "You don't need permission if you want to visit Garen. You're a free person. You can come and go as you please. Just think about it. If you want to return with me when I leave, you're welcome."

From the look on her face, he had her tempted at least. All Otto could do now was hope for the best.

᧡

The trip back to their suite was as easy as the walk to the armory. Aside from the still-sleeping guards, he didn't encounter another soul. Once inside, he let his invisibility spell fade. Hans and Corina were engrossed in a game of cards, seeming perfectly at ease, which was exactly how he wanted them to look.

Corina looked up from her hand. "Did you have any trouble, Master?"

"None. The guards at the armory were happy to see me. Apparently Illsa was having trouble smelting the mithril. I gave her a few pointers and hopefully planted a seed. Now I need to take a little trip outside." Otto patted his pockets and was annoyed to find he didn't have a coin on him. "Hans, do you

158

have a copper piece?"

"I have one!" Corina dropped her cards and dug a coin out of her pocket.

"Thank you."

Otto gathered a little ether around his thumb and rubbed the coin until both sides were smooth. Next he inscribed a rune on it and charged it with ether until it glowed. He didn't put as much in as he would have for a permanent marker. Hopefully a passing wizard wouldn't notice the coin.

Now he just needed to find a place to hide it.

He took a seat between Hans and Corina then sent his sight flying out of the building. Somewhere near the embassies would be best. They were all clustered about eight blocks from the administrative building. Except for Bandon's, all the embassies had guards out front.

He couldn't get too close, or he'd be spotted appearing. Otto pulled back and found a park a block east. It wasn't huge, maybe fifty yards square with a fountain in the center. He looked closer and smiled. Much like in Garen, they had a habit of throwing copper coins into the fountain. Perfect.

Otto found an empty alley not far away, marked the place with a thread, and returned his sight to his body. The moment he returned he moved away from the table and became one with the ether.

An instant later he was in the alley and invisible. He made the walk to the park and scowled when he found a mother and two kids gathered around the fountain. The mother, a tired, but seemingly happy woman in her early thirties handed each of the kids a copper coin.

The boy threw his in at once, but the little girl held hers clutched to her chest for long seconds.

Come on! He needed to return before someone showed up.

At last she made her wish and tossed the coin in. The mother led them off. Otto waited until they were out of sight and tossed his coin in. His wish was that he wouldn't need to use this backup plan. He dearly hoped it came true.

CHAPTER 14

Otto and his brother, along with the rest of the Garenland contingent, had gathered in the courtyard before sunup. A hundred Audin soldiers were busy loading supplies into wagons pulled by mechanical horses. A floating load carrier at the rear of the column held all of the Garenlanders' gear. No wizard had transferred control to Otto yet, but he assumed it would happen soon.

"Did you get some sleep under your wobbly roof?" Otto asked.

Axel shrugged. "Some. It felt like camping in enemy territory so I set a guard rotation. I don't think the guys appreciated it."

Otto understood the sentiment. Father had drilled caution into them since birth and now it was as natural as breathing. "Did you and Mother do anything interesting after I left?"

"Not really. We mostly talked. I'm worried about her."

Otto frowned. She'd said nothing to him that suggested out-of-the-ordinary problems. "Why?"

"It sounds like Father and Stephan are fighting worse than usual this time. I fear what she might return home to."

Father would never do anything to Mother. Otto felt certain she was the only person in the world he truly loved. In that case... "You're afraid Stephan might hurt her."

"Father's tough, but he's not getting any younger." Axel looked away from the packing and into Otto's eyes. "You know our brother as well as I do. Eventually he's going to make a move to seize the barony. If he kills Father, he might view Mother as a threat. He's just insane enough to kill her too."

Otto's frown deepened. He wished he could say Axel was totally off target, but he wasn't. With Stephan, no act was out of bounds if he felt it necessary. That made him a useful weapon, but a dangerous one that risked twisting and hurting the hand that wielded it.

"Our business here will be wrapped up long before fall. When we're back in Garenland, I'll take a trip home and have a chat with Stephan. If he harms a hair on Mother's head, I'll rip him apart an inch at a time."

"What about Father?" Axel asked.

"Do you care?"

"Not especially. At least not about the man himself, but I do worry about the people of the barony with Stephan in charge."

"You want to take his place?" Otto asked. "I could kill him and you could leave the military. Setting you up as the new baron wouldn't be difficult. It would be good for the empire as well. Having a madman ruling one of the central baronies is just asking for trouble."

Axel winced at the suggestion. "Becoming baron myself wasn't what I had in mind."

Otto nodded, unsurprised. Whatever ended up happening, this wasn't the time to solve the problem. The wagons were nearly packed. Movement out of the corner of his eye prompted him to turn toward the administrative building. Renna had emerged and was hurrying their way. She had sturdy traveling gear on and a pack over her shoulder.

No mention had been made of the woman joining them. Once again his fear of betrayal flared to life.

"Is she married?" Axel asked, jarring him out of his worries.

"Renna's high up in the Audin secret police. She's not the sort of woman you want to involve yourself with."

Axel grinned. "Might be fun for a night or two."

"Until she decides to cut your throat."

Otto walked away from his brother and met Renna partway to the caravan. "Will you be joining us?"

"Yes." Did her voice hold a hint of nerves? Otto might have been imagining it. "August wanted me to go along to make sure everything went perfectly."

"That's very considerate. Your timing is excellent. The soldiers are nearly finished loading the wagons."

They found Hans and Corina along with the rest of the scouts near the final wagon in line. One of the soldiers was already seated on the bench, ready to guide the metal horse.

"Load up!" Axel said.

The scouts clambered in followed by Hans and Corina. Otto turned to Renna. "Will you be riding with us?"

"No, you look full. I'll find a place elsewhere." She hurried off, bringing an abrupt end to the conversation.

Otto shook his head and climbed up beside Corina. The feeling of impending doom wouldn't leave him even though he had nothing to base it on but instinct, and that wasn't terribly reliable.

When the last person had boarded their wagon, the driver snapped the reins and they were off. Death and glory awaited.

Otto just hoped they got the glory and someone else the death.

♈

The caravan spent the first day traveling through rolling plains not unlike those in Rolan. Otto had few good memories of Rolan, but Corina gazed off with a wistful expression. Hopefully she was remembering good times with her parents and not the stuff that came later. They passed dozens of large farms, grazing cattle, and fields of growing corn.

No threats presented themselves. Not surprising given how close they were to the city.

Three days out, they reached the first settlement, a smallish town with a single street and two inns. Camp was made outside of the town, but everyone was permitted to visit the stores and taverns as long as they didn't end up drunk. Everyone except Otto and his group.

That suited him perfectly well. As soon as his tent was set up, Otto slipped inside and settled on his cot. He'd barely started centering himself for a bit of spying when Corina poked her head in. "Will you be joining us for supper or should I bring it in?"

"I'll get something when I'm finished. Did you notice if the magical engineers went into town?"

"Yup, about ten minutes ago. They left a squad to keep an eye on us, but everyone else is gone, including Renna."

Otto nodded to himself. Just as he'd figured, this was the perfect chance for her to speak to the officer in command of the replacements. If August was planning treachery, hopefully she'd reveal her plan tonight.

"See that I'm not disturbed."

When Corina had withdrawn, Otto closed his eyes and sent his vision up and out toward the nearby town. He studied it from on high and considered where he would go if he wanted to have a private meeting. A room at one of the inns was most likely.

He swooped down into the nearest and began checking the rooms one by one. None of them was at all remarkable or occupied at the moment. A quick peek at the common room found it full of locals and soldiers from the caravan.

No sign of Renna.

Otto repeated the process at the next inn with equal results. Frowning now, he wracked his brain trying to think where to check next. The answer came to him a moment later. Every town had to have a town hall where the mayor or whoever ran the place took care of business.

He found it at the end of the street and passed through the rear wall. Sure enough, there was Renna along with the company commander and two other soldiers, probably his subordinates.

A quick effort of will sent his hearing to join his sight.

"I don't like it," the commander said. "What you're suggesting is a breach of protocol."

"What's more important, protocol or your lord governor's orders?" Renna countered.

"Oh, I'm not questioning my orders, ma'am. Just registering my dislike of them. Keeping two companies at the fort for an extended period will look like aggression to Montage."

"Why would they even know?" Renna asked. "It'll only be a couple weeks at most. We need to make sure everything goes smoothly with our guest's mission."

"We're not even going into the workshop," the commander

said. "What possible difference could we make from the outside?"

"I meant," Renna said, her annoyance growing clearer by the second. "When they've retrieved the artifact, we'll need the returning company to escort them back to Audin. The survivors would make an easy target on their own. Understand?"

The commander sighed. "Not really, but if that is his lordship's wish, we shall, of course, obey."

"Good. Now, go enjoy yourselves. I'm going back to camp to make sure our guests are settled in."

Otto returned his senses to his body and considered what he'd learned. Was Renna planning to attack them on the road back to Audin? You could read her words that way, but you could also read them as simply acting as a concerned ally. He still had no real proof that his so-called friends were planning to betray him, he just couldn't shake the feeling he got from August. There was no way the man's greed would allow him to just let an artifact from Colt's Workshop pass without making a move to seize it.

The biggest problem was that if Otto made the first move, August would be fully justified in carrying out his betrayal. But if Otto hung back and reacted, he might end up in a really bad spot at best and dead at worst. With that in mind, Otto resolved to set his backup plan in motion. He just needed a few more details.

‹›

When Renna arrived at their camp, Otto had emerged from his tent, settled in a folding chair, and accepted a bowl of reasonably edible stew from Corina. He swallowed a mouthful of tough meat and asked, "Everything okay?"

"Fine. The men are having a grand time in town. I'm sorry you couldn't join them. The next sign of civilization is the fort and that's a good ten days away."

"I'm surprised some enterprising people haven't set up way stations for the soldiers traveling between the city and fort. Seems like easy coin."

Renna smiled. "We only do shift changes once a month and this road gets little other traffic."

"I see. There was one other thing if you don't mind."

"Of course. I am at your service."

"Who is Montage? I heard some of your men muttering about them. Is it some sort of bandit gang?"

Her pretty face twisted in distaste, whether at her imagined chatty soldier, or at an enemy city-state, Otto couldn't say. "Montage is the name of the city-state whose fort is closest to ours. It's a backwater state that produces little beyond timber, wheat, and furs. Their armor is at least two generations behind ours and rumor has it the king's son and heir to the throne is a vain idiot."

"Audin isn't on good terms with them then?"

"We have little to do with them, but there is no outright animosity between our nations. You needn't be concerned about them troubling us. They keep an even smaller force at their fort than our one hundred."

Otto nodded. "I appreciate you taking the time to explain. The balance of power in Colt's Land is far more tangled than what we ever had to deal with back home. I find it much easier to know who my enemy is and destroy them."

She sighed. "If only life were so simple. Excuse me, I find I'm weary and we leave at first light."

"I didn't intend to hold you up. Sleep well."

When she'd trudged off Otto stood as well. "Hans, do you have your coin? The special one I prepared for you?"

"Always, my lord." Hans dug the rune-marked silver coin out of his pocket and held it out to Otto.

"Thank you. I have an errand to run. Whatever happens, no one is to enter my tent until I give you the all clear."

"Understood, my lord."

Otto ducked back inside and set the coin in the center of the largest open spot on the floor. Next he went to his tiny portable desk, gathered his writing material, and jotted a brief note for Montage's ambassador from a concerned citizen eager to maintain the balance of power.

When the ink had dried, he became one with the ether and rushed to Audin. He appeared in the park where he'd hidden the enchanted coin and wrapped himself immediately in a cloak of invisibility. It was dark and not a soul moved in the streets. That would make his job a little easier anyway.

Otto had only gone a block toward the embassies when he stopped. In all of his planning he'd neglected one important thing. He had no idea which building belonged to Montage. Delivering his note would be a serious challenge without that particular bit of information.

He set out again, careful to keep to the center of the street where he wouldn't have to worry about running into a suddenly opened door. A five-minute walk brought him to the embassy district. The first building had light coming from some of its windows. Unfortunately, there were no guards outside to question.

Looked like he'd have to check them one by one. He found a quiet spot in an alley beside a tavern, closed his eyes, and sent his vision flying. The nearest embassy was also the largest and most decorated. That didn't match the description of Montage Renna had given. From the sound of it, they were low on funds, so the smallest and most ordinary building would be the place to start.

A minute of searching brought him to a single-story building without a hint of ostentation. He nearly dismissed it as not an embassy, but it had to be given its location.

One way to be sure. He flew through the wall and into a large room holding ten chairs. A lonely desk along the far side was covered with papers. He conjured a speck of light and read the top one. Sure enough, it was addressed to Montage's ambassador, one Jas Cornen. Otto didn't even know if that was a man or a woman. After a moment, he decided it didn't matter.

Using the ether like a pair of invisible hands, he opened a window and carried his message scroll through, placing the unrolled scroll directly under the topmost piece of paper. Satisfied, he locked the window and returned his senses to his body.

Mission complete, Otto willed himself back to his tent.

"Lord Shenk is not to be disturbed," Hans said from outside.

Otto frowned, picked up the rune-marked coin and slipped it in his pocket before pushing the flap aside. "What in heaven's name is all the noise? Can't a man sleep in peace?"

Renna and the unit commander stood facing a scowling Hans who had his arms crossed so that his right hand was only inches from the hilt of his sword.

She shifted her gaze from Hans to Otto. "There's a problem. Raiders hit the town while our soldiers were celebrating. It was a smash and grab. One of our magical engineers was taken and three soldiers killed."

Otto shook his head as if trying to clear the sleep from his mind. How did this all happen in the time he was gone? The trip back to Audin hadn't taken more than twenty minutes.

"I'm sorry to hear that." Otto tried his best to sound like he cared. "What exactly do you want me to do about it? You have a hundred men and three more wizards. If that's not enough to hunt down some grubby bandits, you've got serious problems."

"Our magical engineers aren't trained for battle," Renna said. "They have some combat ability, but not much and we have only two scouts, one of which was killed in the raid."

"So, what, you want me and my team to hunt them down and retrieve your engineer? Will you provide me with replacements for the trip into the workshop if some of my people are killed?"

Renna glanced at the commander who shook his head.

"We don't have forces to spare," he said.

"Neither do I." Otto turned back to his tent.

"Wait!" Renna said.

He faced her again and quirked an eyebrow.

"May I speak to you alone a moment?"

He frowned, but she wasn't stupid enough to try and seduce him again much less threaten him. "Fine."

He held the flap open and she ducked in ahead of him.

Otto stopped one stride inside and crossed his arms. "I'm listening."

She sat on his cot and patted the cushion next to her. "I don't want anyone to overhear."

Otto conjured a silence ward. "I could strangle you to death and no one would hear your cries for help. Now, say what you have to say."

"My orders are to seize whatever you bring out of the workshop on the way back to Audin."

Otto feigned surprise. "And you're telling me this, why?"

"I think it's a stupid idea that will accomplish nothing beyond getting a lot of people killed, many of them on our side. All that interests me is the wellbeing of Audin. We can't spare engineers. The truth is we don't have enough as it is despite what August might have told you. The man taken was the leader of this team. His loss would force us to get someone else from the city, someone that would be better used designing new weapons not sitting in a fort in the middle of nowhere."

"What's your offer?"

"Save our engineer, and I guarantee you safe passage back to Audin. What August might do when you arrive is beyond my control."

Otto stared at her, trying to figure out if she was sincere. It felt honest and he saw no sign that she was lying. Renna seemed to legitimately fear him and no doubt figured, correctly, that she would be the first to die if she betrayed him. Accepting her offer would at least eliminate one potential threat.

Besides, how hard could it be to free one engineer?

"Very well, I accept your terms. Which way did the bandits take your man?"

"West, toward the desert."

"What's out there?"

"I don't know. Nothing of value, certainly. Audin doesn't patrol the area."

"Wonderful, we're going in blind then."

ᖆ

Otto and every member of the team he'd brought from Garen made their way west from camp. The night was clear and the moon bright so they had no trouble seeing. On one hand this was good since they could see the enemy coming, on the other hand that worked against them as well. Otto would have preferred to wait until morning, but heaven only knew how far the bandits might go by then.

They were swinging wide of the town in hopes of picking up the bandits' trail on the far side. The flat prairie made for easy walking at least. There was hardly a tree worthy of the name for miles. So different from home, but not unpleasant for all that.

"Why are we doing this again?" Axel was walking beside him at the head of the small group while one of his men ran ahead to look for tracks.

That very question had been running through Otto's head since he agreed to Renna's deal. There was no guarantee she would even keep her word, though she'd be insane to betray him now that she had warned him of her plan.

"Think of it as a goodwill-building exercise. If we save one of their own, it will make it that much harder for them to betray us."

Axel snorted. "A good soldier will obey orders regardless."

Otto turned his head a fraction to take a better look at his brother. Axel had grown a beard during his time in Straken and his eyes had lost some of their wariness. He hadn't been in a fight in months. Otto would never accuse Axel of losing his edge, but this little exercise would be a good refresher.

"That's true, but even the best soldier will hesitate to kill someone that saved their life or the life of a comrade. That second or two might make the difference between us living or dying. Besides, I hate bandits. Miserable vermin, the lot of them."

"Lord Shenk." Otto and Axel both turned to look when Cobb spoke. "Colten's waiting just ahead."

"He must have found their trail," Axel said.

They reached the tracker a minute later. Colten saluted then said, "They made no effort to disguise their trail. The bandits are headed due west at a quick march."

"Numbers?" Axel asked.

"Best guess, a dozen or there about. They're all on foot which gives us a chance to catch up."

The bandits had a nearly two-hour head start. Otto doubted they'd stop until they reached their camp or base. It seemed they had a long night of hiking ahead of them.

Otto's thought proved prophetic when three hours later they reached the edge of the desert. It didn't look like Otto expected. Instead of hills of sand there was nothing but hard-packed gravel and dust.

"Tracking's going to be hard in this," Colten said.

"I'm going to have a quick look around." Otto closed his eyes and went scouting.

His sight flew a hundred yards up before sailing out across the desert. It was a miserable landscape. He couldn't imagine how it supported life. At the very least there was little in the way of ambush spots.

From on high he spotted a light in the distance. Since it was the only sign of life in the area, he went for a closer look. Fourteen men, one of them bound with rope, sat around a campfire. Some four-legged creature about the size of a house cat roasted over the flames. Their prisoner didn't appear injured at least. They probably wanted to ransom him back to Audin.

The ether swirled oddly around one of the bandits. Not like

a wizard. Not like anything Otto had ever seen. Now what had he stumbled across?

He had barely begun to study the bandits' camp when the one with the strange magic looked right up into his invisible eyes.

Otto ended his spell instantly. "I found them. A little under a mile northwest of here. One of the bandits spotted my extended vision. I don't know what his abilities are, but let's be cautious."

Axel barked orders and they quick-marched toward the bandit's camp. It didn't take long for the smell of smoke and glow of the fire to reach them.

At Axel's gesture the scouts split off to surround the bandit camp. Otto fully expected to find it empty, but was surprised to notice everyone sitting exactly as he left them. The bandit with the odd connection to the ether stood but made no move to reach for the axe hanging at his side. The bound magical engineer sat between a pair of bandits, but neither made a move to threaten him.

"You were the ones spying on us," the bandit said. "I sensed the danger at once."

More curious than worried Otto asked, "If you knew you were in danger, why didn't you run?"

"More danger if we ran. Waiting was safest."

Otto scratched his cheek as he tried to figure out the man's plan, assuming he had one. "You're not a wizard, yet you're connected to the ether. You saw my invisible eyes."

"I saw nothing," the bandit said. "I sensed danger from above. When I prepared to give the order to withdraw, I sensed worse danger. That's how the gift works. There was danger in raiding the town, but I misread what it meant. Now, I suppose we pay with our lives."

"Who taught you how to use your power?" Otto asked.

"No one. I was born with it. The power works when it wants to, gives no details, only feelings. It's a small advantage, but one that's kept my band safe for two years."

"Amazing." In all his reading, Otto had never come across something like this. An individual with a unique magical ability that worked outside of their conscious control. He'd have to ask Lord Karonin about it when he got home. At the very least it would be a shame to waste such a unique magical talent by killing the man.

"We won't resist," the bandit said. "I only ask for a clean death for my men and I."

Otto shook his head. "I'm not going to kill you. I only want your prisoner. Turn him over and you're free to go."

The bandit stared at him, clearly not trusting his good fortune. "I will not lead you back to my village."

"I'm not interested in your village. Hans, cut our friend free."

When Hans stepped toward the bound prisoner, the two bandits beside him shifted out of the way. Otto had spent far more time hunting bandits than he would have liked, but never had an encounter gone like this. It was bizarre. Not that he planned to complain. Completing the mission without losing any of his men was a good day. Finding a unique magical phenomenon was a bonus.

"Are there more like you in your village?" Otto asked.

"Not now, but one is born now and again." The bandit shifted and when he did the firelight hit his eyes, revealing lines like white lightning in them. The ether was focused there. "Why are you letting us go? No soldier of Audin has ever spared a bandit."

Otto had never spared a bandit before either. "You interest

me. And I am no soldier of Audin. Get going and don't attack that town again for a while."

"On my honor I will not." The bandit held out his hand and Otto grasped his wrist. They shook and a moment later the bandits vanished into the desert. Oddly enough he had no doubt the bandit would keep his promise.

"Heaven bless you, Lord Shenk," the engineer said. "I feared those savages would kill and cook me. I can't figure out why you let them go."

"Neither can I," Axel said. "We had them dead to rights. They weren't even going to resist. In my experience, the only good bandit is a dead one."

Otto shrugged. He wasn't about to explain his reasoning with so many people around, especially a wizard from Audin. "This isn't our country. We were asked to do a job and we did it. The fate of thirteen half-starved desert rats isn't our concern. Let's head back. I'd like to sleep at least a little before we leave in the morning."

The group set out and Otto kept to the rear. As they walked, he sent threads of ether into the sand. There had to be something out here that explained the bandit's magical ability. Half an hour later he found it and nearly laughed.

The fools in Audin said they had no mithril, yet there were streaks of powdered mithril running through sections of the desert. That had to be what triggered the bandit's magical ability. The mithril must have strengthened the ether around their village enough to alter the children born there.

"Master?" Corina asked. "Is everything all right?"

"Everything's fine." Better than that, Otto had found a new mystery to research. He'd have to become immortal just to answer all the questions he had bouncing around inside his head.

CHAPTER 15

The fort didn't impress Otto. The wood-and-stone structure looked sound enough, but somehow, after seeing the wonders of their armory, he'd expected something a bit more magical. A simple wooden wall about thirty feet tall surrounded a two-story stone fortress. A single gate, fifteen feet tall, allowed entrance. Four guard towers manned by archers kept watch over the surrounding territory. Of Colt's Workshop, there was no sign.

Only a few hours remained before dark. A hot meal, heaven willing a bucket of warm water to wash up with, and a good night's sleep would be wonderful. Though whether he could sleep with his ultimate destination so close was another question altogether.

"Lord Shenk," Hans said. "Someone's watching us."

Otto tore his gaze away from the fort and followed Hans's finger to a lone mounted soldier little more than a speck on the horizon. Silhouetted by the setting sun, the figure was easy to spot. Which suggested he was making a point of revealing his presence.

"Good eye." Otto turned to the driver. "Who's keeping watch over us?"

The driver spared a glance to his left and grunted. "Montage scout. They never come close enough to be a problem."

"And the workshop?"

"Two days further north."

Clearly conversation wasn't the soldier's strong suit so Otto left him in peace. He'd expected the fort to be closer to his destination. How did you guard something out of your sight? On the other hand, since no one had ever gone inside and emerged alive, there was probably no reason to be overly concerned they'd miss something. Either way, it worked to Otto's advantage.

Otto looked back just in time to see the rider wheel around and ride off. No doubt to report their arrival. He couldn't help wondering what the Montage ambassador made of the note he'd left on his desk. Given what happened with Bandon, they had to at least take it seriously. As long as any attack came after Otto and his team were inside the workshop it would work to his advantage. If they attacked early, that would pose a problem.

Fifteen minutes after spotting the scout, the wagons rolled into the fort. When the last wagon was through, a heavy timber was put in place, sealing them in.

Otto and the others clambered down from their ride. Axel eased his way over, hand resting on the hilt of his sword. "What now?"

"According to our driver, the workshop is another two days north. We'll rest here tonight and set out at first light."

"Gonna be tight." Cobb looked around in distaste.

He wasn't wrong about that. Any thought Otto had about a

night of comfort before leaving was gone the instant he laid eyes on their temporary home.

Over his brother's shoulder Otto spotted Renna approaching. He met her halfway to the group. "I fear it's another night of camping for all of us," she said by way of greeting.

"I suspected as much. Assuming we can have a hot meal and warm water to wash off the dust, I won't complain."

She smiled. "That, at least, I can promise you. I can also offer a word of caution."

Otto quirked an eyebrow.

"Montage has been more aggressive with their scouting over the last several days. I doubt they'd be stupid enough to enter our area of operation, especially within the thirty-mile zone around the workshop, but you should keep your guard up at the halfway point."

"I always have my guard up, but thank you for the warning. Have there been issues with your neighbor to the west before?"

"Nothing serious. The city-states are constantly skirmishing along the borders. One of us claims a valley here and another claims a hill there. The borders are constantly moving. As long as there isn't a full-scale war, no one thinks anything of it."

"I'll leave you to set up. We've cordoned off an area near the northern wall. You'll see it roped off. Dinner will be brought to you at sunset."

Otto nodded his thanks, his mind occupied with thoughts of Montage raiders. The irony that he might be killed by a force he'd set in motion wasn't lost on him. Still, more threats made it harder for anyone to focus on them.

Hopefully it would be enough to get them all safely home.

○

Otto stood in the fort's yard with the magical engineer he'd rescued from the bandits. The man's name was Ghent and he spent most of five minutes babbling about how grateful he was for Otto's help. Keeping a smile on his face had nearly broken Otto, but he managed it. Every bit of goodwill he could build now made it that much more likely that they succeeded with the mission.

Hovering beside the two wizards was the eight-foot-long load carrier. The device really was a fascinating bit of magic. If he had more time, Otto would have loved to learn how to make one himself. As it was, he was content to bind this one to his will.

"Okay, Otto, stretch out with the ether and find the carrier's crystal," Ghent said.

Otto did as he was bid, and soon he had the blue crystal surrounded by ether. "What now?"

"Since I've already severed the connection between the carrier and its former master, all you need to do is build a tether between you and the gem. Put two threads of ether into the gem. You'll find an ethereal construct shaped like a hoop. Tie your threads to that."

Otto frowned and guided the threads into the crystal. The construct was easy enough to spot even though he'd never seen anything like it. Tying the knot took little effort, but it was awkward. He usually used the ether to augment or transform the real world. Fusing two bits of ether together when he only controlled one took all his concentration.

When at last the knot pulled tight he let out a breath. Otto had fought battles that left him less tired. And yet he also felt exhilarated. The new magic reminded him how much remained to learn.

"That's very good," Ghent said. "I didn't think you'd manage it on the first try. It took me four the first time I bound a gem to my will. Now, do you want to practice some basic commands?"

The sky was getting brighter by the minute, but Otto figured he'd better learn everything possible while he had the chance.

"Okay. What do I do?"

"The carrier's default setting is 'follow.' Walk toward the fort and then back."

Otto strode off and the carrier followed about ten feet behind. It was a bit like a hound at heel.

When he reached Ghent Otto asked, "What else can it do?"

"You can command it to remain in place or come to you from a distance. It's not a terribly advanced construct, so that's about it."

"And how do I give it commands?"

"Picture what you want it to do, in this case stay where it is. Visualize it not moving. When the image is strong in your mind send it through the ether to the gem."

If connecting to the gem was awkward, this was worse. How did one send an image through the ether? Picturing the carrier not moving was easy enough, but transmitting that image to the crystal balked him.

Finally he settled on focusing his will. *STAY!*

Otto took a few steps and the carrier followed after. Swallowing a curse Otto returned to Ghent. "It didn't work."

"You just need more practice. Forming your thoughts into a shape the crystal understands is difficult. It may take some time to master."

"Otto!" Axel called from beside the wagon Renna had provided for their journey. "We're ready."

"Seems I'm out of time. I'll practice some more when we make camp tonight. Thanks for your help."

"There's one more thing. Another wizard can sever your connection to the carrier, by cutting the ethereal cord you tied around the crystal. Bear that in mind if you leave it behind while exploring."

"I will." Otto strode over to the rest of his team, the carrier following along like an obedient puppy.

"You always wanted a pet," Axel said when he arrived. He held out a hand and Otto let his brother pull him up into the back of the wagon.

"I wanted a dog, not a magical floating box." Otto sat beside Corina and searched for a place to put his feet amidst all the supplies. They had enough food for two weeks. If they hadn't found the chamber by then, they probably weren't going to.

"You know Stephan would have just strangled any pet you had." Axel sat across from him. "Okay, Cobb."

On the driver's seat, Cobb snapped the reins and the magical horses set out for the open gate. Renna stood on the wall above the gate and waved to them as they passed underneath. Corina waved back.

Their first day of travel passed without incident. The magical horses were tireless and devoured ground at an amazing rate. What Otto wouldn't give for a hundred of them along with matching suits of man-sized enchanted armor. The combination would make an unstoppable cavalry. Of course, since they had no one to fight at the moment, there was little point in building such a force.

As dark approached, the group reached the campsite Renna mentioned during their last meeting. Audin's forces had cleared it out back when they imagined making regular trips to loot Colt's Workshop. After all these years it was little more than a dirt clearing off to the side of the road.

"I like these metal horses," Cobb said as he climbed down from the driver's seat. "Don't have to feed 'em. Hell, we don't even have to unhitch them."

Otto walked around a little, trying to work the stiffness out of his legs. The carrier followed him around, keeping a constant three paces behind.

He stopped and turned to glare at the thing. Time for another test. He imagined the carrier staying where it was until he had the image perfectly in his mind. Then he wrapped the image in a bubble of ether and sent it down the thread that bound the carrier to him. When he resumed his hike, the carrier stayed where it was.

Though he gave no outward sign, pleasure at this small success filled him. Now that he understood the principle, he should be able to give the carrier any other command he might wish.

Half an hour later, the tents were pitched, a fire burned, and a stew pot bubbled over it. Hardly fine dining, but once they reached the workshop it would be cold jerky and dried fruit. Otto shook his head and dropped to the ground between Hans and Corina.

"Do we have time for a lesson, Master?" Corina asked.

"Have you practiced extending your sight?"

"When it was safe. I can manage a hundred yards or so."

"That's not bad. Why don't you try your hearing instead? The process is exactly the same only with your ears instead of your eyes."

Otto watched her guide threads of ether into each ear then back out. She sent them into the dark and he smiled. Soon enough she'd be able to detach each of her senses and extend them. These were useful spells that would serve her well for life.

Only seconds later Corina ended the spell. He was about to ask why she quit so quickly when she said, "There are people out there. I heard their footsteps."

Otto expanded the ethereal barrier that protected him to enclose Hans and Corina. Across the camp, Axel and Cobb were bickering about something. Otto extended his voice and whispered in Axel's ear. "Company coming."

Using hand signals, Axel directed his men into fighting position. Otto trusted his brother to manage that while he sent his sight, augmented by a dark vision spell into the sky. He spotted the strangers at once, ten of them. Though rendered in shades of gray, they were clearly armed soldiers sneaking up on the camp in hopes of taking them by surprise. If Corina hadn't heard them approaching, they certainly would have succeeded.

The fact that there were only ten of them meant they either didn't know who they were dealing with or didn't want a fight. Since they had drawn their swords, Otto assumed the former.

"Orders, my lord?" Hans asked.

"Stay still and let them make the first move. If they only want to talk, then we'll talk. If they prefer violence, well, they've come to the right place."

Otto enhanced his senses but didn't extend them again. Soon enough he heard the tall grass rustling. He caught Axel looking at him, nodded, and mouthed the word "close."

His brother quirked an eyebrow.

Otto held his hand palm down in what he hoped was the signal to hold position. He really needed to learn the sign language the scouts used, especially if they were going to serve as his personal troops.

The soldiers burst into the clearing and one of them shouted, "No one move. If you resist, you die."

They wore green and gold uniforms which argued against bandits. Nevertheless Otto said, "The bandits in this part of the country are better dressed than most."

The man that spoke bristled at the insult. "We are not bandits, we're Montage rangers assigned to the nearby fort. My commander ordered us to find out your purpose in approaching the workshop. You will come with us for questioning."

"No, I don't think we will," Otto said. "My visit to Colt's Workshop has been delayed enough as it is."

"Don't be foolish," said the man Otto thought of as the enemy leader. "I have a hundred men encircling your camp right now."

Corina stiffened beside him but Otto just shook his head. "That's a good bluff, but I checked, you're all alone out here. I doubt there are even a hundred soldiers stationed at your fort. Now go away, our supper is almost ready."

The leader tightened his grip on his sword. "I have my orders. One way or another, I will have answers."

Otto despised dealing with stubborn fools. He flicked his iron ring and ten threads of ether shot out, binding the rangers in place.

"Axel, would you and your men be so kind as to disarm these idiots? Be sure and search them thoroughly. I don't want anyone doing anything else stupid."

Half an hour later the ten rangers had been stripped to their smallclothes, their weapons piled off to one side. Axel glanced at Otto. "That thorough enough?"

"Indeed, thank you." Otto stood and strode over to the

commander. "Just out of curiosity, what did you want to know?"

"Your purpose. The workshop is a death trap. Teams beyond counting, many far larger than yours, have entered and not returned. What's in there that could tempt you to such a risk?"

"I don't think I'll tell you that. Anything else?"

"Is it true you exchanged mithril for access? If so, how much?"

"That is true. I gave August half a ton of raw ore as a down payment with another half ton when we return. What that will yield in pure mithril I can't say."

The commander's jaw dropped. "That will double or even triple their force of magical armor. Do you have any idea what you've done?"

"I made a deal. If August honors his end, I'll honor mine. Very simple." Otto took a step closer. "I'm going to let you go now. But if I see either you or your comrades again, you won't walk away from the encounter. Understand?"

"I do."

Otto released his spell and the rangers hurried away as quickly as their feet would carry them. He watched them with his magical sight until they mounted their steel horses and rode off.

"Are you sure letting them go was a good idea?" Axel asked.

"I thought you were the one that said I shouldn't be so casual about killing people. Anyway, I'm hoping the other city-states will attack Audin. We should be able to sneak through the chaos and escape through the portal."

"And if they don't?"

"Then we'll have to fight our way through whatever trap August sets."

"That's a workshop?" Axel said.

Otto shared his brother's incredulity. Colt's so-called workshop looked more like a small city made of steel. Six towers jutted above the metal wall surrounding the place. Nothing moved on the battlements, but Otto didn't doubt for a second it was defended. He silently cursed his master for neglecting to mention that the workshop was actually a city.

They'd arrived within sight of the massive place three hours before sunset. Nothing and no one had tried to interfere with them after they sent the rangers on their way the night before. Now that they were here, Otto wasn't sure how to proceed. In his mind he'd envisioned a single tower like his master's armories or perhaps a large citadel. But this?

Two weeks' worth of supplies might not be enough to search half of it. Since they'd been traveling, Otto had seen no signs of animals and the few birds he spotted were small, certainly not enough to feed thirteen people.

Otto sighed. He'd worry about food later if they had to. Right now they needed some way inside. The wall facing them had no gate.

"Let's ride around the perimeter," Otto said. "Everyone keep a sharp lookout. I don't want to be taken by surprise by some automated defense. Corina, keep an eye out for any magical reaction. I'm going to have a look inside."

Otto closed his eyes and sent his sight flying towards the workshop. Directly above the wall he struck an invisible barrier his magical eyes couldn't pass through. Some defensive spell of Lord Colt's to keep out spies no doubt.

He blinked his vision back. Looked like they'd have to do this the hard way.

Halfway around the city Corina said, "Master, there's something in the metal."

Otto looked closer and sure enough there was an ethereal construct built into the wall. It resembled the eye hook that allowed him to control the carrier, only it was shaped like a door ring.

"Stop here, Cobb," Otto said.

When the wagon had clattered to a stop, Otto climbed out and moved closer to the wall. Nothing attacked him so that was a good sign.

"Why are we stopping here?" Axel asked. "It's just a blank section of wall."

"To you perhaps, but I can see a bit more. Prepare your men. I'm going to try and open it."

Otto shaped the ether into a ten-thread tentacle and sent it to wrap around the ring. First he yanked, but nothing happened. A twist to the left brought the same result. When he tried to the right, something happened. The ring twisted a fraction, but not nearly enough.

Ten more threads shot out to reinforce his construct and he tried again. This time it turned ninety degrees and stopped. No reaction from the wall.

Frowning with concentration, Otto added ten more threads, nearly his maximum output. Brow furrowed and sweat pouring down his face, Otto twisted with all his might.

The ring turned a full one hundred and eighty degrees and a vibration ran through the ground. A hole opened in the ground and a lever rose out of it.

Otto checked it for traps and found nothing. He walked over, grabbed it, and yanked. It quivered but didn't move.

"Hans, give me a hand."

Together the two men pulled until Otto's jaw ached and his shoulders screamed.

All at once the lever gave. He nearly fell on his face with the sudden release. A section of wall directly in front of them melted away like the metal was liquid, granting access to the city. The lever vanished back into the ground.

The scouts shouldered their laden packs and Otto led the way inside. The six towers he'd seen from outside were actually the tops of much larger buildings. The only six buildings inside the walls. Each of them covered what Otto guessed was about ten blocks. In the center, a large, open plaza of some sort filled the space between them.

"Master!

At Corina's anxious shout Otto spun in time to watch the wall close up behind them. He had a moment of panic that faded when he spotted the lever jutting out of the ground to the left of where the opening had appeared.

"It's alright. At least we won't have to worry about anyone coming up behind us."

"Unless they know how to open the wall," Axel said.

If Axel had realized how much power it took to turn that ring, he wouldn't have worried about it. Besides, anyone after them would be more apt to wait outside in ambush than to follow them into what the locals considered a death trap.

"Let's see if we can find a way into one of those buildings," Otto said

"We'll look for a door," Axel said. "You keep watch for any magical threats."

Otto nodded and the scouts split up to look around. Hans and Corina remained beside him.

"I'm surprised you'd let your brother take charge," Hans said.

"This is exactly what I brought Axel and his men for. They're scouts. What I know about sneaking around wouldn't fill a very big book. I just turn invisible and try to walk softly. Better to let those who know what they're doing handle this."

Otto closed his eyes, but when he tried to extend his vision the ether refused to obey. Frowning, he summoned lightning around his fingers and it instantly crackled to life. Fire obeyed as well. The wards must only restrict spying magic. Annoying, but not the end of the world.

He had taken a single step toward the city center when Axel and his men came sprinting from behind the left-hand tower. He didn't have a chance to ask what the problem was before it appeared: a metal construct shaped like a spider twenty feet long with foot-long fangs that dripped with acid.

The spider had a crimson gem imbedded in the first segment of its body. Otto sent thirty threads' worth of ether to wrap it up.

The construct slowed but didn't stop. If Otto couldn't break its link to the ether with thirty threads, there was no way he could defeat it magically.

Axel stopped beside him, panting for breath.

Otto ignored him and turned to a young man with a bow. "Put an arrow through that glowing gem in its chest."

The spider kept coming and it overwhelmed Otto's magic. If his ether barrier failed, that thing would tear them apart.

Corina moved over beside him and added her four threads to the spell. While it made little difference, Otto appreciated the effort.

The archer fitted an arrow to his now-strung bow and loosed.

His mithril-tipped arrow hit the gem and skipped off. It

wasn't much, but Otto found a tiny flaw in the crystal. He shoved ether into it and squeezed.

The crystal shattered and the spider crashed to the ground ten feet from them.

Otto blew out a long breath. That had been far too close.

He squeezed Corina's shoulder. "Good job."

"You too," he added to the youthful archer.

"I didn't do much," the archer said. "The arrows are too pointed. I need something blunt to shatter a crystal."

Unfortunately, forged mithril was nearly indestructible. Otto had neither the time nor the equipment to alter the shape of his arrowheads.

"You did enough. That tiny crack you made gave me an opening to destroy it. Don't forget to recover your arrowhead before we move on."

"I guess we know why no one ever made it back with any loot," Hans said. "That thing probably tore them to pieces."

"But we beat it," Corina said. Her face was pale from exerting herself so much. "It should be safe now, right?"

Axel snorted. "If that's the only guardian, I'll kiss Stephan's wife. I suggest we stick together from now on."

Otto nodded his agreement. "And make sure everyone with a bow keeps it ready. A few seconds might mean the difference between life and death."

CHAPTER 16

As a diplomat and spy, Renna had more than her share of patience. She shouldn't be worried about Otto and his team yet. In fact, they probably only reached the workshop today. Thinking about their reaction to the size of the place made her smile, but it didn't last. They could all very well be dead by now. Colt's Workshop didn't come by its deadly reputation for no reason.

Despite her training, she couldn't relax, so instead she spent most of her time pacing atop the battlements. Her gaze never wavered far from the direction of the workshop. Her desire to know what was happening would have to stay unfulfilled. She was no wizard and the gift of far sight was beyond her.

Dragging her gaze away from the north to the northwest she froze. In the distance, a force of soldiers, some mounted on steel horses but most on foot, were headed directly for the fort. Four massive, twenty-foot-tall suits of armor stomped along with them. Given their approach vector, they had to be from Montage.

"Commander!" she shouted.

The garrison's leader had been overseeing a drill in the training yard. He stopped what he was doing and looked up at her.

"Enemy forces approaching. Looks like Montage's entire garrison."

He scowled, ran for the nearest set of stairs and joined her on the wall. "What are they thinking?"

"If their scouts spotted Otto and his team leaving, they might have found out they weren't from Audin. It wouldn't take much to learn where they came from and that we defied the will of the council. They might even have permission from the other city-states for an attack. Of course none of that actually matters at the moment."

"No, it doesn't." The commander left her and ran down the wall to the nearest alarm gong. Soon a cacophony of noise filled the air.

Soldiers poured out of the barracks and ran for the armory. Their magical armor would be the first thing readied for combat. One advantage they had was the double garrison. Montage would be facing twice as many soldiers as they expected.

Renna was content to leave the soldiers to their work. She hurried down from the wall and dashed for the fort. She needed to get to the communications room and contact August. If Montage had made a move here, the other city-states would be in motion as well. And while none of them had an army close to Audin, once they decided to act, it wouldn't take long to move their forces into place.

She dodged a pair of soldiers who came running out of the main gate and slipped inside. The central room served as the fort dining hall. The communications room was a small chamber off that. A single hard rap on the door brought the magical engineer on duty to the entrance.

The nervous young wizard licked his lips and asked, "Ma'am?"

"I need to reach Audin."

He moved aside to let her enter. A silver-framed mirror hung on the wall and he hurried over to it. While he did whatever magical thing was required to activate the mirror, he asked, "I heard the noise outside. What's going on?"

"Montage has sent its forces against us. Whether they set a siege or attack directly, time will tell."

He swallowed then turned slowly, his face pale and sweaty. She found it hard to believe he was the same age as Otto. The foreign nobleman held himself with a calm confidence that would have been impressive in a man twice his age.

"This is my first deployment outside the city. Are we going to die?"

She was spared having to answer when Lord Audin appeared in the mirror. Renna glanced at the wizard. "Wait outside, please." He scrambled out and shut the door.

"What is it?" he asked.

"Montage is attacking the fort. If they've somehow become aware of our deal with Otto, they may have alerted the other city-states. I recommend putting the military on full alert."

He grimaced. "How could they have learned the truth? Otto erased the Bandon ambassador's memory and she hadn't told anyone else what she learned."

"Maybe someone else at the embassy overheard something. It doesn't really matter how they found out. The important thing is being ready when their forces strike."

"You are right, of course. We'll need to move aggressively. If we can hit the enemy's forces before they link up, we might have a chance. Thank you for the warning. But don't forget your other mission. Whatever Otto brings out of the workshop, I want it."

"I remember, my lord." She bowed as the lord governor faded from view.

Double-crossing Otto would be more dangerous than fighting the forces besieging the fort. However, those forces would at least serve to provide an excuse for why she failed.

〇

Otto stared at the tower they had just circled as if he could force an entrance to appear by sheer force of will. Pity it didn't work that way. In fact, he had no idea exactly how it did work. There were no handles, no hidden magical switches, no seams, nothing that indicated an entrance. He considered and rejected trying to cut an opening with his mithril blade. Not so much because he feared damaging the sword as because he doubted such a crude method would work.

He scratched his cheek and turned away from the frustrating building to face his companions who stood waiting for some brilliant suggestion about their next move. He wished he had one.

Since only one place remained to check he said, "Let's head to the city center. Maybe we'll find something there."

"It's empty," Axel said.

Otto shrugged. "I'm open to suggestions."

When no one offered any, Otto set out. The steel streets were wide enough for a wagon and perfectly smooth. No sign that they had ever been used marred their surface. As they walked, everyone's gaze darted all around. Even though they hadn't seen another guardian since defeating the metal spider, they all expected an attack at any moment.

Happily they reached their destination unmolested. In the city center they found a round, sunken area that brought to mind a fighting pit. Like everything else in the city, the walls and floor were solid steel. What interested Otto were the six portcullises built into the walls of the pit. Each one lined up exactly with a tower.

"There's our way in." Otto leapt down, using the ether to slow his fall.

"How are we supposed to get down there?" Axel asked. "I don't fancy breaking my legs in a sixty-yard fall."

"Form two groups of six. Stay close together."

When they had formed up as he wished, Otto conjured a platform under the first group and carried them down. The second joined them a moment later.

Now that they were assembled, he went to the first portcullis. A cursory examination revealed no way, either magical or mundane, to lift the barrier. The steel wasn't actually that thick. Otto drew his sword. A handful of powerful, horrendously loud hacks carved an opening four feet wide in the portcullis.

He stepped back and listened. If there was a guardian, that noise should bring it running.

Five minutes later nothing had shown itself. Otto looked at Corina. "Would you like to conjure us a light?"

Her smile was nearly enough to brighten the tunnel on its own. A moment of concentration brought a pair of glowing, white orbs into existence. She sent one down the tunnel ahead of them and kept the second overhead.

At Axel's command, five of his men with Cobb in the lead started down the tunnel. Otto, Corina, Hans and Axel himself made up the second group, and the remaining five scouts brought up the rear. Their steps echoed as they marched down the passage. Otto tried to guess their position relative to the tower they were approaching. He estimated five hundred yards separated the side of the pit from the tower's wall.

Keeping up a cautious pace, surrounded by menacing darkness, the group continued their way under the workshop.

The lead scout froze ahead of them.

"What is it?" Axel asked.

"I don't know what it is," Cobb said. "But I don't want to touch it."

Otto saw nothing in the ether that worried him. He brushed past the front row and stopped cold. The remains of a construct blocked half the tunnel. It looked like it might have been an ant, but now its rear legs had been torn off and its central body segment ripped in half. He shuddered to think what could have done that to something made of solid-steel plates. Hopefully whatever it was didn't await them further down the tunnel.

A silent command left the carrier behind as he eased his way around the deactivated construct. He found a cavity in the center of its head where no doubt its power crystal had rested. Perhaps Lord Colt had salvaged the crystal but never returned to recover the rest of the ant.

Otto shook his head. It was all conjecture and irrelevant in any case. He wasn't interested in playing with metal bugs. They needed to find the chamber and get out of here.

"It's safe," Otto said. "You can come around."

When the others had joined him, they got moving again. Only a few minutes later they stopped again, this time in front of a metal door the exact same size as the tunnel. Unlike the portcullis, this one had a magical handle. Otto only needed twenty threads to turn it. The instant he did, the door slid into the floor.

Axel glared at him. "A little warning next time."

"Sorry. Want to go first?"

The brothers stared into the darkness. Silent as a tomb and black as death, the entrance didn't invite company. Oblivious to the tension, Corina guided one of her light orbs past them into the room.

Nothing instantly attacked them. In fact, there was nothing threatening inside what looked like a workshop. Two steel tables big enough to hold the broken ant construct filled most of the room. Tools hung from boards attached to the wall and shelves were covered with parts whose function Otto couldn't begin to guess. At the rear of the room, another door led deeper into the building.

The chamber clearly wasn't here and they were wasting time gawping around. Otto led the way through the workshop. He ignored everything, making his way directly to the door. He checked it for traps, found nothing, and tugged on the handle. It swung silently open, the hinges still perfectly maintained after all these years. How that was possible was another question, one he didn't care to explore at the moment.

Beyond the door, a hall stretched out before them. Two doors were visible just at the edge of Corina's light.

Otto glanced at Axel. "Time for your scouts to earn their pay. Let's try and clear this level before calling it a night. Once you've determined there's no threat, I'll search each room for the item I'm looking for."

He conjured lights and anchored them directly above each soldier's head. Axel organized his men and soon they were off. They checked the two closest rooms before moving deeper into the complex. Since there was no reason to delay, Otto headed for the first room.

As they walked Corina asked, "Master, why isn't there a portal here?"

"Security I assume. Besides, as an Arcane Lord, Colt wouldn't have needed a portal to travel anywhere he wanted to go. Given the magical protections around this place, privacy was important to Lord Colt."

"He couldn't have worked here alone," Hans said. "The place is too big for one man."

"I'm sure he had plenty of apprentices, the same as Lord Karonin and the others. I suspect that workshop we just left belonged to an apprentice rather than the master. What I seek will be wherever Colt himself worked."

"Then why search here at all?" Corina asked.

Otto shrugged and stopped outside the first room. "Because I could be wrong."

Otto wasn't wrong. They spent most of three days searching the tower from bottom to top and found no sign of the artifact. The found many other fascinating items, including a library that Otto would have happily spent months exploring. But he didn't have months. He had at most two weeks, or now ten days. Exploring all the towers before they ran out of food seemed a dubious prospect.

At least no other constructs had attacked them. In fact, while there were enough parts and crystals to build heaven only knew how many of the magical devices, they'd found none complete.

All that remained to search was the top of the tower. Otto stopped in front of the closed door and scratched his chin. Half a week of stubble covered his chin, which reminded him of his time as a prisoner of the Wizards Guild, not a pleasant memory to be sure.

As had become his routine now, he checked the door for magical traps, found none, and tugged on the handle.

It didn't budge.

"What's the holdup?" Axel asked.

"The door's locked. It's the first one we've found sealed in the whole tower. That has to mean something."

"What?" Corina asked.

Otto wished he had an answer. He wished he wasn't just hoping it meant something because he was starting to lose faith. He shook his head and focused on the ether. It took a moment to spot a small circle right above the door. It had a spiral design on the center.

At his mental command, ether flowed into the spiral. It started to glow, the energy making its way around and around until it reached the center and the door popped open. He pushed it the rest of the way and stepped through.

Crystals imbedded in the ceiling crackled to life. The white light revealed an open room with a magical circle engraved in the center. Otto crouched to examine it. While the runes were drawn in a more jagged, almost mechanical style, they still very much resembled the ones around the portal that he knew so well.

Unfortunately, this circle wasn't connected to the portal network so none of Valtan's power flowed through it. It had to work on the same principle. The runes were even filled with mithril. The main problem was, Otto had no idea how to activate something like this and even if he did he didn't know where he might end up.

"This is the last room," Axel said. "What do we do now?"

Otto debated for only a moment then said, "Now we try a different tower."

↻

The second tower was identical to the first. Every room, hall, and staircase exactly the same. Even the books in the library were the same. They only needed two days to search this one and at the top they found another circle. It was perfectly clear to Otto that if he wanted to find the chamber, he would have to risk trying to activate the circle.

"Hans, you have your coin, right?"

"Yes. What are you planning, my lord?"

"I'm going to see where the circle takes me. If I run into trouble, I can teleport back here."

"Are you certain?" Hans asked. "You mentioned magical protections. If something prevents you from fleeing, you'll have to fight alone."

"I'll go," Corina offered.

"As will I." Hans removed the coin from his pocket and set it off to one side of the circle. "You can still return safely."

"But I can't bring you two back with me." Otto shook his head.

Axel cut in. "You didn't bring us along to wait here while you went off by yourself."

"Fine, we'll all be fools together. Everybody in the circle."

They barely fit, but somehow everyone squeezed into the rune circle. Four of the scouts ended up riding in the carrier. Now all Otto had to do was activate it and hopefully not dump them all into the ocean or the mouth of a live volcano.

He closed his eyes and focused on the ether. He sent a thread to each of the runes. As ether poured into them, they began to vibrate. When they couldn't hold another drop of power, he cut off the flow and opened his eyes.

Just in time for a wall of white light to engulf them.

The transition lasted only a second. The next thing Otto knew, he stood in a new room, one far bigger than any he'd seen yet. It was another workshop. Tables and shelves laden with all manner of tools filled every corner. At least more of the magical crystals lit the place. They wouldn't have to stumble around in the dark or rely on the tiny motes of light Corina conjured.

Otto took a few deep breaths to steady himself. When the last rune faded to darkness, he stepped across the circle. Nothing reacted, which in this case he took as a good sign.

"Do we fan out or stick together?" Cobb asked.

"Stick together," Axel and Otto said at the same time.

"Where do we look first?" Axel asked.

Otto wasn't certain. Unlike the towers, this room had no rhyme or reason to its layout, at least not one discernible to Otto. It felt like Colt had simply finished or abandoned a project and left it where it was.

"Let's try and follow some sort of grid pattern. I don't want to miss anything," Otto said.

They worked their way through the mess until they reached one of the walls. From there they maneuvered along a path through the junk to the corner of the room. They swept along the wall, the line of searchers covering a path twenty paces wide. At times they waded hip deep through scrap metal. Taking a step without getting cut to ribbons was a challenge by itself.

The search went on for hours, until Otto's back and legs ached and it took all his willpower just to put one foot in front of the other.

"There's an open space just ahead, Master," Corina said.

Sure enough, directly in front of them, the junk thinned out and an opening appeared. Even if they found nothing, this would be a good place to take a rest and eat. At the edge of the open space Otto froze.

Dead center, lit from above by a glowing crystal, sat the chamber. Eight feet tall and made of thick glass with a mithril tripod at the top, it perfectly matched the description his master had given him.

"At last." Otto stepped into the clearing and a previously invisible rune flared to life.

Otto strengthened his defensive spells in preparation for an attack. Instead, a six-foot-tall image of a man as much metal as flesh appeared.

"Who the hell is that?" Axel asked.

"Quiet. That has to be Lord Colt. This may be some sort of test. Keep your distance and let me approach the illusion alone."

Otto moved closer and the illusion turned its head to follow him. A few feet away he stopped. How exactly did one address the illusion of a long-dead wizard? It was clearly aware of him. Whether it was actually intelligent or not was the question.

"Who are you?" the illusion asked, ending his mental debate.

"My name is Otto Shenk. I'm one of Lord Karonin's apprentices."

"And why has that witch sent you to my workshop when I'm away?"

Otto winced. It seemed Lord Karonin and Lord Colt weren't on the best terms. He'd assumed all the Arcane Lords were at least collegial if not friendly. Clearly that had been a mistake.

"She asked me to retrieve the Chamber of Eternity. Lord Sur has found a new candidate to join your number." Otto hoped invoking the specter of the first lord would convince the illusion that he had the right to claim the chamber.

"Liar! If a new lord had been selected, Amet would have mentioned it at our last gathering. I think you're a thief taking advantage of my absence to loot my workshop. I don't know how you slipped past my apprentices, but you won't make it out of here alive."

The illusion vanished. The next thing Otto knew he was surrounded by soldiers.

"That didn't sound good," Axel said.

"No. Load the chamber into the carrier. We need to go." A tremor shook the workshop. "Right now."

He didn't need to give the order twice. A quartet of scouts wrestled the chamber to the carrier. It fit with six inches to spare. The rear gate slammed into place and they ran for the rune circle.

Piles of metal and parts crashed down around them as the tremors grew worse. It took all of Otto's focus just to maintain his balance.

"What's going on?" Corina asked.

Otto wished he knew. He doubted the workshop would collapse on them, not with so many valuable items strewn about the place. But something was clearly happening.

A quick glance behind him revealed something rising out of the heaps of scrap. He couldn't make out exactly what it was and he didn't want to get close enough for a better look.

The group sprinted into the central clearing and gathered in the circle like before.

Otto poured ether into the runes.

Nothing happened. The mithril remained dark. The runes refused to absorb his magic.

The construct he'd seen earlier rose in the distance. A single glowing red eye focused on them.

"Get us out of here!" Axel said.

"I can't. Whatever defensive spell we triggered has rendered the circle inert. We're trapped."

CHAPTER 17

Eddred kept a careful grip on the ship's wheel. Even in calm weather the currents made holding the ship steady tricky. He'd been spending a few hours every day manning the helm, mostly to help break the tedium. If anything happened he immediately handed control back to the captain.

They had to be at least three-quarters of the way home by now, maybe more. Other than a day-long squall a couple weeks ago, the trip had been smooth enough. Supplies were holding up despite the extra mouths to feed. All in all their situation was as good as could be expected. The future, on the other hand, felt totally out of control.

Try as he might, Eddred had come up with no new ideas about how to deal with Otto and his new empire.

He hauled the wheel a fraction to the right. Maybe they should just take up work as traders. There was plenty of demand for ships and it wasn't such a bad life.

"Your Majesty!" Lilly came boiling up from the lower deck. "Your Majesty! Lord Valtan wishes to speak with you."

Eddred's heart skipped a beat. If Valtan wanted him now, it couldn't be good news.

"I'll take the helm, Your Majesty." Captain Carter moved to relieve Eddred of his duties.

"Thank you, Captain." Eddred hurried across the deck and down the stairs, hope and despair warring within him.

In his cabin, he found Adam seated on his cot with the magic mirror in his lap. He held it out to Eddred then he and Lilly left without a word. They were well trained and he appreciated their professionalism.

"Lord Valtan?" Eddred tried not to stare at the wizard's pale, pained face.

"I thought we had more time. I knew what he planned, but the artifacts are well hidden. It should have taken him years to collect them all."

"My lord, perhaps if you explained what's happened."

"Yes, of course." Valtan cleared his throat and seemed to bring himself under control. Eddred had never seen him out of control before and the sight shook him to the core. "Otto has activated the wards protecting the first artifact of the Chamber of Eternity."

Eddred had never heard of such a thing and said so.

"It's a device that allows a wizard to make the transition to an Arcane Lord. To my shame I helped create it. If Otto succeeds in getting all three pieces, he'll become like me only without the restrictions I've placed on myself."

That might be the most horrifying thing Eddred had ever heard. "Are you certain he succeeded in claiming the item?"

"No, but I must assume the worst. If he's found Colt's piece already, he must know where the others are located. Much as I hate the idea, I need you to contact the assassins and accept their offer. I'll gather the gold. Tell them to travel to South

Barrier Island. The payment will be waiting. Otto must be stopped."

"And Wolfric?" Eddred asked.

"If the new emperor is killed, that will at least slow Otto while he holds the nations together. The risk of Otto Shenk becoming an Arcane Lord is too great. Any chance must be taken."

"Very well. I'll contact Naja and tell her we accept her terms."

"Good." Valtan vanished, leaving Eddred to his own devices. If the Arcane Lord was that shaken, the danger must be even greater than he first feared.

Hopefully, the assassins were as skilled as Naja claimed. They might be the world's last hope.

$\backsim$

Axel gripped the hilt of his mithril sword and squinted into the darkness. Many of the crystals had gone dark when the workshop started shaking and he could only make out bits and pieces of whatever sort of thing was coming to kill them. He should have known the search was going too smoothly. For a few days he'd allowed himself to imagine that the giant steel spider Otto destroyed when they first arrived might be the only guardian in the place.

That was clearly a terrible mistake.

"It's getting closer," he said.

"I can see that, thank you," Otto replied.

"Don't you think we should run?" Axel asked.

"Where, exactly, do you want to run to? We're in a sealed box. Unless I can figure out how to open it, there's no escape. Keep that thing busy while I try and find the exit. Have your archers target its crystal. If that doesn't work, aim for the joints. Remember, you're wielding mithril. Cutting through steel is perfectly possible."

Axel barely heard his brother add, "Assuming Lord Colt hasn't enchanted it."

Great, buy time on the off chance Otto could pick the lock holding them in here. Axel couldn't very well complain. He'd volunteered for this mission after all.

"Colten, take the archers and try to smash that thing's crystal. Cobb, take a squad left. I'll take the other right. Hit-and-run tactics. We do not want a stand-up fight with this thing."

His men broke up and three fell in behind Axel as he led them right. They all knew what they were doing. He took comfort in that. His decision not to bring any of the less-experienced scouts seemed genius now. The last thing he wanted was a green rookie at his shoulder as they fought some magical living statue, or whatever the hell these things were.

As they moved closer, their opponent became clear. Though he still didn't know what it was. The monstrosity had six legs holding up an armored body. Two massive claws flanked a mouth filled with spinning blades that looked like they'd grind a man up in a hurry. A tail tipped with a foot-long steel spike arched over its back.

The legs had exposed joints. If they damaged a few of them, that might buy them a minute or two.

An arrow came whistling in, hammered into one of the glowing eyes, and skipped off into the darkness. So much for easily blinding it.

The monster turned toward Colten's archers. The moment it did, Axel lunged in and hacked at the nearest leg joint.

His mithril sword bit into the metal, but didn't shear it off cleanly. Still, he felt it cut, which meant that a couple more hits should bring it down. He hoped, anyway.

The rest of his squad managed hits of their own before the steel beast spun toward them.

As Axel's team leapt back, Cobb came at it from the other direction. The screech of mithril on steel hurt Axel's ears.

The two groups kept at it, harrying the metal monster, narrowly avoiding its claws, and generally scrambling to stay alive. Only its lack of speed kept them a step ahead. But Axel's arm grew heavier by the second. They could maintain this pace for minutes at most. If Otto hadn't found the way out by then, they'd be torn apart.

♍

"What are we going to do?" Corina asked as Axel led his men toward the approaching construct.

That very question was at the front of Otto's own mind. Their survival depended on him coming up with a good answer, quickly. The first sounds of battle reached him. Axel wouldn't be able to hold the construct off for long. If they had five minutes Otto would consider them lucky.

"Look around, through the ether. If you see anything at all tell me. There must be a way out of here."

"Unless this is a death trap," Hans said.

"Even then, Lord Colt had to have a way to reset it." Otto had to believe that. Otherwise their situation was completely hopeless.

He searched the floor around them first and found nothing beyond the lifeless magic circle. The walls were too distant to have anything of use. He looked up. In the distance, the sounds of battle grew more intense.

The area directly above them was clear. That didn't bode well.

Otto expanded his search area.

"Master, I found something."

Heaven be merciful. "Where?"

"Ten paces to the right and fifteen feet off the ground. I don't know what it is."

Otto focused where she indicated and sure enough a concentration of ether hung in midair. He cursed himself. He was thinking too much like a non-wizard. You could place an ethereal construct anywhere. There was no need for it to be built into a wall or the ceiling.

Forming crude hands, he reached in and pulled the exterior shell apart. Sure enough, another lever lay hidden inside. That had to be the way out.

Otto wrapped a thread around it, turned toward where his brother fought, amplified his voice, and said, "I found it! Get back here!"

He wrapped every thread at his command around the lever and eased it down partway.

A vibration ran through the floor.

"Master, the circle," Corina said.

He looked down and sure enough the circle had raised up about an inch. Otto and the others moved so that they were standing inside of it.

When his brother arrived Otto said, "Everyone in the circle, quickly. Climb into the carrier if you have to."

Axel waved his men in and they hurried to clamber aboard. Beyond them, the construct was coming slowly toward them, one of its legs dragging behind it.

Cobb was the last one to arrive. As soon as he was in the circle Axel joined them. Otto yanked the lever the rest of the way down. The circle rose up on a metal pillar. Above them, an opening appeared revealing a section of sky.

"Where's your sword?" Axel asked.

Otto was so focused on escaping, he hadn't even noticed that Cobb was unarmed.

"I left it in that thing's leg joint. Why did you think it was dragging?"

Axel clapped his second on the back. "Good thinking."

"Yes," Otto agreed. "But the cost of that sword is coming out of your pay."

Axel and Cobb both stared until Otto smiled. He didn't know where the joke came from. Maybe just hysterical relief that it seemed like they might escape in one piece and with the chamber.

The pillar rattled and a horrific screech filled the air. Their rise slowed.

Hans peered over the edge. "It's got its claws in the metal."

Otto pushed his way through the soldiers and joined Hans. Sure enough the construct was trying to pull them back down. It wasn't having much luck, but at this rate it would take forever to reach the exit.

As he watched, the monster was lifted off the floor as it clung to the side of the pillar. To Otto's horror, it began to climb.

He shared a look with Hans who asked, "What do we do?"

Otto was beginning to wish people would stop asking him that. But he was in charge and getting them out of this mess was his responsibility.

Elemental attacks would be a waste of time. He formed an ethereal tentacle and tried to rip the construct's claws out of the pillar.

Moving a mountain would have been easier. Something in

the magic that sustained it weakened Otto's own attack. It felt like Colt had built the thing specifically to kill wizards. And maybe he had. Who else was likely to show up and try to claim the chamber?

"Corina, how close are we to the top?"

"Halfway, Master."

The construct would reach them before they cleared the lip. Otto needed to speed the pillar.

Threads of ether shot out and sank into the metal.

There had to be a power source.

Come on, where is it?

Long seconds later he found it, a crystal built into the floor under the pillar. Otto poured ether into it and they sped up. He focused on maintaining a steady flow. Too much and he risked shattering the crystal. Not enough and the scorpion would reach them.

"Almost there!" Corina said.

"Ten feet below us, my lord," Hans added.

Otto released his spell and staggered away from the edge. Hans caught him and they rejoined the group.

"Move everyone away from that edge," Otto said, his voice barely audible.

Hans repeated his order in a sergeant's bellow. The scouts hastened to move and not a moment too soon.

One of the construct's claws popped over the edge and slammed down where one of the men had stood only moments before.

The lip of the exit was in sight, only four feet to go.

The pillar screeched to a halt

Otto looked over his shoulder. The construct had its claws between the platform and the exit and wouldn't let them rise any higher.

"We have to climb out," Otto said.

Axel heard him and waved his men into motion. The nimble scouts quickly leapt and pulled themselves up and over the edge.

No way was Otto going to manage that. He could barely stand on his own after powering up the lift. Hans had to help him shuffle over to the edge. Once there, Axel grabbed his wrist and pulled him the rest of the way out. He focused his mind enough to summon the carrier and it flew up over beside him.

They ended up in the middle of the pit where they started.

"What do you say we take a rest?" Axel asked.

Otto liked that plan, but there was no way he dared follow it. "I wish. We have to keep moving."

Another shriek of tortured metal emphasized his words. Soon enough the construct would force its way onto the platform and into the pit. If they were still here when it arrived... He didn't want to think about what would happen.

"We need to get out of the workshop," Otto said.

"First we need to find a way out of this hole," Axel countered. "We have grappling hooks, but there's nothing for them to catch on."

"We don't need grappling hooks. Put five guys in the carrier. Corina, keep an eye on our metallic friend. If it reaches the platform give a shout."

"Yes, Master." Corina darted over and stared into the opening.

Cobb and his squad clambered into the carrier. Now Otto needed to focus. With every speck of clarity he could summon, he pictured the carrier rising up to the top of the pit. When he had the image perfected, he sent it through the link.

The carrier shuddered, but slowly rose. Too slowly by the sounds coming from behind them.

"Corina?" Otto asked.

"It's got both claws onto the platform and is wriggling the rest of its body into place. Two, maybe three minutes."

Two minutes? He'd be lucky if Cobb's group made it to the top by then.

"Hans, come here."

"My lord?"

"Gather whatever rope you need and tie it under my armpits. You'll have to drag me up the side."

"Why will we have to drag you?" Hans asked.

Axel ignored the conversation and started collecting coils of rope from his men.

"Because, I'm liable to pass out after I finish lifting you all out of here. I'm barely staying on my feet as it is. Assuming I do lose consciousness, you'll have to carry me to the exit. You shouldn't need magic to open the door, just pull the lever we saw when we arrived. Once the wall seals behind us, we should be safe from the construct. Clear?"

Hans nodded. "Perfectly, my lord. You get us out of this hole and I'll take care of the rest. On my life, I swear."

"Lift your arms up," Axel said.

Otto complied and a loop was dropped over his shoulders. Axel snugged it up.

Satisfied, Otto reached out with the ether. No Bliss greeted him this time, only the dull, grinding pain of overuse. He ignored it and focused on the carrier's power source. A pair of threads shot out and pumped ether into the crystal.

The carrier's speed doubled and in seconds it reached the top.

The scouts hastened to climb out.

The instant they did, Otto recalled the carrier. "Everybody inside. You too, Corina."

She left the edge of the pit and hurried to climb in beside Hans. "It's almost there, Master. Less than a minute I'd guess."

Otto grimaced against the pain and this time sent ten threads into the crystal.

A blinding headache nearly put him on his knees.

Focusing through the pain, he sent the climb order through his link. This time the chamber practically flew to the top of the pit.

The last thing Otto saw was the carrier settling down and the others climbing out. Then the world went black.

⌒

Hans leapt out of the carrier and spun back toward the pit. Lord Shenk lay on the cold steel, his body limp and unmoving. From the circular entrance to the lower chamber, a pair of claws waved around as the metal monster fought to free itself. They didn't have much time.

Even as he thought it, the construct ripped free and rose out of the hole.

"The rope!" Hans grabbed it from Corina and started pulling. One hundred and seventy pounds of deadweight didn't move easily.

A moment later Axel grabbed on behind him and together they hauled with all their might.

"It spotted him!" Corina shouted. "Hurry!"

Her voice was shrill with fear. That told Hans all he needed to know.

Redoubling his efforts, Hans pulled with all his might. Foot by foot he dragged his unconscious master closer to safety.

A few feet further on and the weight grew heavier.

Hans nearly lost his grip.

"He's to the wall," Corina said. "That thing is only fifteen yards away."

Hans lurched back, hauling Lord Shenk up four feet in one go. Together he and Axel trudged step by step. The scouts had formed a defensive perimeter in case the noise of the construct below should draw unwanted attention.

A heavy blow rattled the ground.

"Corina?" Hans asked.

"It's okay. The monster can't reach him. Twenty yards more and he'll be out."

Hans grunted. Twenty yards might as well be a mile. His shoulder screamed and his legs burned. He never would have imagined pulling an unconscious man would be this hard.

"Come on, old man," Axel said. "Don't tell me you're done already."

"Who are you calling an old man?" Hans pulled harder. He owed Lord Shenk a great deal, including his life on several occasions. He would not fail him now.

Hans was aware of nothing but the weight on the line and where he placed his feet. Foot by foot, stride by stride, nothing else clouded his focus. Until all at once the weight was gone.

"He's up and he's breathing!" Corina shouted.

Hans finally relaxed. They'd done it.

More heavy blows from below shook the air. Corina left Lord Shenk and peeked over the side. The blood had drained from her face when she turned back.

"It's climbing the wall."

Hans ground his teeth in frustration. Lord Shenk must have known it could do that. That's why he told them not to stop until they escaped the city.

Axel pointed at Cobb and another man built like a brick wall. "You two carry my brother. We're leaving this place, right now."

No one argued and soon they were on the move. Even though Lord Shenk was unconscious, the carrier still followed along right behind him. Hans gave a light shake of his head. He'd seen enough magic to last a lifetime, yet he seriously doubted he'd seen even a fraction of what Lord Shenk planned to reveal.

He glanced back, but there was no sign of the construct. Hopefully it would slide back into the hole and stay there.

Ahead of them, a youthful scout led them back toward the exit, quick-marching down the streets, never hesitating. At least not until they rounded a corner and found the construct standing between them and the wall. Its glowing red eyes glared at them with all the hatred of a demon.

"How?" Axel trailed off as if unable to force the useless question out.

"Why isn't it attacking?" Corina asked.

Hans had been wondering exactly that himself. It was like it only wanted to stop them from escaping. That was a change of pace since it had been doing its best to crush them to pulp earlier.

There was a groan and Lord Shenk said, "Set me down."

Hans hurried over to support him with Corina only a step behind. "Are you well, my lord?

"No, but I am alive thanks to all of you. What's the situation?"

"It's a standoff. The creature is between us and the wall. It's not attacking, only blocking our way. It's as if it's waiting for something."

Lord Shenk grunted and said, "Well, let's go find out what it wants."

Hans stared for a moment, certain he'd misheard. "My lord?"

"I don't think that's a good idea, Master," Corina chimed in. "It nearly killed you in the pit."

"And yet now it's content to stare me to death? No, something's changed and we don't have forever to wait. Help me over there."

Lord Shenk delivered that last sentence in his "time to stop arguing and do as you're told" tone. Hans knew it well enough to understand that the discussion was over.

Hooking Lord Shenk's arm over his neck, Hans helped him walk toward the looming construct. Out in the sunlight, this was the best look Hans had gotten of the monster. It measured nearly thirty feet long and its needle-sharp tail loomed fifteen feet above them as if poised to run them through.

Hans considered himself a brave man, but it took every ounce of his will to put one foot in front of the other. Whether by dint of exhaustion or some understanding Hans couldn't comprehend, Lord Shenk never hesitated with his weak stride.

At last they stood directly in front of the construct and it still made no move to slay them.

"Lord Colt," Lord Shenk said. "Do you wish to speak with me further?"

A new glow appeared just above the creature's red eyes. Hans feared some attack, but instead a light shot out and a shining figure three feet tall appeared in the air in front of them. It was the same machine man from below.

"Congratulations," the apparition said. "Escaping the workshop was your first test. Finding the courage to approach my guardian was the second. You have proven yourself worthy of the chamber. I wish you the best of luck in acquiring the final two pieces of the puzzle. Be assured that my tests were the easiest of the three."

The image vanished and the construct clattered aside, allowing them free passage to the exit. Lord Shenk waved to his brother and the weary group trudged to the wall and outside without further incident.

"Do we camp here or put some distance between us and the city, my lord?" Hans asked.

"Camp here. Anyone that might threaten us is terrified of this place."

Not without good reason. Hans kept that thought to himself. They'd survived and completed the mission. That was enough for him.

CHAPTER 18

Renna stood on the battlements of Audin's fort and stared out over the forces surrounding them. She'd expected Montage to do something, but sending five hundred soldiers to besiege them wasn't it. They didn't have nearly that many soldiers garrisoning their fort and she couldn't help wondering if some of the other city-states hadn't contributed troops. She squinted against the morning glare at the tiny figures moving around.

The enemy had set up well out of bow range and showed no sign of attacking. They must have found out about Otto's mission and were positioning themselves to intercept him when he returned with whatever artifact he sought. Assuming, of course, that he actually survived Colt's Workshop. A decidedly large assumption on everyone's part. Over a week had passed since he set out with neither word nor sign one way or the other.

"Rather more than the spies claimed Montage had manning their fort." The commander had slipped up beside her so quietly, Renna jumped when he spoke. She needed to be careful. That sort of lack of attention could get her killed in another setting.

"I'll wager a week's pay more than one of the other city-states provided men to this siege," Renna said. It made sense too. None of the others would want to risk anyone else claiming the artifact for themselves. The stupid balance and all that.

"What are our orders?" the commander asked.

Renna shook her head. She had no orders for the man. Her mission was to return Otto to Audin with the item. Technically, she was supposed to steal it from him on the way back, but she'd already made up her mind not to do that.

"I recommend letting them make the first move," she said at last. "Our forces aren't enough to break the siege, correct?"

"Not a chance," the commander agreed.

"Then our options are limited. Are we in any danger of running out of supplies?"

"None, not after the load you delivered. Even with the extra men, we can last months."

"We won't need to. If Otto isn't back in eighteen days, he won't be coming."

♈

Otto came awake delighted to find his headache gone and his body only mildly stiff. Considering how roughly he'd treated it, that was a miracle. Judging from the amount of light streaming into his tent, the day had gotten well under way.

He tossed his thin blanket aside. Everything that happened after they escaped the city remained a blur. He vaguely recalled collapsing in his cot the moment the tent was raised, but after that, nothing.

Someone had pulled his boots off at least. He yanked them back on and collected his sword from its spot leaning against the tent wall. Before stepping through the flap, Otto reached out to the ether. Threads appeared at his command and no discomfort assailed him. Good. He was ready to face the next part of the mission, somehow getting them to the portal and home in one piece.

"Master!" Corina came running toward him but stopped short of her usual enthusiastic hug.

He smiled at her worried look and patted her shoulder. "I'm fine now, don't worry. How long did I sleep?"

"All night and half the day. Hans was getting worried." She added in a whisper, "So was I."

"Take it as a cautionary tale," Otto said. "Overusing your magic comes with a price."

He turned toward the fire where the scouts had gathered. His main interest was the pot bubbling over it. Nearly a full day had passed since he last ate and his stomach didn't appreciate the neglect. Cobb scooped him out a bowl of stew without comment and passed it over. Otto nodded his thanks and took a bite. Surprisingly decent, though that might have been hunger talking.

Hans stood a little ways off near the carrier and its precious cargo. He started towards Otto who waved him off. He needed nothing for the moment.

After devouring half the bowl of stew Otto asked, "How are our supplies holding up?"

"About four days' worth left," Axel said. "Five if we don't overdo it."

That gave them plenty of time to reach the fort and absolutely ruled out heading straight for Audin. Things stood exactly as he expected, for better or worse. "Let's set out as soon as the meal's finished."

"Good idea," Axel said. "Even sealed up that city, or whatever it is, gives me the creeps. I almost feel like someone's watching us."

Thinking of Lord Karonin and her magic mirror, Otto couldn't rule out the possibility that Lord Colt had a similar arrangement here. Not that it mattered. From their new home in the netherworld, the long-dead wizards were no threat to anyone.

It took an hour to break down the camp and then they set out. No rangers from Montage troubled them this time. After two nights and a day, they reached the vicinity of the fort. Smoke rose in the distance, too much smoke to be from just the kitchen.

"Something's wrong," Axel said, speaking Otto's thoughts out loud.

"I'll take a look." Otto closed his eyes and went scouting.

From on high the source of the extra smoke quickly became clear. A small army had the Audin fort surrounded. Otto flew down for a closer look, but something smashed his ethereal construct to bits. His sight returned to his body rather more suddenly than he expected, leaving his vision blurry for a moment.

"Our friends have a problem," Otto said. "About five hundred soldiers have them surrounded. No way we're sneaking through. They also have at least one wizard. Not a magical engineer either, but someone that uses magic the way we do."

"How strong?" Axel asked.

Otto shook his head. "No way to say from here. If they're

alone, I'm not worried. The soldiers are another matter. I could obliterate them, but it would probably leave me in the same shape I was in yesterday and I don't want to risk it."

"So what's the plan?" Axel asked.

"I'm thinking hammer and anvil. We have Renna and her people attack from the fort then hit them from behind. We'll smash them between us."

"Good plan," Axel said. "Will she play along?"

"I think so. Getting us back to Audin so the lord governor can rob us is her main priority. With that in mind, don't give it your all. We want to win, but wearing down Audin's numbers wouldn't hurt anything."

"Cold-blooded, little brother, absolutely cold-blooded."

Otto shrugged. Maybe it was, but you didn't concern yourself with the well-being of a thief, even one supposedly on your side.

He extended his sight a second time, swooping well wide of where he encountered the wizard before approaching the fort. His ethereal eyes made it through without issue this time. Renna stood on the battlements, arms crossed and looking rather troubled with the situation.

Otto added his voice to the link and said, "We've arrived within sight of the fort."

She jumped six inches when he spoke, put a hand to her chest, and grimaced. "If you're trying to scare me to death, you made a good effort. How did it go?"

"We survived. Do you have a plan for dealing with your situation?"

"We're outnumbered nearly three to one. Forcing our way out will be a problem."

"How about you draw their attention, then we attack from behind?"

She sighed. "No offense, Otto, but the thirteen of you aren't exactly enough to worry the enemy."

Renna couldn't see his smile, but hopefully she heard it in his voice. "I assure you, when the time comes, we'll worry them plenty. And it's not like we have a ton of options here."

"Fair point. When do you want to do this?"

"As soon as you're ready. The longer we wait, the better the odds that they spot us."

"Alright, say an hour? We need to prep our knights."

"Fine. As soon as they move to engage you, we'll hit the rear of their line."

Otto severed the threads.

"Well?" Axel asked.

"One hour." Otto worked a crick out of his neck. He still tensed up when his sight was out of his body. Probably he always would. "Remember, let them fully engage before we strike. I'll lead with a couple fireballs to soften them up."

"What about me?" Corina asked.

"You will stay here and protect the chamber."

"But—"

"No buts. I'm not leaving it unprotected. If you get into trouble, you know how to contact me."

She pouted for a moment before saying, "Yes, Master."

Otto nodded. Having her stay behind would free him to fight without worrying about protecting her. How long had it been since he really let loose with some destructive magic? Too long.

He was looking forward to blowing off some steam. Pity for the enemy, but someone had to be his target.

A little over an hour later, Otto and the scouts were crouched behind a clump of heavy shrubs within sight of the fort. The enemy forces didn't seem overly concerned and he hadn't noticed anything magical from the opposing wizard. As far as he could tell, they remained unnoticed.

"What's the holdup?" Cobb grumbled.

He had a new sword commandeered from an archer. He'd been forced to endure a bit of ribbing along with an admonition from Axel not to lose this one. Otto understood why his brother enjoyed the army. There was an easy camaraderie that you didn't get at court and you certainly wouldn't find in the Shenk household. You also had to obey orders, which Otto wouldn't have liked nearly as well. Having gotten out from under Father's thumb, he had no desire to end up under someone else's.

"There." One of the scouts, Colten, Otto thought, pointed at the fort's gate as it slowly opened.

A mad scramble ensued as the besieging force rushed to form up and move their magical armor into the forefront. They weren't completely disorganized and before the Audin soldiers could press forward, the enemy was ready to meet them.

Otto drew his sword and prepared his spell. Ether flowed through the mithril, gaining power as it did.

The magical armor came together with a massive clash. Even from a distance the noise hurt Otto's ears.

"Otto?" Axel asked.

"Not yet."

He watched and rubbed his fingers together, building up heat.

The front rows of infantry engaged, their shields pressed tight, nearly shoulder to shoulder.

Otto stood and sent out three targeting threads. He kept them well behind the Audin forces. Another thread joined the heat of his fingers to the ether he'd been building up.

A moment later, three huge fireballs shot out, detonating in the midst of the enemy forces.

Bodies flew and men screamed.

Axel led the scouts out as soon as the fires died. The ten men went roaring into the stunned enemy formation.

"Should we join them, my lord?" Hans asked.

Otto shook his head, but didn't take his eyes off the battle. The wizard that destroyed his ethereal eyes had to be here somewhere. He needed to be ready to eliminate them as soon as possible lest Axel and his men suffer the same fate as the enemy.

♍

Axel gripped his new sword and watched as the Audin forces battered against the besieging force. He glanced at Otto, but his brother clearly had his mind on something magical. Letting an ally fight alone, even an unreliable ally, went against all of his training. Only supreme self-control and a desire not to get hit by whatever spell Otto had planned kept him holding his position.

He glanced back again. This time a reddish-orange glow had formed around Otto's sword. Any moment now...

A second later three fireballs shot out and exploded amidst the attacking forces. Axel was reminded once again why he liked being on the same side as his brother.

As soon as the flames died and smoke cleared he shouted, "Charge!"

The scouts leapt out from their hiding place and sprinted toward the disoriented forces.

His first opponent didn't look like he'd ever shaved much less swung his sword in anger. A right-to-left overhead chop cut the kid in half. The mithril blade sheared through heavy leather armor, flesh and bone with equal ease. It felt like cutting butter.

Axel spun and took a charging man's arm off at the elbow. His back cut sent his opponent's head flying.

A quick glance around the battlefield revealed the others having similar results. Axel had never fought using mithril weapons before. It almost felt like cheating, assuming such a concept had any place in war.

He hacked down two more men, one of them dressed in a mail coat that offered no more protection than the first kid's leathers. It made little difference what he set the edge of his sword against, nothing so much as slowed his blade.

A tingle ran up his spine.

Axel spun and found himself facing a woman dressed in a simple brown robe with long, wild hair.

Lightning crackled around her hands.

He winced, waiting for the pain.

Energy shot out at him.

The blast struck something and stopped a foot before hitting him.

Every hair on his body stood up straight.

Before he could process what happened, the woman's chest burst outward and a fist-sized hole appeared. She collapsed and didn't move.

He looked back and Otto gave him a thumbs-up.

Axel blew out a sigh and turned back to the fight. When they got home, he'd have to buy his brother a very expensive thank-you drink.

⟡

Corina stalked back and forth in front of the carrier, listening to the sounds of battle, and scowled. She knew her master didn't trust her in battle. She didn't really blame him either. Even Corina could acknowledge that she'd been pretty squeamish during the battle in Rolan and afterward. But how was she supposed to improve if he never let her fight?

She kicked a stone and sent it flying out of the clearing. It wasn't fair! She'd come a long way since Rolan. But she couldn't prove herself if he never gave her a shot.

A shiver ran through her when her master touched the ether. He was so strong she couldn't help sensing it whenever he cast a serious spell. Whatever he just did qualified. In her mind's eye she pictured the battlefield and the smoking craters where his spell impacted.

A scuff of boots on gravel dragged her focus back to the clearing. Three men dressed in brown leather emerged from the nearby woods. They carried straight, bladed swords and didn't appear to have shaved in weeks. She could almost see the stink rising off them.

"Only one guard, and a pretty one at that," the center man said. "Maybe we have a bit of fun before we take the item?"

Why did the first person to ever call her pretty have to be a filthy thief?

"No," the man on the right said. "We only got until the battle ends. Let's make this quick."

"You're no fun," the center man said as he took a step toward Corina. "If you run along, we won't hurt you, girl."

As if she'd do that. Running away without a fight would guarantee her master never trusted her in battle. "My master placed the safety of this item in my hands. Flee or face the consequences."

They shared looks before busting out laughing.

Corina would make them pay for that. A targeting thread shot out and she sent lightning immediately after.

The spell was rushed and she hit the center man in the gut instead of the heart. He went down twitching, but wasn't dead.

The other two sprinted toward her.

Cursing her carelessness, Corina flicked her iron ring and bound the two men as she'd been taught. One fell flat on his face when he lost control of his muscles. The other somehow stayed upright, but neither could move a muscle.

She'd done it! Corina smiled. Wait until her master saw the thieves she captured. He'd be so proud of her.

Her smile withered. No, he wouldn't be proud of her for capturing these three men.

She reached for her dagger.

The reason he didn't trust her to fight by his side was he doubted her ability to do what was necessary. That she would hesitate to kill her enemies. If she really wanted to impress him, she needed to fully eliminate the threat. And there was only one way to do that.

Corina took a step towards the bound men. The tip of the dagger trembled as she drew nearer and she snarled, forcing it to stay still.

She wouldn't be weak. Not this time.

The still-standing man's eyes stared at her, seeming to burrow into her flesh. Her spell kept him from even blinking.

Corina imagined the fear, the absolute terror that must have filled him. Then she reminded herself that he'd come to take what didn't belong to him and if he'd had to, no doubt he would have cut her throat without a second thought.

"I'm sorry," she whispered.

She brought herself up short as soon as she said it. Don't be sorry. Be strong! She could hear her master's voice in her head. If Corina really wanted to take her place at his side, something like this couldn't reduce her to a trembling mess.

The dagger rose again. As she fought to force herself to take another step, the third man slammed into her. He'd recovered from her botched lightning spell while she dithered.

He drove her to the ground with all his body weight. Her dagger went flying on impact.

He clamped his big, calloused hands around her neck.

Corina's concentration wavered and she felt the spell holding the other two waver with it.

Lose control and you're dead!

Turning her focus inward, she used her little remaining magic to summon lightning, running it through her body and into the thief on top of her.

He howled and released his grip.

She wrapped a thread around his heart and sent every bit of power she could muster arcing into him.

The thief twitched and shuddered as her spell burned the life out of him.

Corina steeled herself and didn't stop until he was dead.

When the thief finally collapsed, she let out a long sigh. Her stomach twisted and she felt like she wanted to throw up. A few deep breaths calmed her roiling insides.

At last she collected her dagger and stood up straight. Before she could think about it, she cut both men's throats.

When they finished bleeding out, she tossed the dagger away and wept.

○

The quiet after a battle always felt jarring to Otto. The crash of swords and the screams of the dying still rang in his head. It didn't last, but for a little while the fear and excitement lingered. When at last his inner silence matched the outer, he went looking for Renna.

As they picked their way across the battlefield Hans asked, "Did the battle go as you hoped, my lord?"

Otto took a moment to consider his answer. The besieging force was crushed, which was good insofar as it allowed Otto and the others access to Audin's fort and fresh supplies. Audin's force had suffered losses, but fewer than he'd hoped. Only about forty men on that side had died in the fighting. Otto had hoped for closer to eighty or ninety.

At last he said, "It went well enough. Hopefully my little display will be enough to keep Renna and her associates in line, at least until we reach Audin. After that, all bets are off."

When they neared the fort, Axel and the scouts came striding his way. No one appeared injured, which had been Otto's only real concern.

"Thanks for the save," Axel said. "I thought that wizard was going to fry me."

Otto nodded. He'd been watching for precisely that moment. The enemy only had one of what Otto considered a standard wizard. "How did you like the mithril swords?"

Axel grinned. "They make fighting almost too easy. Towards the end, I almost felt bad for the men I was cutting down. I certainly can't argue with their effectiveness."

"Good. Did any of your archers fire arrows? We'll need to collect them. I don't want to leave any mithril for the scavengers."

Axel turned to his men. "Arrow count!"

While the archers started going through their quivers Axel said, "Finding specific arrows in this mess won't be easy."

"Yes, it will. I'll make the arrowheads light up. All your guys need to do is go around and collect them."

"Seven arrows fired, Lord Shenk," Cobb said.

Otto paused and let the ether flow out of him and across the battlefield. He ignored everything around the enemy knights. Soon enough he located the arrowheads. They glowed like stars in the night sky to his magical vision.

"I see them!" one of the scouts said.

"Pick them up and join us at the fort," Axel said.

The archers hurried to carry out the order while the rest of them continued on to the main gate. Renna waited just outside along with the commander that had traveled north with them.

"I stand corrected," Renna said. "Clearly the enemy noticed your arrival. I'd heard stories about war magic, but I've never seen it used. Your spells rattled them. As soon as they lost focus, the battle was all but won."

"It wasn't just the magic," the fort commander said. "Each of your fighters strode through the battle like The Reaper himself. I hope to never face you in battle."

Otto shot Renna a knowing look. "As do I, Commander. It's been a difficult few days. Perhaps a night's rest before we depart for Audin?"

"Of course," Renna said. "We'll have a victory meal prepared. If you'll excuse me, I need to contact Lord Audin and let him know the battle is over."

"Certainly. I need to collect Corina and the carrier. Excuse me."

Otto started back toward their camp. When Axel moved to join him Otto whispered, "Stay here and keep an eye on them. I don't want to return to a nasty surprise."

"And I thought Father was paranoid. Fine, but be careful. You don't want to walk into an ambush."

Otto appreciated his brother's concern, but anyone stupid enough to ambush him and Hans would very soon wish they hadn't. Besides, he doubted there was anyone still alive to attack them.

Just as he figured, no one bothered them and about ten minutes later they strode into the clearing that served as their temporary camp. Three bodies lay on the ground, two with their throats cut and the third with the telltale signs of light-ning damage. The dead men wore rough brown leathers and nothing to mark them as serving one side or the other.

"Master!" Corina came out from behind the carrier. "I stopped them. They snuck up on me and tried to steal the chamber, but I stopped them."

"I can see that. Very well done." Otto chose to ignore her red eyes and pale complexion. Clearly the fight had shaken her. But in the end she did what was necessary and that was all that mattered. "I told you your job was important."

She looked down. "I thought you just didn't want me with you during the battle."

Otto wanted exactly that, but didn't say so. Instead he put a gentle hand on her arm. "Of course not. While it certainly would have been dangerous to have you at my side, eventually you'll need to face the battlefield again. Today simply wasn't that day. Did these three say anything that might indicate who they served?"

"No, Master. They didn't say much of anything really."

"Well enough. Let's have a quick look at them." Otto gestured and the ether rushed out, swirling around the bodies and searching for anything magical. He found that something only seconds later. In the pocket of one with a cut throat, something glowed in his magical vision.

"What is that?" Corina asked. She must have seen it as well.

Otto shrugged then bent to collect the item.

What he pulled out of the man's pocket couldn't have looked more innocuous. A three-inch disk of polished silver engraved with runes and housing a small blue crystal in the center. While it didn't prove anything, that was the same sort of crystal Audin's magical engineers used. Of course, for all Otto knew, every city used the same type of crystal.

"Lord Shenk," Hans said. "We should probably return."

"Yes, we should. Wouldn't want to worry Axel." Otto conjured ethereal tentacles that lifted the bodies onto the carrier. "We'll see how Renna reacts when she sees the bodies. That should at least tell us if our friends from Audin sent them."

"Do you think they would?" Hans asked.

Otto shrugged. "Can you think of a better chance to steal the chamber? Of course, those rangers must have reported that we were headed for the workshop. We can't rule out Montage sending someone after it. Heaven above, I can't wait to get home and set the chamber up in the palace basement behind every magical barrier I can conjure. Let's head back."

At Otto's mental command, the carrier floated along behind him. Corina walked at his side, head held high. He couldn't have been more proud of his apprentice. She still had a long way to go, but today she took a big step in her journey as a wizard.

CHAPTER 19

As soon as Otto turned to go collect the carrier and his apprentice, Renna quick-marched back to the fort. She needed to speak to Lord Audin and the sooner the better. Having seen how powerful Otto's magic was, she had to warn him not to go through with his betrayal. They probably had enough soldiers to wear him down, but what would remain of the city guard wouldn't have strength enough to stop a company of bandits. Whatever they gained wouldn't be worth the cost.

She nodded to the guard on duty as she slipped through the main gate. No one questioned her as she made her way to the communications room. One of the engineers was always on duty, just in case an emergency arose.

Well, one had certainly arisen. Renna hammered twice on the door and the wizard opened up. He took one look at her and hastened to make the connection to Audin. As soon as the link had activated he hurried out of the room, closing the door behind him.

Half an hour later, she had nearly chewed her fingernails to the quick. Finally Lord Audin appeared in the mirror. "What is it?"

"You need to call off whatever you have planned when Otto returns to the city. I've seen his power and it is substantial. You'll lose hundreds. The soldiers with him are skilled and armed with weapons that cut through armor like it was paper. No treasure could be worth the cost."

Lord Audin's frown had deepened as she spoke. Renna knew from the start that he wouldn't like her advice. But she had to offer it for the good of the country.

"Your orders are to seize the treasure before he even reaches the city. Was I not clear about that?"

"You were perfectly clear, my lord. But given our losses during the siege, the only way I could succeed is to leave the fort dangerously undermanned. If your orders stand, I will, of course, obey to the best of my ability. But I feel it is my duty to make you aware of the situation."

Lord Audin's angry expression softened. "I understand and you've never steered me wrong. Perhaps I was rash in my decision-making. Leave them alone on the journey back. I'll decide what to do next when you arrive."

The tightness in Renna's chest loosened a fraction. That was basically the best she could have hoped for. "As you command, my lord. We leave for the city in the morning."

"Very good. I look forward to seeing you again." The lord governor's face vanished.

The crisis had been averted for the moment. Now if she could just get Otto through the portal before Lord Audin's greed got the better of his good sense, maybe Audin would come out ahead on this deal after all.

As Otto led his companions toward Axel and the rest of the scouts near the fort entrance, he glanced across the battlefield. No mithril glowed in the field save the thin bands running through the fallen magical armor. Good, the archers had found all their arrowheads.

"I'm beat." Corina stifled a yawn.

"That's the aftermath of the fight," Hans said. "The more experience you have, the less it bothers you."

Otto ignored them and focused on his brother. "Any trouble?"

"None. Everyone's been on their best behavior. You?" Axel gave the corpses in the carrier a close look.

"Corina took care of this lot. Whether they end up being trouble or not is to be determined. Let's set up and eat. I want to make an early start tomorrow and I'm sure you're all tired."

They entered the training yard just as Renna emerged from the keep. She strode toward them at a quick walk.

Axel got his men working while they waited for her and said, "Actually, as battles go, this one wasn't bad. Compared to the fighting in Straken, we barely broke a sweat. The mithril weapons made a huge difference."

"Excellent. They'll be your permanent gear from now on. Including a replacement for your second."

"Cobb will appreciate that."

"I've just spoken with Lord Audin," Renna said when she reached them. "He was well pleased to hear of your success."

"I'll bet," Otto said. "Three thieves tried to take our prize during the battle. Are their faces familiar to you?"

Renna moved closer to the carrier. A bit of magic adjusted the bodies so all their faces were visible. She looked closely at the dead men and Otto looked closely at her.

"They're rough characters, but not ones I know." She wasn't lying which implied the thieves worked for Montage. "Did you think I sent them? Even after what I told you?"

Otto shrugged. "I know you meant it when you said it, but that was then and this is now. Things change. I'm not foolish enough to think otherwise."

She shook her head. "So young and yet so cynical. I'll be traveling back to Audin with you so you can keep an eye on me."

"Fair enough." Otto spotted Ghent crossing the yard. "Would you excuse me?"

He left Axel and Renna behind and hurried over to catch the magical engineer.

"Lord Shenk." Ghent slowed to let him catch up but didn't stop as they made their way to the fort's armory. "I fear I can't talk long. Several of our armor units were damaged in the battle plus we need to salvage the enemy units."

"I won't keep you," Otto said. "I was just wondering if you'd go over with me how to disconnect from the carrier once I'm finished with it. I'm assuming the lord governor will want it back."

"Ah, of course. It's very simple. You just find the connection point and disconnect your threads. Essentially you're reversing the process." They entered the armory and Ghent finally paused. "Was there anything else?"

"Just one more thing." Otto pulled the disk he took off the thief's body out of his pocket. "Do you know what this is?"

Ghent took the disk and studied it. "It's an override disk. You attach it to a magical device under someone's control and it breaks the link and establishes a new one with a person designated by the wizard that created it. It even allows a non-wizard to control a magical device. Where did you find it?"

Otto took the disk back. Clearly Ghent hadn't given it to the thief. "Before I tell you, does this device belong to Audin?"

"The design is pretty standard. I suppose it might be one of ours. Why?"

"I took it off a thief that was trying to steal the carrier or more precisely the artifact."

"And you fear one of us is responsible?"

"The thought crossed my mind. Can you find out?"

"No. The only way to know for sure would be to check if one of the devices is missing from our magical storehouse. Only the unit commander and the chief magical engineer have access."

Otto cocked his head. "Isn't that your position?"

"It will be, when the current chief returns to Audin. For now, I'm officially the second-in-command. He still has the key."

"I see. Well, I'll let you get to work. It was good to meet you."

"Same, and thank you again for saving my life." Ghent bowed then moved deeper into the armory in the general direction of a battered suit of armor.

Otto took his leave and crossed the yard to where the scouts were busy setting up their tents. Hans had his tent up and was working on Corina's. His apprentice sat in a folding chair, mouth partly open, sound asleep.

Hans glanced his way as he lifted the tent flap. "I don't wish to be disturbed."

"Understood, my lord."

Inside, Otto settled on his cot and extended his sight. He should have asked Ghent where the magical storehouse was. Oh well, too late now. If it was full of magical items, he should have no trouble locating it.

Outside of the fort itself, Otto found nothing magical beyond the armory. His ethereal eyes slipped through the wall of the fort and soon enough he spotted a bright collection of magical items. Quick as thought he soared down the halls until he came to a narrow, closed door behind which the magical emanations emerged.

Fearing a trap, he conjured ethereal tentacles and probed the door and frame. Aside from an ordinary steel lock of exceptional quality, he found nothing of interest. Steadying himself, Otto slid through the door into a modest closet filled with a chest of drawers. The tentacles formed again and pulled the drawers out one by one.

At the fourth one he found two more of the disks as well as a third depression where the one currently in his pocket would reside. Returning his sight to his body, Otto considered what to do with this new information. Assuming Ghent had told him the truth, only two people could have sent those thieves.

He'd best kill them both tonight. Just to be sure.

Otto woke early, determined to be ready to march at first light. He was so close to the finish line now he could taste it. Apparently he wasn't alone. When he ducked out of his tent, Axel, the other scouts, and Hans were already up and packing. Only Corina still slept. Since the sky remained dark, he resolved to give her ten more minutes.

Unfortunately, two minutes later, a shout of alarm went up from the fort. Otto moved over closer to the fire and held out his hands. A pot of porridge was warming. Otto gave it a sniff, but the bland mush didn't offer much hope for a flavorsome breakfast.

Hans took down the last pole of his tent and said, "What do you suppose that's about?"

"Who knows. As long as our departure isn't delayed, I don't care."

Soldiers went running toward the fort. Axel and his men kept their hands close to their weapons, but no one gave them more than a passing glance.

Corina finally emerged from her tent, her tan sleeping clothes in total disarray, and looked blearily around. "What's all the noise?"

Otto shrugged and Hans started taking Otto's tent down.

"Did you sleep well?" Otto asked.

"Better than I expected." She yawned. "Home by the end of the week, you think?"

"I sincerely hope so. I've had enough of this land to last the rest of my life."

Cobb had just begun serving up bowls of porridge when Renna approached the camp. She seemed pale and her usually flawless dress was wrinkled and smudged with dirt.

"Breakfast?" Otto asked.

"No, thank you." She spoke like she was still partly asleep.

Otto suspected it was shock at finding the fort's commander and chief magical engineer dead in their beds. Stopping their hearts with a burst of lightning last night had been remarkably simple. There were no magical defenses around either of their rooms or the fort itself. Stupid or arrogant, he didn't know which, but it certainly made his task easier.

"Is everything alright?" Otto asked. "We noticed a bit of excitement at the fort."

She told them about the deaths. "The healer is examining

them now. We'll be leaving as planned, only two men shorter than I expected."

Otto nodded, pleased by the lack of delay. "You have my condolences for the loss of your people."

"Thank you. Will you be ready to leave within the hour?"

"We will."

She wandered off without another word, seemingly without a destination.

"Is she okay?" Corina asked.

"She will be. Come on, eat up. We still have a little packing to do."

An hour later a caravan of sixty soldiers, along with Otto and his people, set out for the city. Renna rode in the front wagon while Otto stayed in the last. He'd heard nothing about the deaths and doubted their healers would know what happened even if they cut the bodies open and examined their hearts directly. His spell would have left at most a little scarring on the tissue.

The killings didn't work especially well as a warning, since he couldn't tell anyone he did it. On the plus side, he assumed one of the dead men had sent the thieves that attacked Corina. They wouldn't be doing it a second time.

"What sort of welcome should we expect?" Axel asked.

"An unpleasant one. Renna as much as admitted to me she had orders to steal the artifact and that she didn't intend to follow them. I very much doubt August will be equally reasonable. I suspect he ordered either the commander or chief engineer to send those thieves. Renna seemed completely in the dark when she saw the bodies."

Axel shot him a narrow-eyed look. "That would be the two guys that died last night. You killed them."

"Of course. They would have been traveling with us. I had

no desire to spend the entire trip looking over my shoulder and waiting for them to order the soldiers to kill us and steal the artifact."

"Look, my lord." Hans nodded toward the west.

Otto squinted against the brightness and spotted a single figure astride a metal horse. "Great, more rangers. I'll take a closer look."

"Can I do it?" Corina asked.

"I think he's a bit out of your range." Otto closed his eyes and soon enough had a bird's-eye view of the area. He checked for a mile in every direction, but saw nothing beyond the single ranger who seemed content to follow them at a distance. "He's alone."

"Will you kill him too?" Axel asked.

"I was debating that very thing. I'd rather capture and inter-rogate him. If the besieging force has been wiped out, I can't figure the point of one guy trailing us. Things I don't under-stand make me nervous. Corina, would you like to try and ask Renna if she's aware of the ranger and what she'd like to do about him?"

She beamed. "Yes, Master."

So young and eager. Otto had felt exactly the same when he started his formal training. He had to fight to remember she was only two years his junior. Sometimes she felt far younger.

Corina's lips moved but no sound emerged. A moment later she said, "If he's still following us when we stop for lunch, she says we can take him."

"A reasonable compromise." Otto took a moment to tag the rider with a thread then returned his sight to his body. Until she decided to betray him, Otto would let Renna believe she was in control of the situation. It would make things easier.

Otto spread a thin layer of ether around the wagon then

closed his eyes to rest. He hadn't fully relaxed in weeks and the strain was getting to him. He needed to maintain his focus for a little longer. Once the chamber had been secured at Castle Garen, he would take a day or two for recovery. Maybe spend some time with his mother before she had to return to Shenk Barony.

With that pleasant thought foremost in his mind he dozed until the wagons rattled to a stop.

His eyes snapped open and he sought the ranger. Sure enough he found the man about the same distance to their west. He seemed content to only watch. Time to find out why.

Otto flicked his iron ring and sent binding magic through the thread he'd used to tag the ranger. He ended up having to use five threads to maintain the magic at such a distance.

When he felt it take hold he turned to Axel, "Would you mind sending a few guys to collect our prisoner? He won't give them any trouble."

"Cobb! Take second squad and fetch my brother's parcel."

"Yes, my lord."

Cobb and five others trotted off to the west while Otto and the rest climbed down. They never bothered with a fire at lunchtime, instead gnawing on jerky and washing it down with tepid water. Dried pear bits at least added some flavor for dessert.

Otto had barely started on his first strip of jerky when Cobb and the others appeared with the prisoner between them. They carried the rigid man like he was an especially heavy table. Otto never thought about the difficulty of carrying someone totally stiff.

They dropped the ranger at Otto's feet just as Renna came walking over. "That was easy. Your style of magic is certainly useful at times."

"Indeed." Otto released the ranger's head and asked, "Why are you following us?"

"Orders."

"I need a bit more detail than that," Otto said.

The prisoner just glared at him. Why did every interrogation go this way? They always resisted and always broke. Just once Otto would like to deal with a reasonable enemy. One that weighed their situation objectively and simply told everything they knew. Was that too much to ask?

Apparently it was, at least today.

"Very well, have it your way." Otto conjured his ethereal probes and asked, "Why are you watching us?"

When that section of the prisoner's brain lit up, he hooked the memory and dragged it out of the man's mouth. "The army wants to be kept appraised of your progress. They want to have Audin fully besieged before you can get inside."

"What army?" Renna asked, her voice high with worry.

Again Otto dragged the information out of the prisoner. "Word of your deal with the outlanders has spread to all the other city-states. A coalition army has been formed of every nearby unit. They are currently marching on Audin at best possible speed."

"I need to send word to August," Renna said. She looked around as if a messenger was going to appear out of thin air.

"Our transport horses aren't designed for speed," one of the soldiers said. "Even if we unhooked one, it wouldn't be noticeably faster than pulling the wagons."

Renna gave Otto a pleading look. "Can you warn him?"

Otto's smile held no humor. "Audin is well beyond my range. And even if I went there, what sort of greeting would I receive?"

She winced. "Fine. Everyone into the wagons. We're moving."

Otto drew his sword and finished the prisoner with a stroke to the neck. Everyone clambered back into the wagons and they got underway.

"Is this good for us, or bad for us?" Corina asked.

"Time will tell," Otto replied.

He tapped his chin as he considered the possibilities presented by an approaching army. He could use that. The only question was, how.

CHAPTER 20

E ddred could hardly believe he was back in the City of Coins already. He felt like a failure coming crawling back to someone that offered him a solution to a problem he couldn't solve himself. Before, the sights and sounds of the city had seemed enchanting and exotic. Now everything felt dull and lifeless. His failure had cost him something. A little piece of his soul died when he fled from Otto in Bandon.

He shook off his morose gloom and crossed the dusty street to take a seat at one of the innumerable cafes that filled the city. While the crew enjoyed some time on land, he'd come alone to contact Naja. Well, mostly alone. Lilly and Adam had followed him despite his orders. Stealth, clearly, wasn't one of their skills. Eddred had spotted them five blocks from the ship. He didn't bother ordering them back and instead pretended they weren't there.

Eddred settled on an empty table and immediately placed the serpent-marked coin in plain view. A serving girl about sixteen came to his table and took his order for a glass of chilled wine. Her gaze lingered a moment on the coin before she hurried away in a swirl of billowing cloth.

Five minutes passed before a sultry voice asked, "Is this seat taken?"

He looked up into Naja's dark eyes. She held a pair of frosty glasses filled with white wine.

"Please join me." Eddred gestured at the empty chair across from him.

She set a glass in front of him and sat. "You look depressed. Business in Colt's Land not what you hoped?"

"No. Bandon and all the other city-states refused to help me. So I came crawling back to you. Lord Valtan will have your payment waiting on South Barrier Island."

Eddred reached for his drink. The moment he touched the glass, Naja's soft, strong hand touched his. "Everyone fails from time to time. As long as you keep trying, nothing else matters. Once we have removed the heads of the empire, you will have another chance at victory. As long as you don't lose heart."

"It's far too late for that. My heart died along with my wife. But your point is well taken. All those who wish to be free of the empire will be ready to act. And thank you for your kind words. When can we expect your agents to collect their payment?"

"Our people on the continent will be alerted as soon as I return to our headquarters. From there, it will be a quick sail to Markane. They may arrive before you do."

"I guess I shouldn't be surprised you have agents on the continent. Did you have anyone in Markane City?"

Her voice was hard and brittle as glass. "Two. Both of them died when the city fell. Had it been otherwise, our price would have been far higher."

Eddred sighed. "Then you have my condolences. It seems everyone has suffered at the hands of that monster."

"We will teach Otto Shenk what suffering is." Naja stood. "I doubt we will see each other again. Be well, Eddred of Markane."

He watched her until she vanished into the crowd. Eddred swirled his wine around and drank it in one long swallow. Getting drunk seemed like a fine idea just now.

CHAPTER 21

The walls of Audin appeared on the horizon. Though they weren't visible at the moment, Otto had seen the approaching enemy army during one of his magical scouting runs. He estimated the force at about ten times the size of the one that besieged the fort. And they had way more magical armor, including five of the massive ones he'd seen in Audin's armory. Whatever happened, August was in for a rough time. Hopefully he'd be smart enough to let Otto and his companions go and focus on his real problems.

Otto hated counting on people to do the smart thing. It seemed he was always doomed to be disappointed. Just to be on the safe side, he'd need to find an edge. What that would be, he wasn't certain yet, but he'd know it when he saw it.

They were about half a mile out when Hans said, "Lord Shenk, the gate is closed."

Otto frowned. It was the middle of the day. The only reason for the gate to be closed was if August knew the army was approaching.

"He's smarter than I thought. Unfortunately for him, August clearly has no idea what a proper wizard can do."

"What are you mumbling about, little brother?" Axel asked.

"He's shut the gates, trapping us between the city wall and the approaching army. August will demand the artifact and probably a bunch more mithril in exchange for letting us in. That's my guess anyway."

"That's a problem, isn't it?" Axel asked.

"Not as big a one as you might think. Since we arrived, I've noticed all the cities' defenses are geared around attacks from magical armor. They have virtually no wards. If he doesn't keep his word, I'll reduce that gate to so much rubble the approaching army will be able to march right through it. Corina, I have a job for you."

"Yes, Master?"

"There will be archers over the gate and on the wall. I want you to destroy their bowstrings."

Her face scrunched up. "How?"

"Simple. Run a thread through the strings then send a stream of fire along it. I've taught you all you need to know to accomplish that. Our survival depends on your success."

She swelled up with pride and thrust out her modest chest. "I won't let you down."

Otto nodded. He'd been exaggerating of course. Arrows were no threat to him, though the scouts were another matter.

"What about us?" Axel asked.

"I need you to keep an eye on the soldiers in front of us. If they do something stupid, it will be your job to deal with them. No misplaced mercy. If they draw their weapons on us, kill them all."

"I know my job. Besides, they saw us fight. Only a complete moron would take on someone armed with mithril weapons."

Otto hoped his brother was right. He didn't fancy having to worry about the soldiers outside as well as the ones inside.

Their little caravan rolled to a halt in front of the closed gates. Just as he'd thought, fifty archers lined the wall and roof of the gatehouse. He glanced at Corina who nodded and began shaping the ether.

"Wait for my signal or any sign they're preparing to attack." She nodded again.

Nerve-racking as it was, he trusted her to handle such a simple spell. Ahead of them, Renna climbed down from her wagon and shouted, "Open the gate! We need to get in before the enemy army arrives."

"We will." August stepped out from behind a pair of archers. Some magic augmented his voice so that it carried easily from his position far above them. "But first I need to speak to Otto about our arrangement."

Otto stared for a moment. How could the fat fool be so stupid that he'd come to the wall himself? Any ruler with a brain would send an intermediary to deliver his message. This would make the job so much easier.

"My lord," Renna said. "We have very little time."

"No, Renna, you have very little time. We are perfectly safe behind the walls. Come now, Otto, let's talk."

Oh, they'd talk alright.

Otto forged three tentacles of ether and sent them racing toward August. He wrapped one around the lord governor's neck, a second around his ample gut, and the third around his ankles. With a thought he yanked the idiot off the wall and carried him toward the wagon.

He felt Corina's spell activate and in a flash of orange fire, every bow on the wall was rendered useless.

Otto lowered August to the dry dirt in front of him. "Now,

what, exactly, did you want to discuss? As you said, the army is coming."

August sputtered and swore. "How do you dare do this to me in front of my own city? I'll have your arrogant head on a spike! I have thousands of soldiers. I—"

Otto tightened the tentacle around his neck, cutting August off in midthreat. "If I see so much as an inch of bared steel, I'll crush your head like a grape. Here's my offer. And this is a 'take it or leave it' sort of thing. You will let us in. We will go directly to the portal and travel home. You will receive no more mithril, but you will survive. Say yes or die where you stand."

Renna stopped well out of reach of a sword. "Lord Audin, the army."

Otto flicked a glance to his left and saw a cloud of dust approaching. "Time is running out."

August's face had gone red with fury. "Very well. I accept your terms. With the proviso that you take this worthless harlot with you. I have no use for a servant that can't follow simple orders."

"My lord?" The pain in Renna's voice sounded genuine. Her devotion to the fat fool baffled Otto, but her choice of master was hardly his concern. Bringing a bitter former enemy back to Garen wasn't wise, but he could always deal with her later if he had to.

August sneered at her then turned to the soldiers on duty. "Open the gate and for heaven's sake, keep your weapons sheathed."

The massive wooden doors creaked and clunked and then swung slowly open.

Otto turned to his brother. "Defensive circle. Stay close and keep a sharp lookout for snipers. Hans, put your sword at his back. Anyone tries anything stupid, gut him. Corina, you're my spare eyes. Keep a close watch."

Axel nodded and arrayed his men. Hans drew his sword and placed the tip in August's side. Corina moved to stand beside him. Renna took a step toward the circle.

"You can follow along from the outside." Otto raised his voice. "You men from the fort, go in ahead of us and keep well out of the way. Your lord governor's life depends on your actions."

The soldiers hurried to obey. When the last of them had passed through the open gate, Otto and his group advanced. The enemy army was close enough that the crash of their magical armor's footsteps rang out loud and clear.

Otto peered between two scouts. The area between the outer gate and the open portcullis was completely free of guards.

"Corina, check behind the murder holes."

A moment of silence then, "All clear."

As soon as they passed through the outer gate, it began to clank shut. Since he had no desire to deal with a second army, Otto raised no objections. Once they passed under the portcullis, that fell with a crash as well.

Inside, the guards had pulled well back. "Looks like they want you to survive this, August. Be sure to thank them after I'm gone."

"You will pay for this indignity, I swear it."

"Yes, yes. Keep quiet."

The group made their way through the streets surrounded by an even bigger force of soldiers. Behind them, the first heavy crash of something slamming into the gate reached them.

A moment later a soldier came running. "The enemy has begun their attack!"

"Deploy our forces," August said. "Do not let them break through into the city. Tell Illsa to activate the new units."

The messenger ran off again.

They were halfway to the portal and none of the soldiers shadowing them had so much as reached for their weapons. So far so good. There was nothing like having the ruler of the nation as your hostage to keep everyone well behaved.

After a long, tense walk, they reached the portal plaza. More soldiers were waiting, but they were keeping a safe distance. It was a wonder they could spare so many men given the army at their gates. Not that it was of any concern to Otto.

They all gathered at the base of the portal and Axel shifted his formation into a semicircle.

Otto reached into his robe to retrieve the control rod.

The moment he looked away there was a scream.

His head snapped up in time to see Renna, a dagger in her right hand, quivering as lightning coursed through her body.

When she finally collapsed, Otto glanced at Corina and raised an eyebrow.

"She drew her dagger and went right at you the second you looked away."

"Well done." Otto finished drawing the control rod, charged the tip, and activated the portal. "I'm afraid you'll have to keep Renna. I have no use for someone that would stab me the moment my attention shifts. Axel, you and your men go first. Corina, you next. I'll send the carrier then Hans and I will follow."

Axel and the scouts needed no further urging. They darted right through. Corina gave him a worried look then jumped through. At Otto's mental command, the carrier flew through the portal.

"On three, Hans," Otto whispered. "One, two, three."

He shoved August away at the same time he transformed the tentacle into a shield.

Six arrows bounced off it before he found himself in the safety of the ether.

An instant later he stepped out into the fort.

A quick touch with the control rod and the portal went dark.

They'd done it. Somehow they'd retrieved the artifact and made it home in one piece. Otto wanted to collapse with relief, but he wouldn't be satisfied until the chamber was locked up and secure.

"We're going to the palace. Axel, you and your men are on point."

"You're not expecting trouble here?" Axel asked.

"No, but after everything we went through to bring the chamber here, I'm taking no chances."

EPILOGUE

"It doesn't look like much." Wolfric had joined Otto that morning as he completed the final adjustments to the chamber in its new home. Three days had passed since Otto returned from Colt's Land and he'd spent most of each day laying spells around the basement room he'd selected to house the chamber.

Otto couldn't argue with his friend's statement. The eight-foot-tall glass cylinder didn't look like much. It sat on a raised, foot-high stone pedestal. Unless you knew how to open it, there didn't even appear to be a door. At the top, a tripod made of mithril poked out. Once Otto acquired it in the Celestial Empire, the Heart of Alchemy would rest on that tripod. Aside from the chamber, the room held nothing in the way of furniture. It was as cold and desolate a room as you might hope to find.

"You're right about that," Otto said. "Considering what it's supposed to do, you'd have thought the Arcane Lords would have added some sort of decorations. How fare matters of state?"

"Well enough." Wolfric yawned. "Taxes flow in. We're not under threat of invasion. The nobles and merchants are all happy. To be honest it all makes me a little suspicious. I keep wondering when everything we've built will come crashing down."

"It's not going to come crashing down. Once the chamber is complete, we'll have the power to live forever. You will rule the empire for all time and I will learn all there is to know about magic. The people will know peace and prosperity. No outside threat will dare attack us and no internal threat will escape my gaze."

"Peace and prosperity forever." Wolfric sighed. "Father would have loved that. If we can truly make that happen, perhaps his sacrifice will have been worth it."

Otto choked off his reply. Without the late king's death, Garenland wouldn't exist as a country much less the heart of an empire. Wolfric seemed a bit maudlin today and Otto didn't want to say anything that might set him off on a grim rant about the late unlamented king. Let him regret if he needed it to sleep through the night. As long as he did nothing to upset the empire's success, Otto didn't care.

"Why don't we go upstairs and have some lunch," Otto said. "All the magic I've been using has left me famished."

Wolfric seemed to shake off his mood and flashed his old grin. "Excellent idea. Let's dine in the old side room, where we used to meet before Father died. It would be alright just this once, don't you think?"

"You're the emperor, my friend. We can eat wherever you'd like."

Otto sealed the room behind them and they made their way upstairs. Palace guards formed up around them as they walked through the halls. Halfway to the dining room one of the pages came running toward them. "Message for you, my lords."

Otto took it and cracked the wax seal. He read the first line and smiled. Captain Wainwright had reached Lux and was tied up at the dock. That was perfect. They could begin refitting the ship for her journey to the Celestial Empire. Hans would need to go and collect his squad as well.

The next stage of his mission would get underway soon enough. Hopefully as soon as the winter was over and storm season ended in spring.

"You seem pleased," Wolfric said.

"Indeed, Your Majesty. I couldn't be more pleased."

ᕲ

A shudder ran through Arcane Lord Valtan. He sat cross-legged in his meditation room and tried to purge the memory of searching through the homes of the rich and powerful for gold to pay assassins to kill his enemies. He felt like some third-rate necromancer looting a moldy crypt. At least he'd gotten what he needed and then some. So much unclaimed wealth filled the homes of Markane's notable citizens, he probably could have hired the assassins five times over.

Despite his best efforts, a hint of rot snuck through his barriers. The many dead had been stewing in the summer heat for months. What little remained of their melted bodies stank worse than anything he'd ever encountered. That was saying something for a man that had visited the flesh pits of Amet Sur's black pyramid.

Something broke one of the wards he'd set on South Barrier Island. The assassins must have arrived. Valtan had ordered Eddred to remain in the City of Coins until the task was done. Until Otto and Wolfric were gone, restoring the old kingdoms would be impossible. Even afterwards, finding members of the royal houses and kicking out the empire's governors would be a massive task.

He shook his head and focused on the moment. The future would take care of itself.

Drawing deeply on the ether, Valtan projected his consciousness out of his body and toward the island. A moment later his awareness focused on two individuals, a man and a woman, approaching the village where he'd left the gold. He appeared in front of them as a ghostly projection.

In the blink of an eye they leapt back and drew their weapons.

"Calm yourselves," Valtan said. "I merely wish to speak with you before you depart with the first half of your payment."

The two assassins straightened but didn't sheathe their weapons.

"What do you wish to know?" the woman asked.

"Your plans. How you intend to accomplish your mission. Slaying the two most powerful men in the empire won't be a simple task."

Wrinkles formed in the man's dark-bronze skin as he scowled. "We will complete the mission. The how won't be certain until we speak to our agents in the empire."

"And if you fail?" Valtan asked. "I assume someone will return my gold."

"If we fail, the Coil will send new agents," the woman said. "If they fail, still more will come. Once the job is taken, either the targets will die, or every member of the guild will."

Valtan nodded his ghostly head. That was exactly what he

hoped to hear. The deaths of those he was supposed to protect would be avenged.

"Take the gold and do your work. The rest will be here when the job is finished." Valtan released his spell and his consciousness snapped back to his body. For better or worse the die was cast. The future of the world now rested on the shoulders of a pair of murderers for hire.

Heaven help them all.

⌒

Having left Wolfric with his harem, Otto became one with the ether and made the instantaneous journey to his master's tower. As always, the unchanging stone walls of the modest tower soothed him. He couldn't honestly say why. Maybe because when he was here, he got to ask the questions instead of being expected to answer them.

Arcane Lord Karonin's ghostly face filled the frame of her magic mirror. The green-tinged skin and floating hair gave away the fact that she was long dead and now trapped in the netherworld.

Nevertheless, Otto bowed and said, "Master, I have retrieved the first piece of the Immortality Engine."

"Congratulations, Apprentice. You had no trouble with Colt's traps and guardians?"

"I had plenty of trouble, Master, but we overcame them. In fact, I even met Lord Colt, after a fashion. Some sort of magical recording lived in the final construct he left guarding the chamber. It spoke and acted like a living being, yet Colt is trapped in the netherworld, the same as you."

"What you encountered was a simulacrum. Colt made a copy of his memories and bound them to the construct to improve its function as a guardian. It's a complex magic and one I never bothered to learn. Amet Sur could do something similar, binding a fragment of his personality to a dead body. His creatures even had the power to wield magic, though not anywhere close to the real thing."

"Fascinating. I can imagine a number of uses for such creations."

"Indeed. When do you depart for The Celestial Empire?"

Otto frowned and tapped his chin. "It's too late in the season to attempt the dangerous journey now. We will make preparations over the winter and depart in spring. Captain Wainwright is eager to attempt the trip given how long it's been since someone successfully sailed that far. There was another thing I encountered that intrigued me."

"Oh?" A hint of amusement filled her voice.

"Yes, there was a bandit with a connection to the ether. Not a conscious one you understand, but a thread ran right into his brain all the time. I've never seen anything like it. He claimed to be able to see the best and worst option in any situation."

"A wild talent. Very rare. Limited precognition is a common ability among them. In all my years I only met five. Even Amet didn't fully understand how their powers worked and he dissected over a dozen."

Otto shivered. "Could you tell me more about the chamber? Does it have any abilities, even incomplete?"

"It has several. Shall I describe them?"

"Please." Otto settled in, eager to learn something new. Secrets that would increase his powers even more.

Was there anything better in all the world?

He thought not.

AUTHOR NOTE

And so we come to the end of The Chamber of Eternity. Otto has finally begun the search for the device he needs to become and Arcane Lord. But the task only gets harder from here and Lord Valtan is determined to see him fail.

I hope you'll join me for the next installment of the Portal Wars Saga, The Heart of Alchemy.

Thanks for reading and I'll see you next time.

James

ALSO BY JAMES E WISHER

The Portal Wars Saga

The Hidden Tower

The Great Northern War

The Portal Thieves

The Master of Magic

The Chamber of Eternity

The Dragonspire Chronicles

The Black Egg

The Mysterious Coin

The Dragons' Graveyard

The Slave War

The Sunken Tower

The Dragon Empress

The Dragonspire Chronicles Omnibus Vol. 1

The Dragonspire Chronicles Omnibus Vol. 2

The Complete Dragonspire Chronicles Omnibus

Soul Force Saga

Disciples of the Horned One Trilogy:

Darkness Rising

Raging Sea and Trembling Earth

Harvest of Souls

Children of Junk

Rogue Star Omnibus Vol. 1

Children of the Black Ship

ABOUT THE AUTHOR

James E. Wisher is a writer of science fiction and fantasy novels. He's been writing since high school and reading everything he could get his hands on for as long as he can remember.

To learn more:
www.jamesewisher.com
james@jamesewisher.com